STAR TREK PICARD

STARGAZER

@IDWpublishing
IDWpublishing.com

COVER ARTIST:
Angel Hernandez

COVER COLORIST:
J.D. Mettler

SERIES EDITOR:
Heather Antos

SERIES ASSISTANT EDITOR:
Vanessa Real

COLLECTION EDITOR:
Alonzo Simon

COLLECTION GROUP EDITOR:
Kris Simon

COLLECTION DESIGNER:
Johanna Guzman

978-1-68405-970-6   26 25 24 23   1 2 3 4

Originally published as STAR TREK: PICARD—STARGAZER issues #1–3.

Nachie Marsham, Publisher
Blake Kobashigawa, SVP Sales, Marketing & Strategy
Mark Doyle, VP Editorial & Creative Strategy
Tara McCrillis, VP Publishing Operations
Anna Morrow, VP Marketing & Publicity
Alex Hargett, VP Sales
Jamie S. Rich, Executive Editorial Director
Scott Dunbier, Director, Special Projects
Greg Gustin, Sr. Director, Content Strategy
Kevin Schwoer, Sr. Director of Talent Relations
Lauren LePera, Sr. Managing Editor
Keith Davidsen, Director, Marketing & PR
Topher Alford, Sr. Digital Marketing Manager
Patrick O'Connell, Sr. Manager, Direct Market Sales
Shauna Monteforte, Sr. Director of Manufacturing Operations
Greg Foreman, Director DTC Sales & Operations
Nathan Widick, Director of Design
Neil Uyetake, Sr. Art Director, Design & Production
Shawn Lee, Art Director, Design & Production
Jack Rivera, Art Director, Marketing

Ted Adams and Robbie Robbins, IDW Founders

Special thanks to Risa Kessler, Marian Cordry, Dayton Ward, and John Van Citters of
Paramount Global for their invaluable assistance.

For international rights, contact licensing@idwpublishing.com.

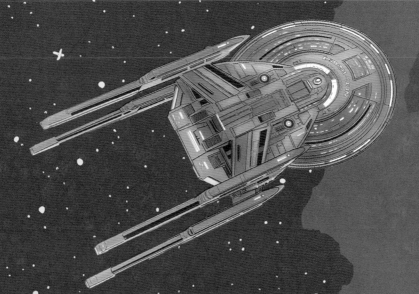

Written by
Kirsten Beyer
& Mike Johnson

Art by
Angel Hernandez

Colors by
J.D. Mettler

Letters by
Neil Uyetake

Based on *Star Trek* created by Gene Roddenberry

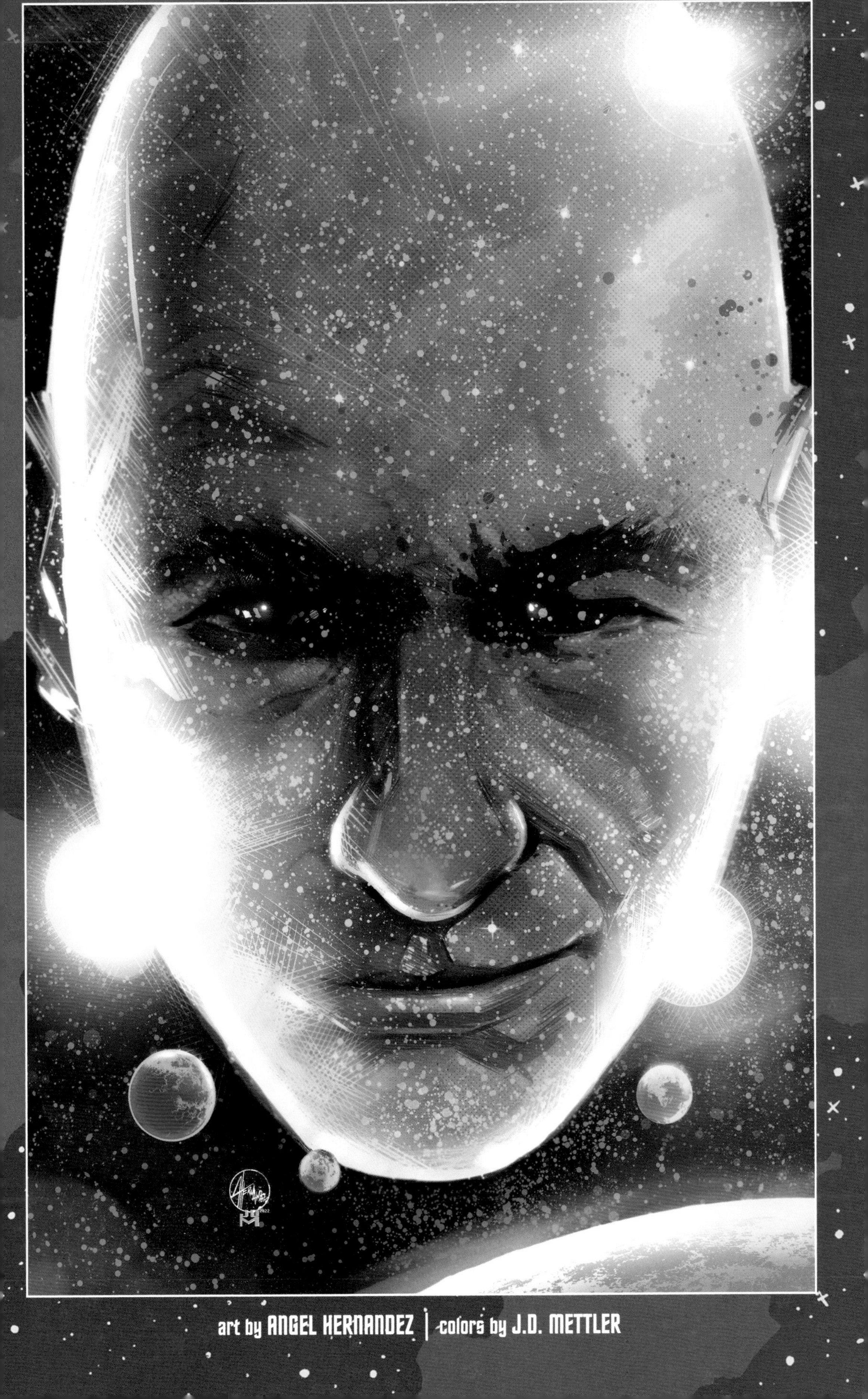

art by ANGEL HERNANDEZ | colors by J.D. METTLER

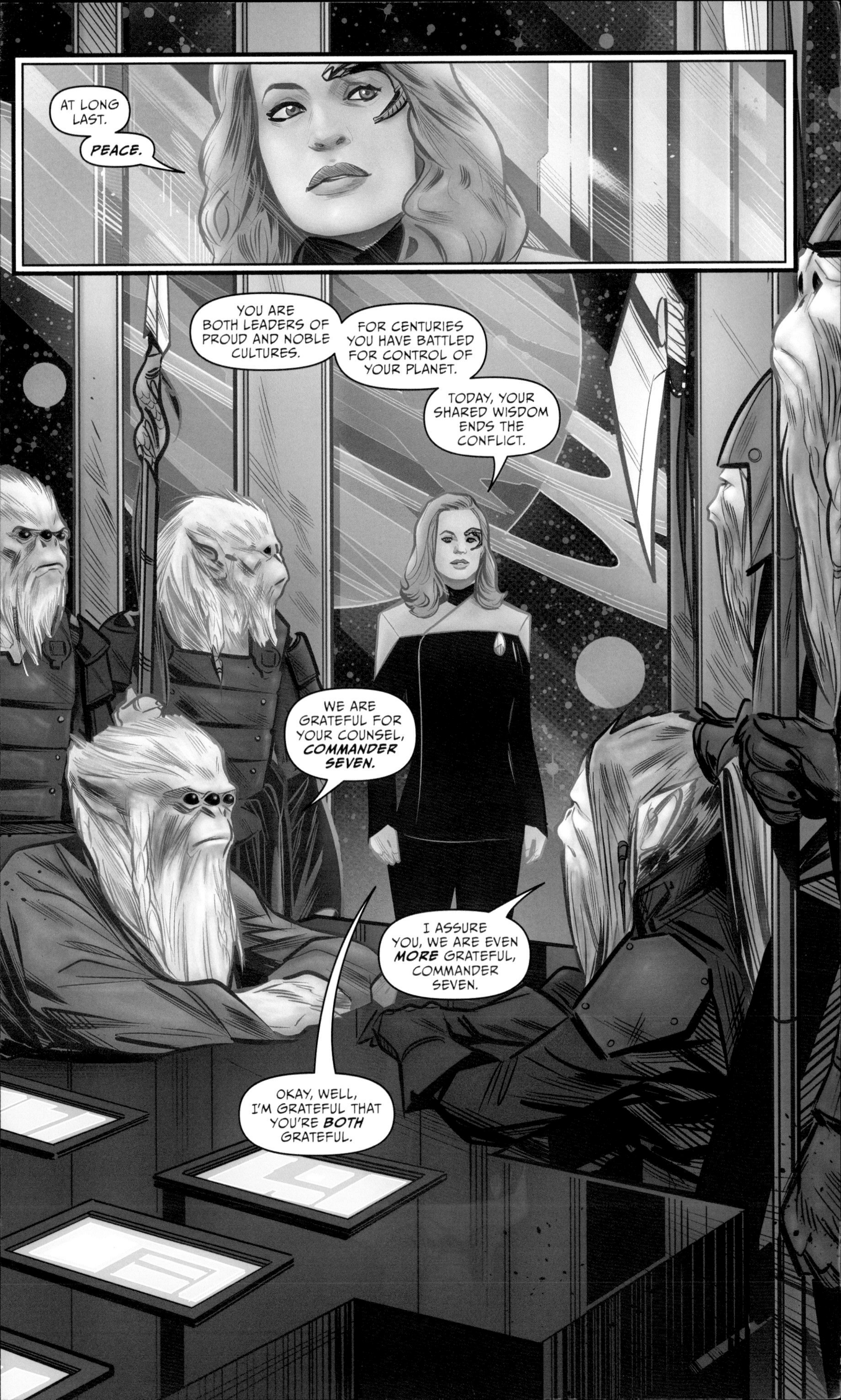

AT LONG LAST.
PEACE.
YOU ARE BOTH LEADERS OF PROUD AND NOBLE CULTURES.
FOR CENTURIES YOU HAVE BATTLED FOR CONTROL OF YOUR PLANET.
TODAY, YOUR SHARED WISDOM ENDS THE CONFLICT.
WE ARE GRATEFUL FOR YOUR COUNSEL, COMMANDER SEVEN.
I ASSURE YOU, WE ARE EVEN MORE GRATEFUL, COMMANDER SEVEN.
OKAY, WELL, I'M GRATEFUL THAT YOU'RE BOTH GRATEFUL.

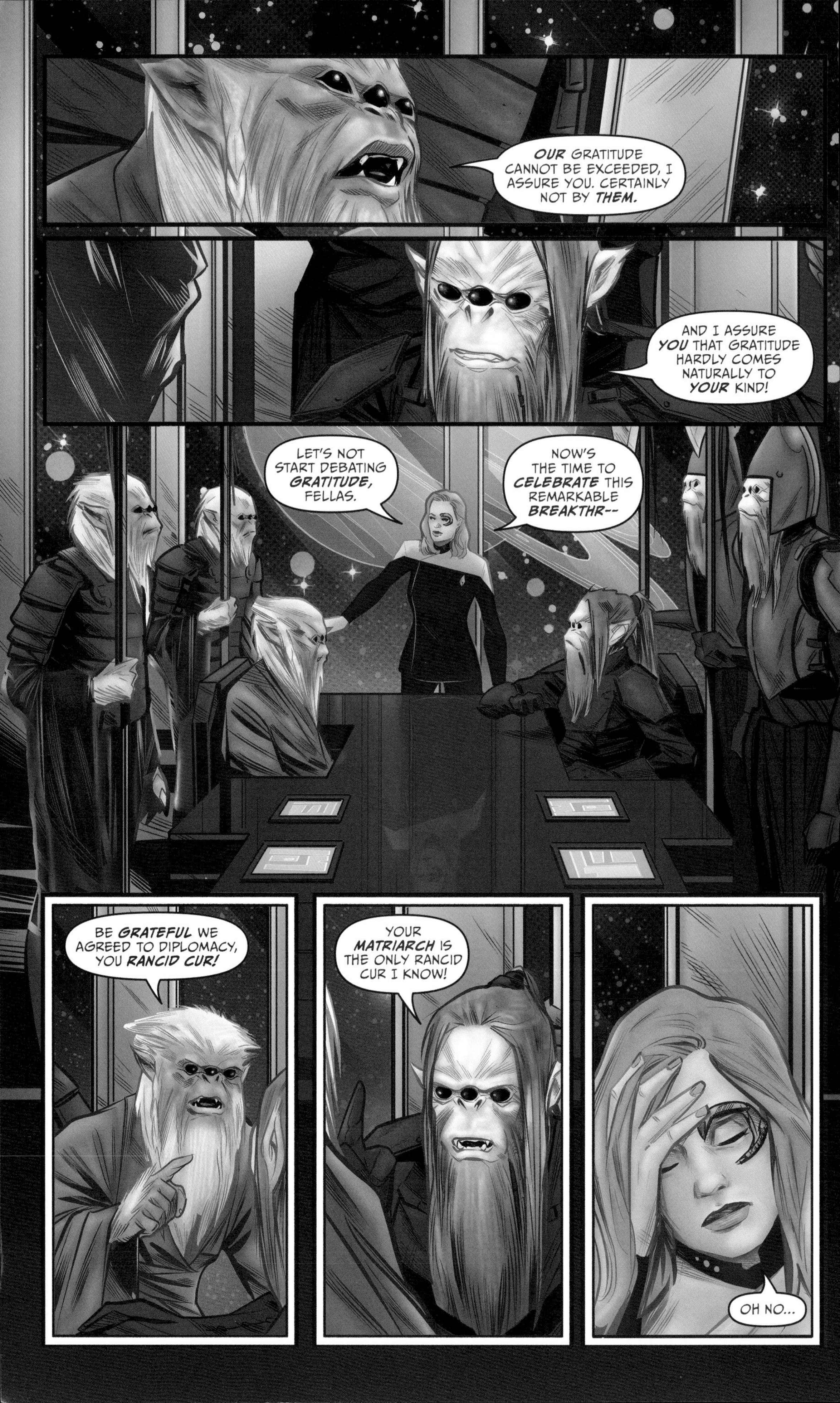
OUR GRATITUDE CANNOT BE EXCEEDED, I ASSURE YOU. CERTAINLY NOT BY THEM.
AND I ASSURE YOU THAT GRATITUDE HARDLY COMES NATURALLY TO YOUR KIND!
LET'S NOT START DEBATING GRATITUDE, FELLAS.
NOW'S THE TIME TO CELEBRATE THIS REMARKABLE BREAKTHR--
BE GRATEFUL WE AGREED TO DIPLOMACY, YOU RANCID CUR!
YOUR MATRIARCH IS THE ONLY RANCID CUR I KNOW!
OH NO...

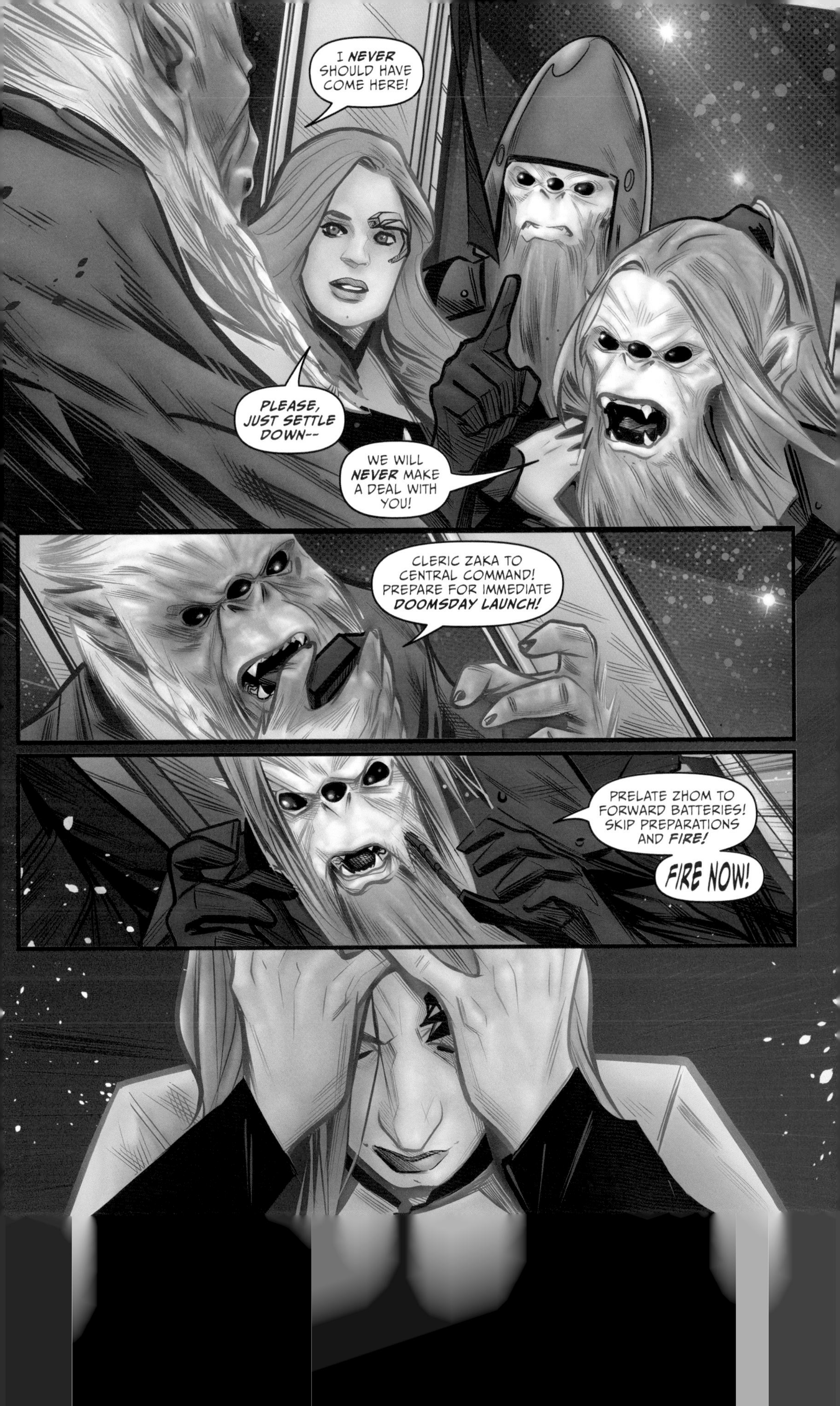

I NEVER SHOULD HAVE COME HERE!
PLEASE, JUST SETTLE DOWN--
WE WILL NEVER MAKE A DEAL WITH YOU!
CLERIC ZAKA TO CENTRAL COMMAND! PREPARE FOR IMMEDIATE DOOMSDAY LAUNCH!
PRELATE ZHOM TO FORWARD BATTERIES! SKIP PREPARATIONS AND FIRE!
FIRE NOW!

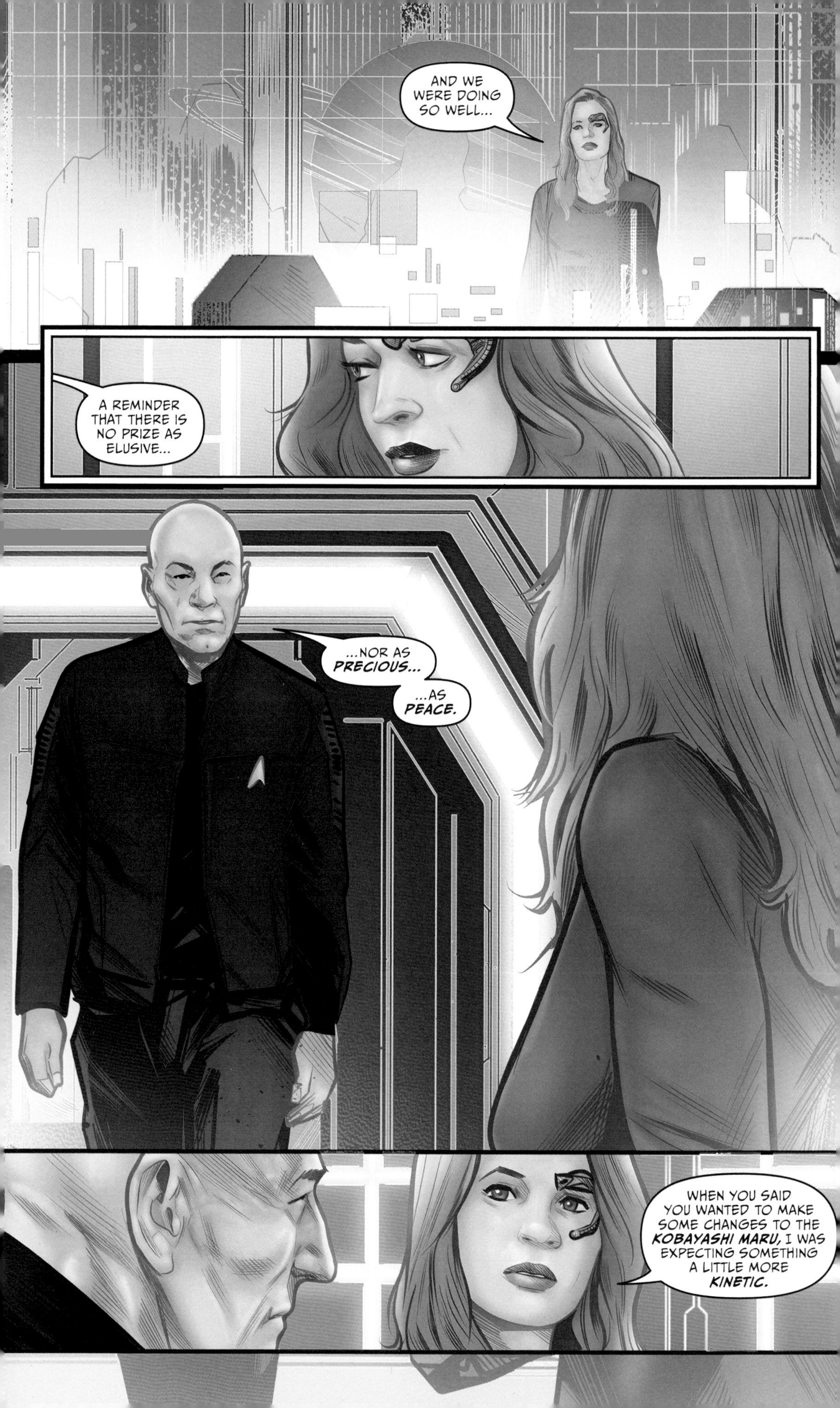
AND WE WERE DOING SO WELL...
A REMINDER THAT THERE IS NO PRIZE AS ELUSIVE...
...NOR AS PRECIOUS...
...AS PEACE.
WHEN YOU SAID YOU WANTED TO MAKE SOME CHANGES TO THE KOBAYASHI MARU, I WAS EXPECTING SOMETHING A LITTLE MORE KINETIC.

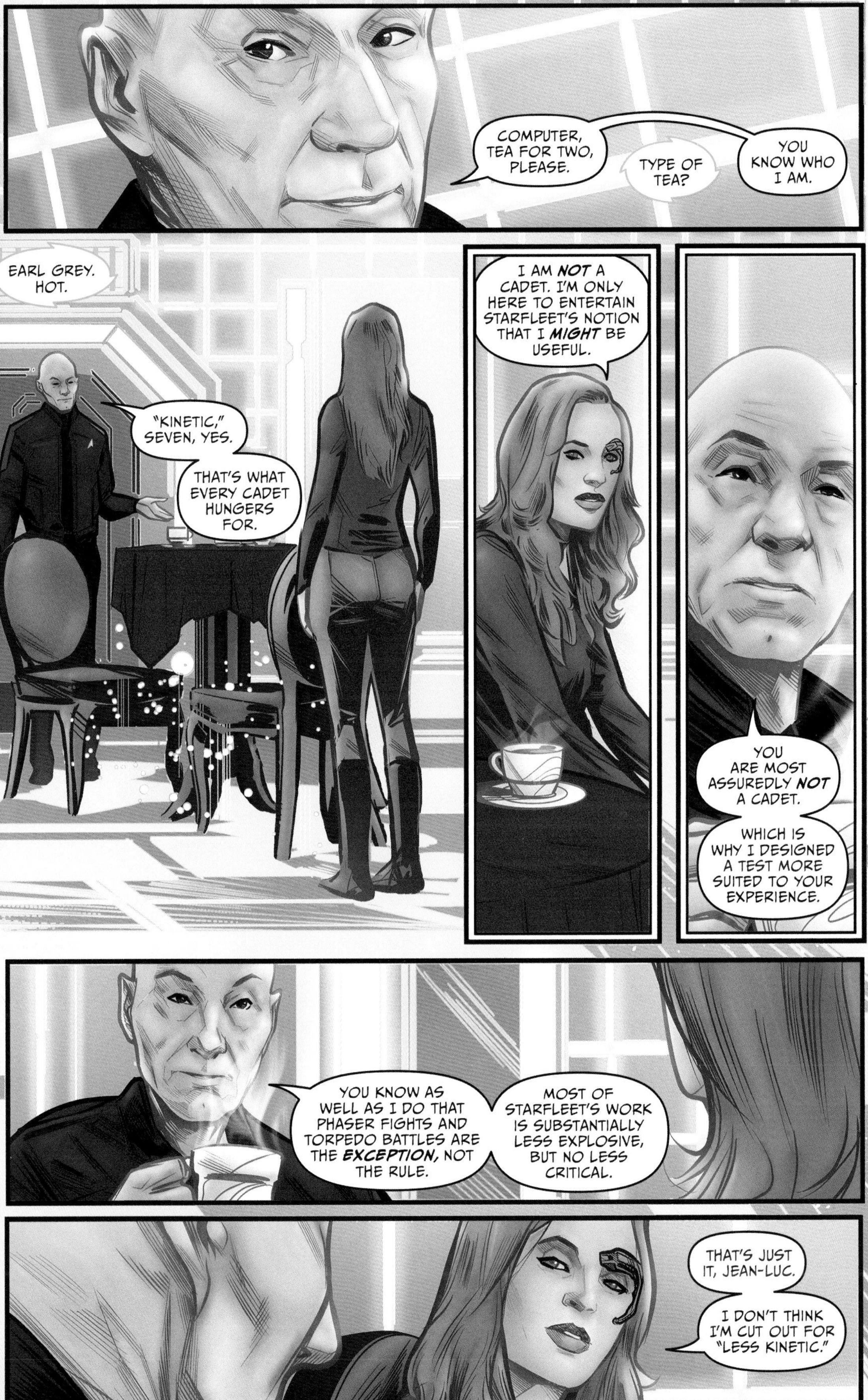
COMPUTER, TEA FOR TWO, PLEASE.
TYPE OF TEA?
YOU KNOW WHO I AM.
EARL GREY. HOT.
"KINETIC," SEVEN, YES.
THAT'S WHAT EVERY CADET HUNGERS FOR.
I AM **NOT** A CADET. I'M ONLY HERE TO ENTERTAIN STARFLEET'S NOTION THAT I **MIGHT** BE USEFUL.
YOU ARE MOST ASSUREDLY **NOT** A CADET.
WHICH IS WHY I DESIGNED A TEST MORE SUITED TO YOUR EXPERIENCE.
YOU KNOW AS WELL AS I DO THAT PHASER FIGHTS AND TORPEDO BATTLES ARE THE ***EXCEPTION,*** NOT THE RULE.
MOST OF STARFLEET'S WORK IS SUBSTANTIALLY LESS EXPLOSIVE, BUT NO LESS CRITICAL.
THAT'S JUST IT, JEAN-LUC.
I DON'T THINK I'M CUT OUT FOR "LESS KINETIC."

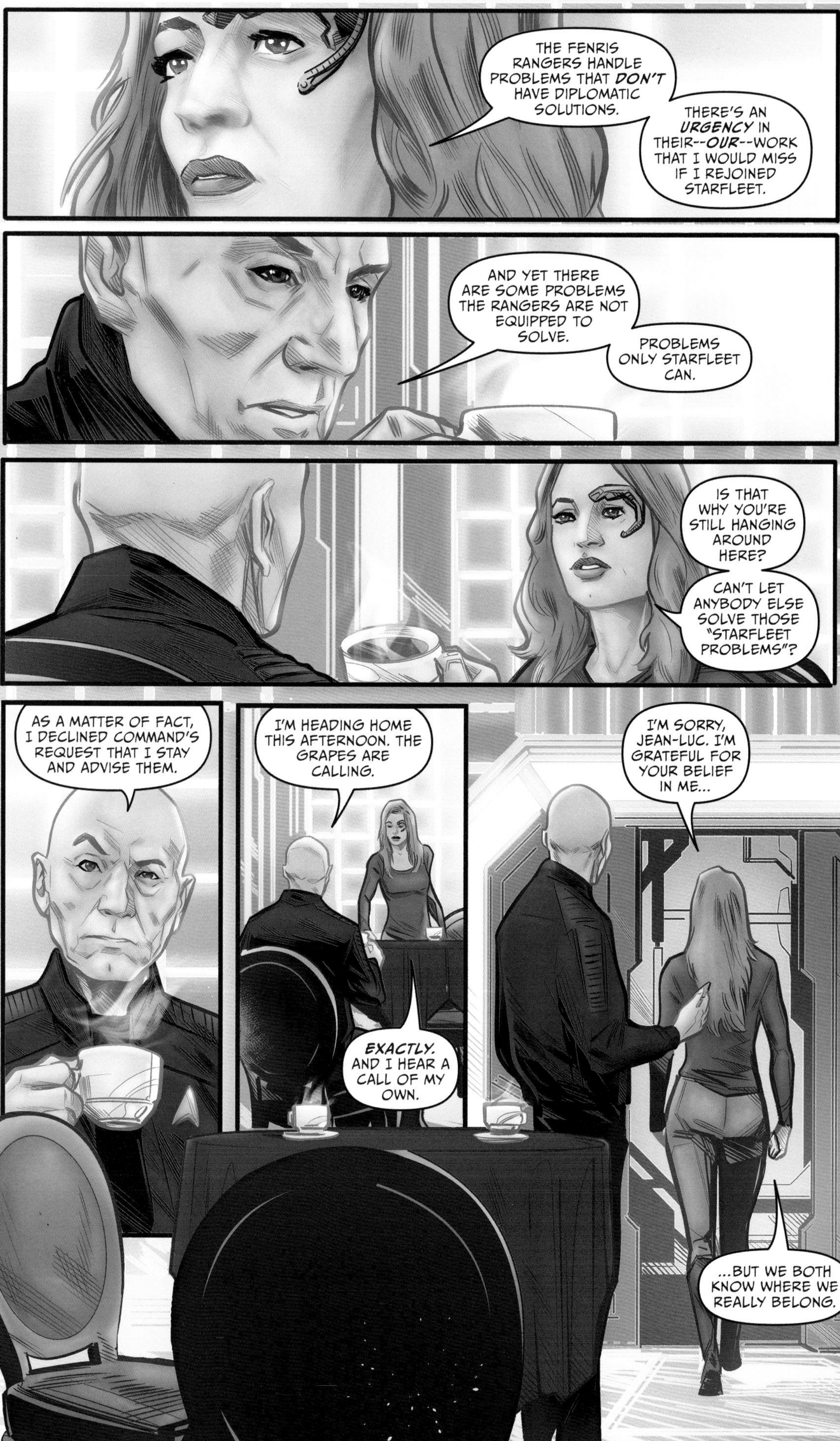
THE FENRIS RANGERS HANDLE PROBLEMS THAT DON'T HAVE DIPLOMATIC SOLUTIONS.
THERE'S AN URGENCY IN THEIR--OUR--WORK THAT I WOULD MISS IF I REJOINED STARFLEET.
AND YET THERE ARE SOME PROBLEMS THE RANGERS ARE NOT EQUIPPED TO SOLVE.
PROBLEMS ONLY STARFLEET CAN.
IS THAT WHY YOU'RE STILL HANGING AROUND HERE?
CAN'T LET ANYBODY ELSE SOLVE THOSE "STARFLEET PROBLEMS"?
AS A MATTER OF FACT, I DECLINED COMMAND'S REQUEST THAT I STAY AND ADVISE THEM.
I'M HEADING HOME THIS AFTERNOON. THE GRAPES ARE CALLING.
EXACTLY. AND I HEAR A CALL OF MY OWN.
I'M SORRY, JEAN-LUC. I'M GRATEFUL FOR YOUR BELIEF IN ME...
...BUT WE BOTH KNOW WHERE WE REALLY BELONG.

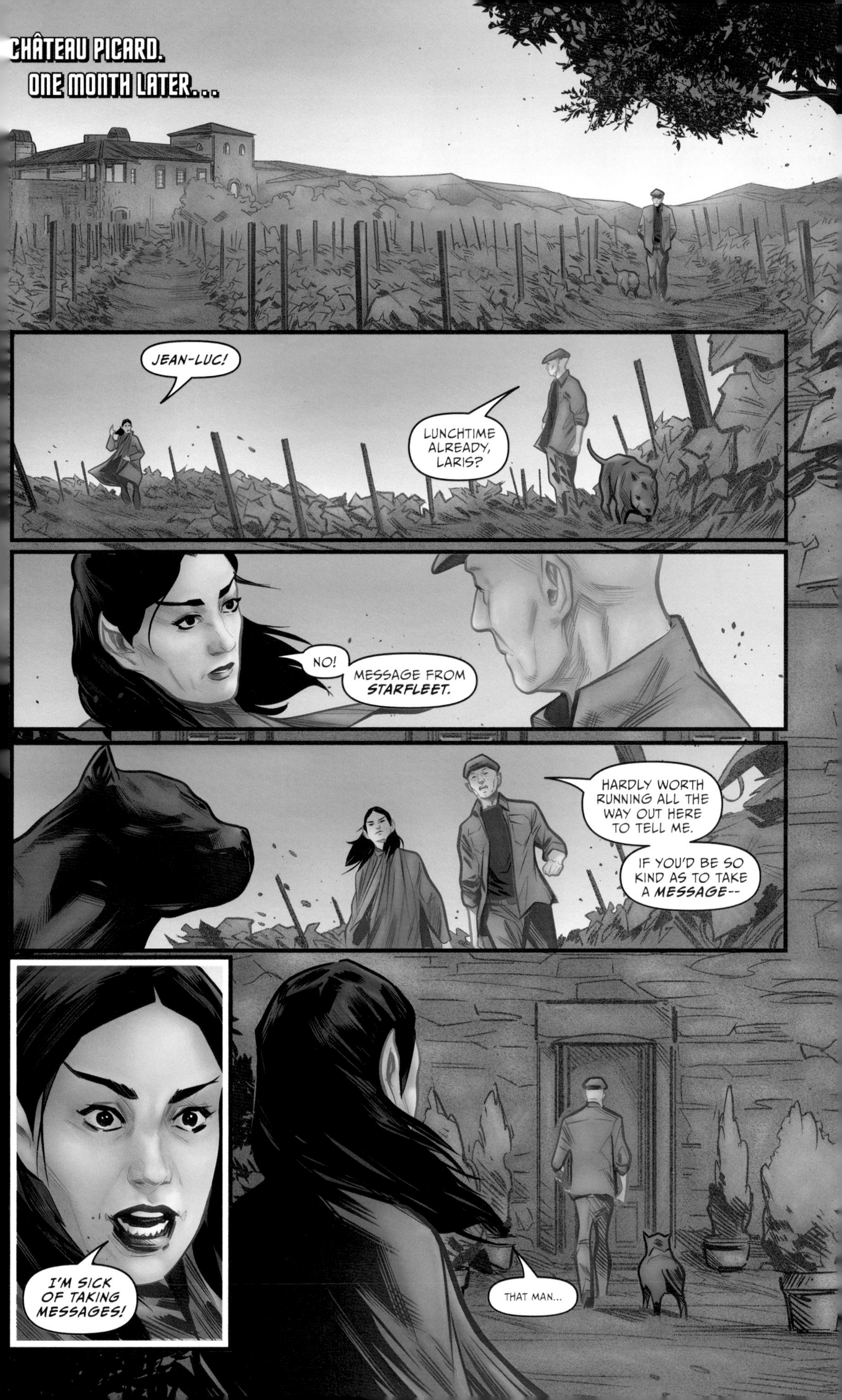
CHÂTEAU PICARD.
ONE MONTH LATER. . .
JEAN-LUC!
LUNCHTIME ALREADY, LARIS?
NO!
MESSAGE FROM STARFLEET.
HARDLY WORTH RUNNING ALL THE WAY OUT HERE TO TELL ME.
IF YOU'D BE SO KIND AS TO TAKE A MESSAGE--
I'M SICK OF TAKING MESSAGES!
THAT MAN...

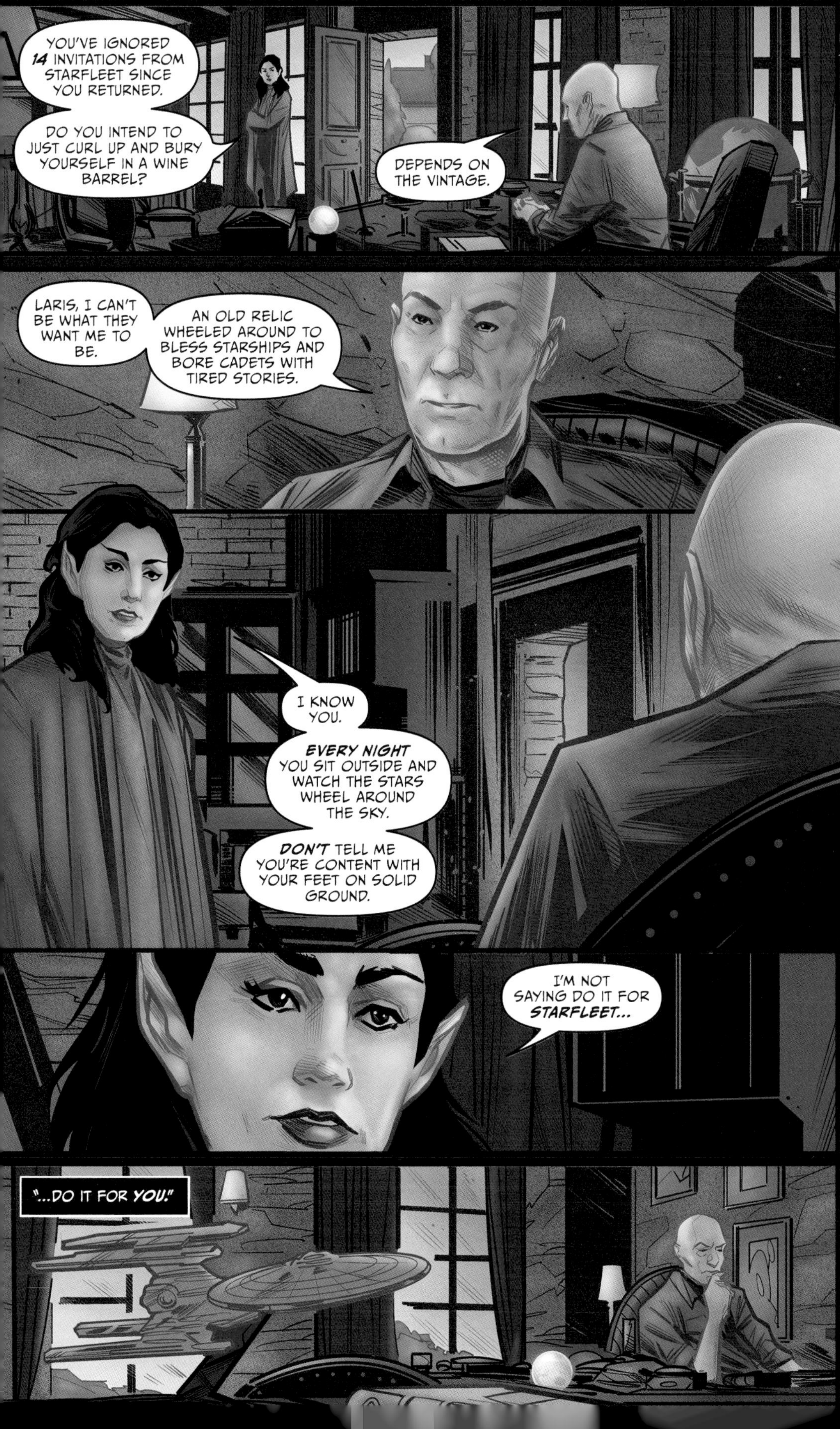
YOU'VE IGNORED 14 INVITATIONS FROM STARFLEET SINCE YOU RETURNED.
DO YOU INTEND TO JUST CURL UP AND BURY YOURSELF IN A WINE BARREL?
DEPENDS ON THE VINTAGE.
LARIS, I CAN'T BE WHAT THEY WANT ME TO BE.
AN OLD RELIC WHEELED AROUND TO BLESS STARSHIPS AND BORE CADETS WITH TIRED STORIES.
I KNOW YOU.
EVERY NIGHT YOU SIT OUTSIDE AND WATCH THE STARS WHEEL AROUND THE SKY.
DON'T TELL ME YOU'RE CONTENT WITH YOUR FEET ON SOLID GROUND.
I'M NOT SAYING DO IT FOR STARFLEET...
"...DO IT FOR YOU."

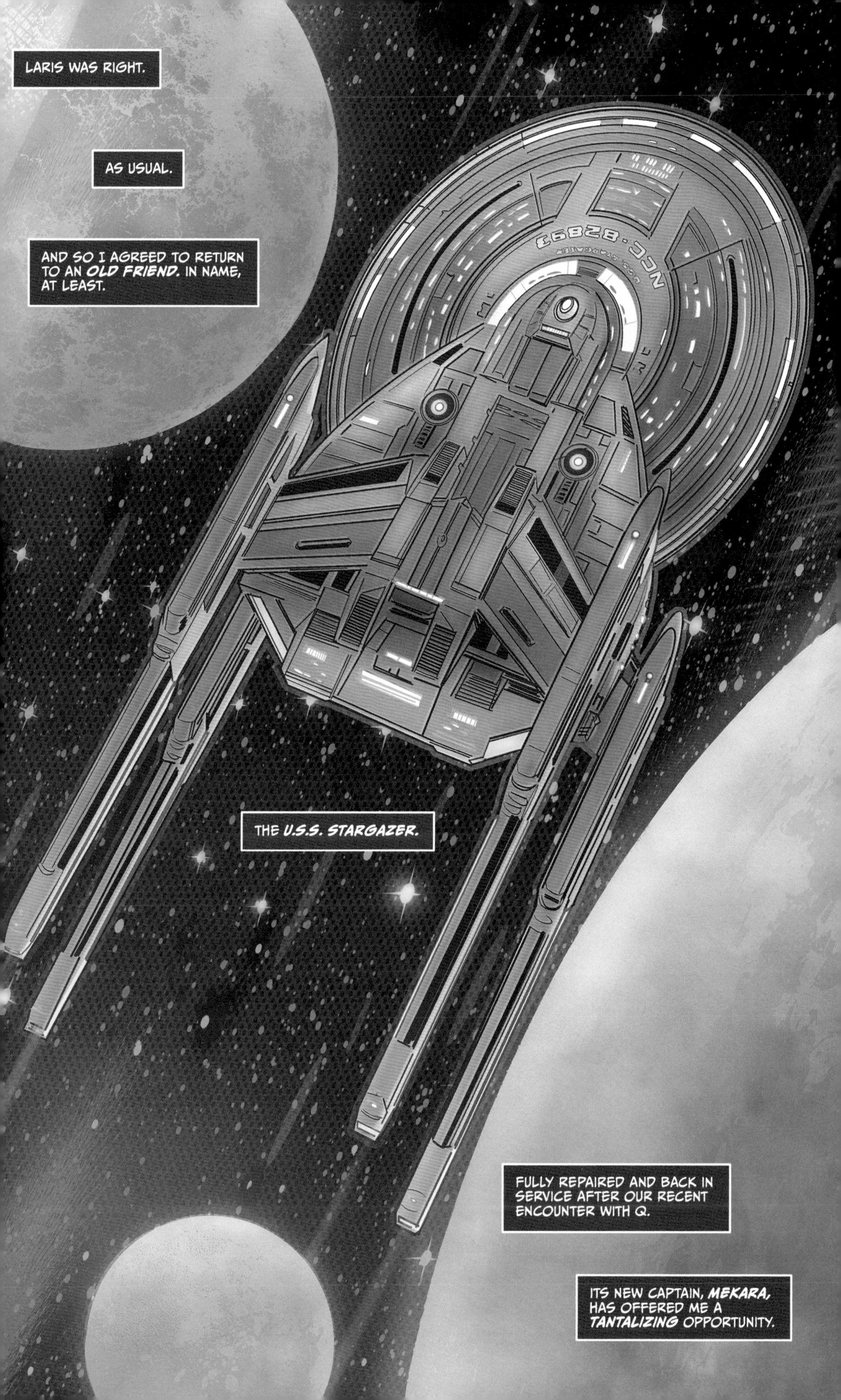
LARIS WAS RIGHT.
AS USUAL.
AND SO I AGREED TO RETURN TO AN OLD FRIEND. IN NAME, AT LEAST.
NCC-82893
U.S.S. STARGAZER
THE U.S.S. STARGAZER.
FULLY REPAIRED AND BACK IN SERVICE AFTER OUR RECENT ENCOUNTER WITH Q.
ITS NEW CAPTAIN, MEKARA, HAS OFFERED ME A TANTALIZING OPPORTUNITY.

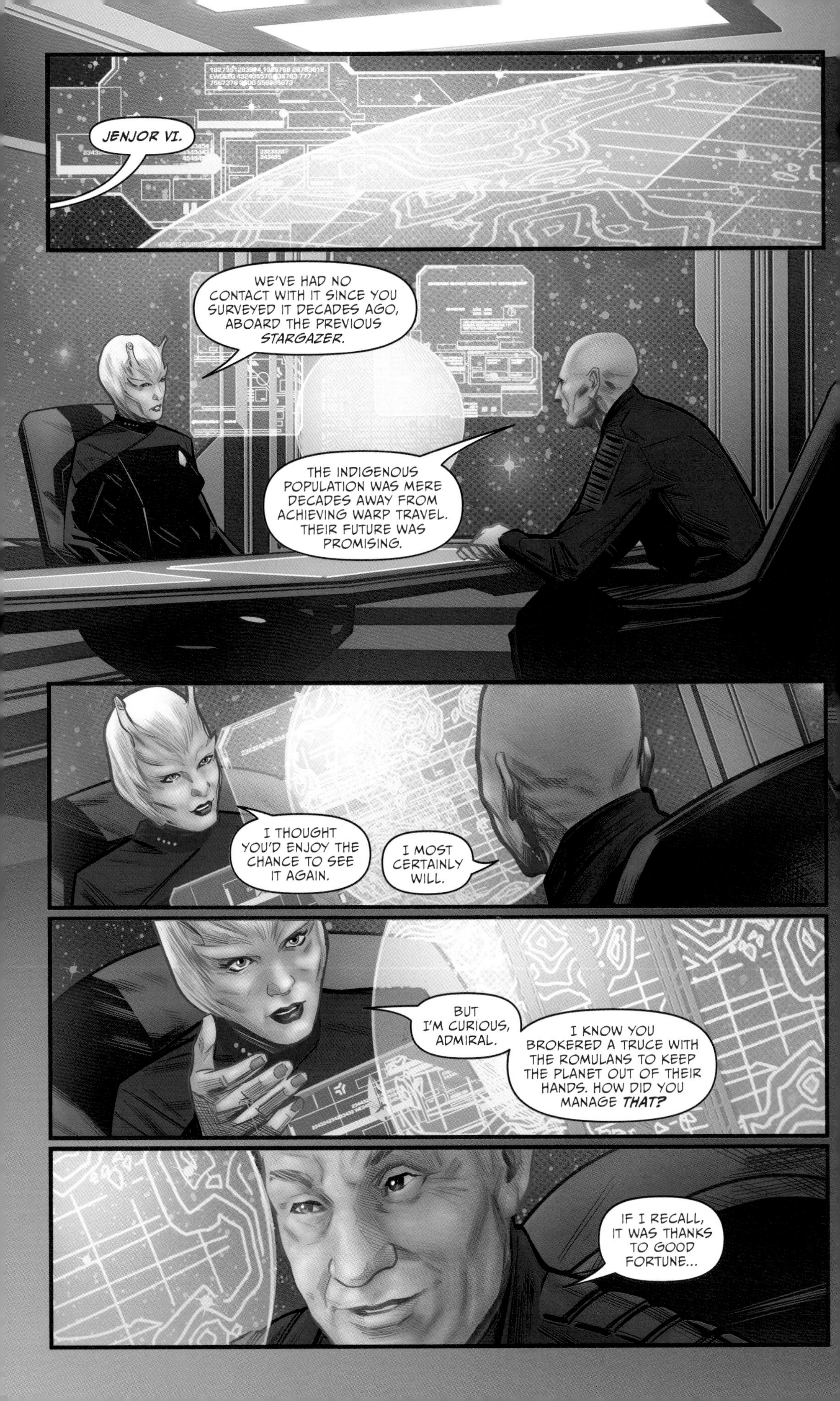
JENJOR VI.
WE'VE HAD NO CONTACT WITH IT SINCE YOU SURVEYED IT DECADES AGO, ABOARD THE PREVIOUS *STARGAZER*.
THE INDIGENOUS POPULATION WAS MERE DECADES AWAY FROM ACHIEVING WARP TRAVEL. THEIR FUTURE WAS PROMISING.
I THOUGHT YOU'D ENJOY THE CHANCE TO SEE IT AGAIN.
I MOST CERTAINLY WILL.
BUT I'M CURIOUS, ADMIRAL.
I KNOW YOU BROKERED A TRUCE WITH THE ROMULANS TO KEEP THE PLANET OUT OF THEIR HANDS. HOW DID YOU MANAGE ***THAT?***
IF I RECALL, IT WAS THANKS TO GOOD FORTUNE...

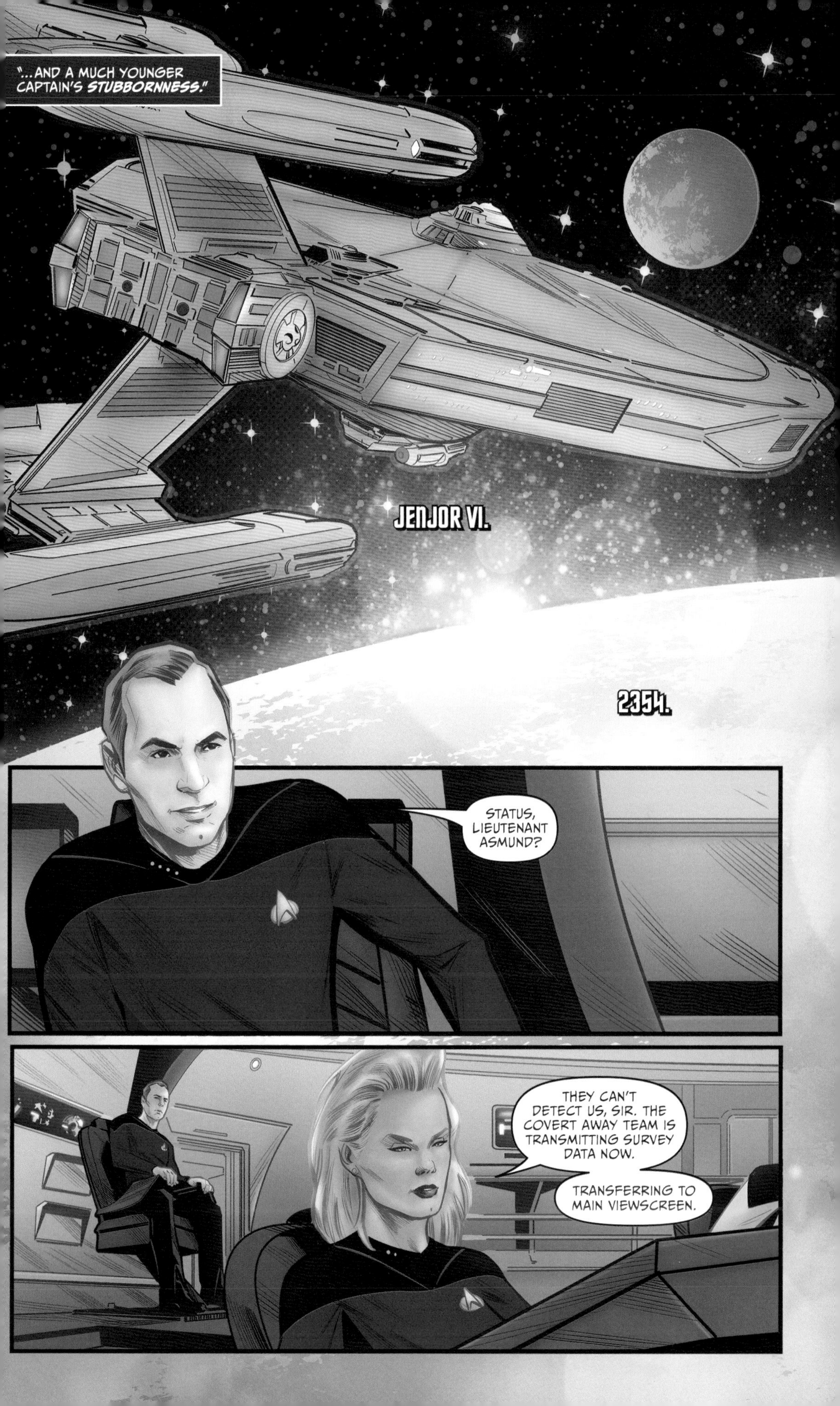
"...AND A MUCH YOUNGER CAPTAIN'S *STUBBORNNESS*."
JENJOR VI.
2354.
STATUS, LIEUTENANT ASMUND?
THEY CAN'T DETECT US, SIR. THE COVERT AWAY TEAM IS TRANSMITTING SURVEY DATA NOW.
TRANSFERRING TO MAIN VIEWSCREEN.

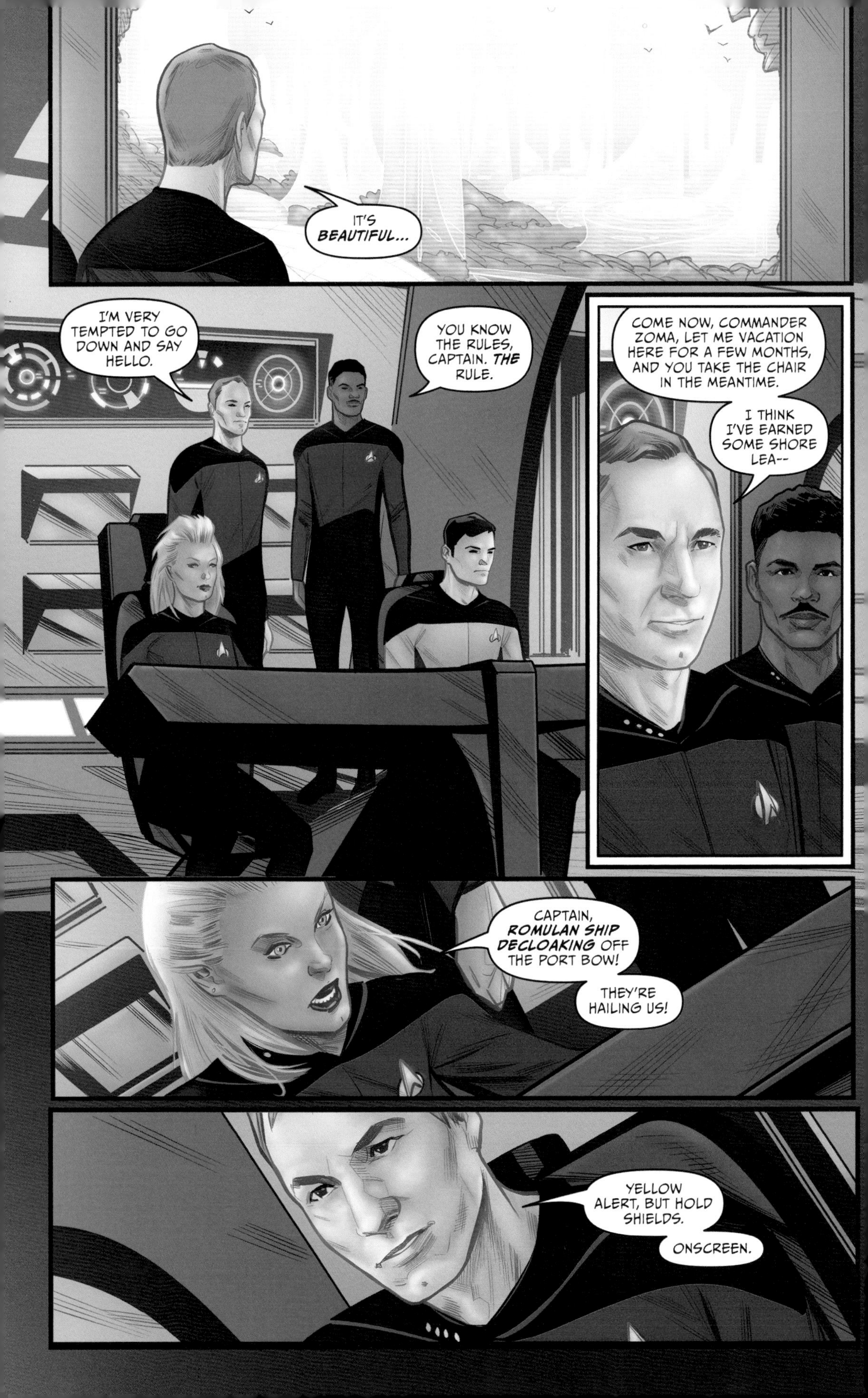

IT'S *BEAUTIFUL...*
I'M VERY TEMPTED TO GO DOWN AND SAY HELLO.
YOU KNOW THE RULES, CAPTAIN. *THE* RULE.
COME NOW, COMMANDER ZOMA, LET ME VACATION HERE FOR A FEW MONTHS, AND YOU TAKE THE CHAIR IN THE MEANTIME.
I THINK I'VE EARNED SOME SHORE LEA--
CAPTAIN, *ROMULAN SHIP DECLOAKING* OFF THE PORT BOW!
THEY'RE HAILING US!
YELLOW ALERT, BUT HOLD SHIELDS.
ONSCREEN.

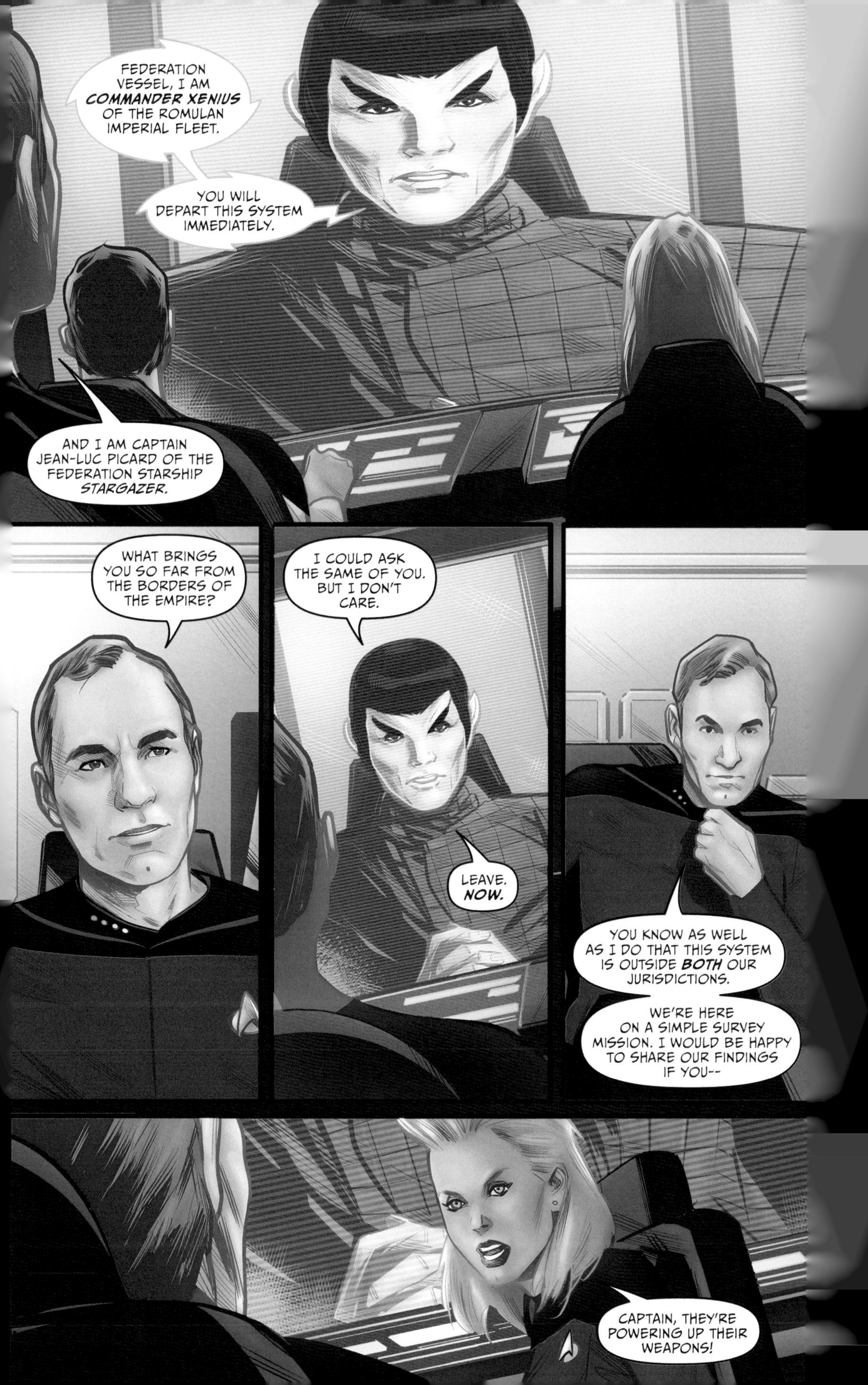
FEDERATION VESSEL, I AM COMMANDER XENIUS OF THE ROMULAN IMPERIAL FLEET.
YOU WILL DEPART THIS SYSTEM IMMEDIATELY.
AND I AM CAPTAIN JEAN-LUC PICARD OF THE FEDERATION STARSHIP STARGAZER.
WHAT BRINGS YOU SO FAR FROM THE BORDERS OF THE EMPIRE?
I COULD ASK THE SAME OF YOU. BUT I DON'T CARE.
LEAVE. NOW.
YOU KNOW AS WELL AS I DO THAT THIS SYSTEM IS OUTSIDE BOTH OUR JURISDICTIONS.
WE'RE HERE ON A SIMPLE SURVEY MISSION. I WOULD BE HAPPY TO SHARE OUR FINDINGS IF YOU--
CAPTAIN, THEY'RE POWERING UP THEIR WEAPONS!

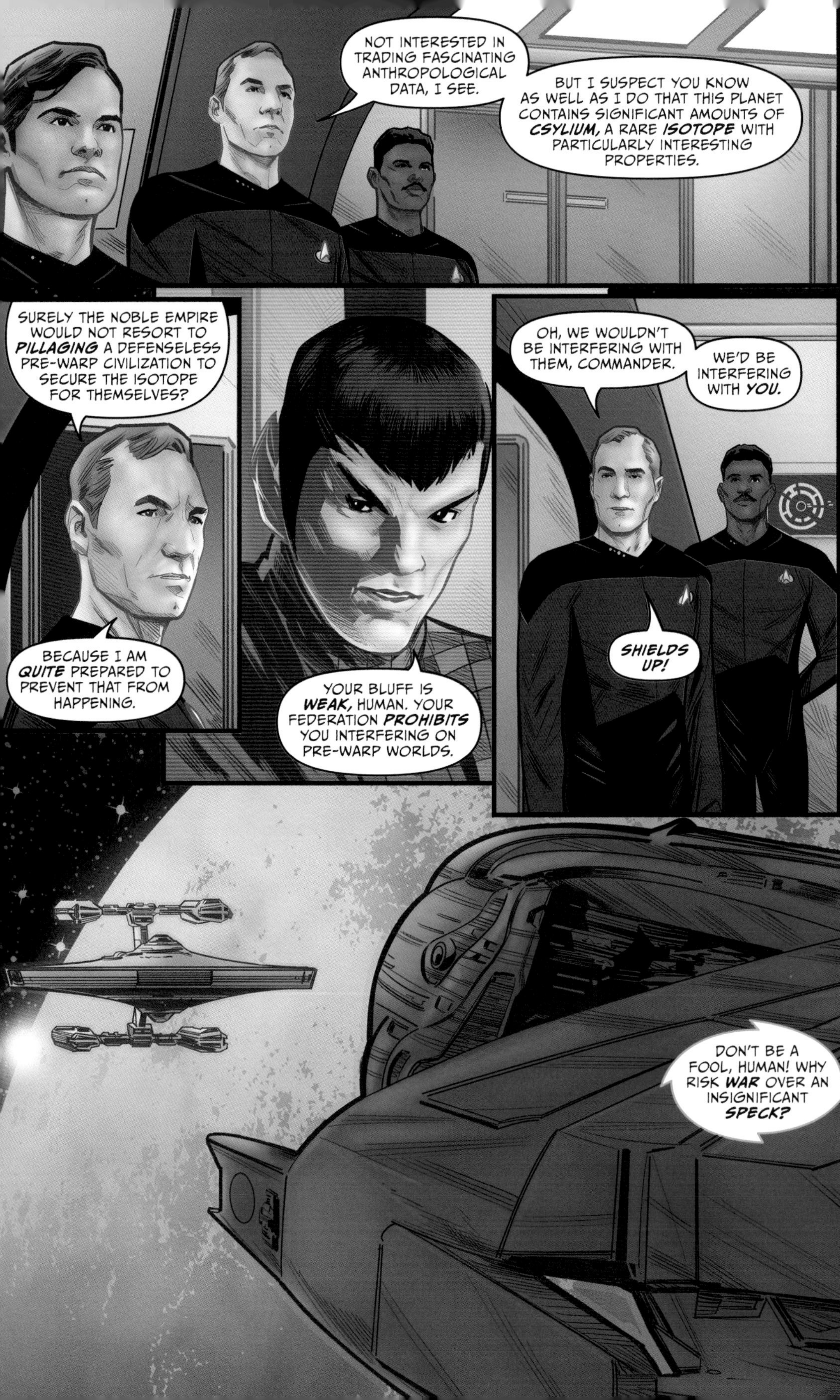
NOT INTERESTED IN TRADING FASCINATING ANTHROPOLOGICAL DATA, I SEE.
BUT I SUSPECT YOU KNOW AS WELL AS I DO THAT THIS PLANET CONTAINS SIGNIFICANT AMOUNTS OF ***CSYLIUM,*** A RARE ***ISOTOPE*** WITH PARTICULARLY INTERESTING PROPERTIES.
SURELY THE NOBLE EMPIRE WOULD NOT RESORT TO ***PILLAGING*** A DEFENSELESS PRE-WARP CIVILIZATION TO SECURE THE ISOTOPE FOR THEMSELVES?
BECAUSE I AM ***QUITE*** PREPARED TO PREVENT THAT FROM HAPPENING.
YOUR BLUFF IS ***WEAK,*** HUMAN. YOUR FEDERATION ***PROHIBITS*** YOU INTERFERING ON PRE-WARP WORLDS.
OH, WE WOULDN'T BE INTERFERING WITH THEM, COMMANDER.
WE'D BE INTERFERING WITH ***YOU.***
SHIELDS UP!
DON'T BE A FOOL, HUMAN! WHY RISK ***WAR*** OVER AN INSIGNIFICANT ***SPECK?***

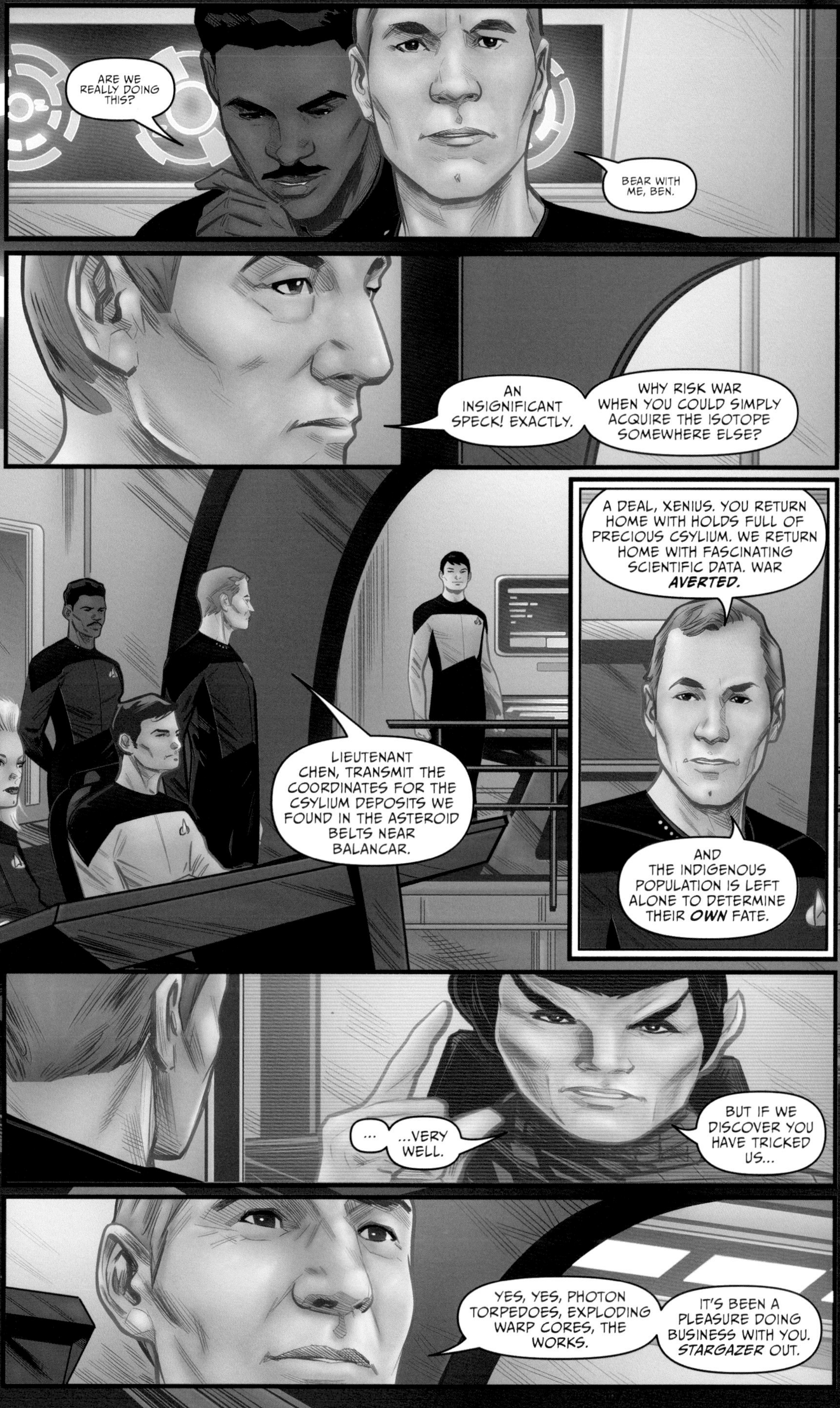
ARE WE REALLY DOING THIS?
BEAR WITH ME, BEN.
WHY RISK WAR WHEN YOU COULD SIMPLY ACQUIRE THE ISOTOPE SOMEWHERE ELSE?
AN INSIGNIFICANT SPECK! EXACTLY.
LIEUTENANT CHEN, TRANSMIT THE COORDINATES FOR THE CSYLIUM DEPOSITS WE FOUND IN THE ASTEROID BELTS NEAR BALANCAR.
A DEAL, XENIUS. YOU RETURN HOME WITH HOLDS FULL OF PRECIOUS CSYLIUM. WE RETURN HOME WITH FASCINATING SCIENTIFIC DATA. WAR ***AVERTED.***
AND THE INDIGENOUS POPULATION IS LEFT ALONE TO DETERMINE THEIR ***OWN*** FATE.
...
...VERY WELL.
BUT IF WE DISCOVER YOU HAVE TRICKED US...
YES, YES, PHOTON TORPEDOES, EXPLODING WARP CORES, THE WORKS.
IT'S BEEN A PLEASURE DOING BUSINESS WITH YOU. *STARGAZER* OUT.

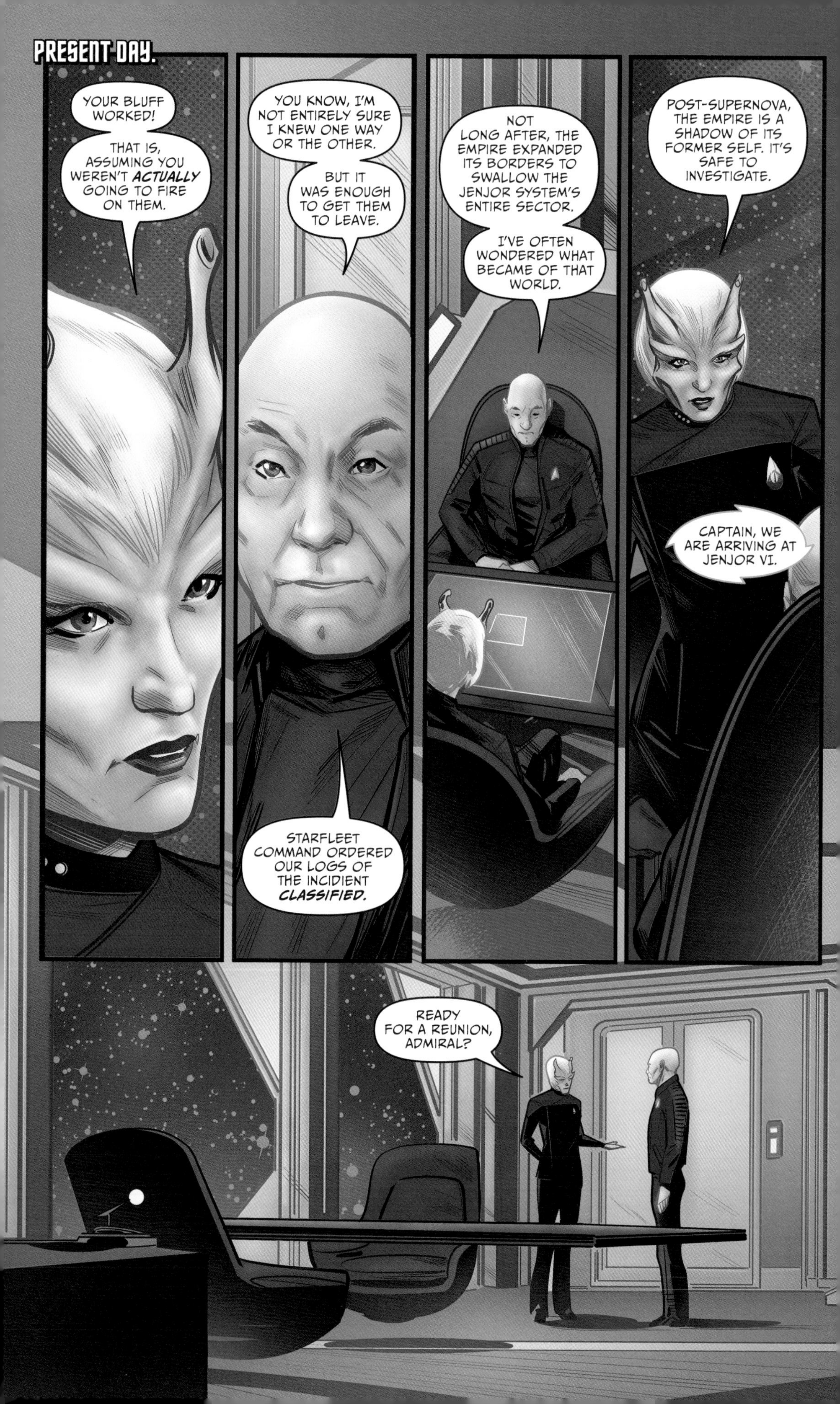
PRESENT DAY.
YOUR BLUFF WORKED!
THAT IS, ASSUMING YOU WEREN'T ACTUALLY GOING TO FIRE ON THEM.
YOU KNOW, I'M NOT ENTIRELY SURE I KNEW ONE WAY OR THE OTHER.
BUT IT WAS ENOUGH TO GET THEM TO LEAVE.
STARFLEET COMMAND ORDERED OUR LOGS OF THE INCIDIENT CLASSIFIED.
NOT LONG AFTER, THE EMPIRE EXPANDED ITS BORDERS TO SWALLOW THE JENJOR SYSTEM'S ENTIRE SECTOR.
I'VE OFTEN WONDERED WHAT BECAME OF THAT WORLD.
POST-SUPERNOVA, THE EMPIRE IS A SHADOW OF ITS FORMER SELF. IT'S SAFE TO INVESTIGATE.
CAPTAIN, WE ARE ARRIVING AT JENJOR VI.
READY FOR A REUNION, ADMIRAL?

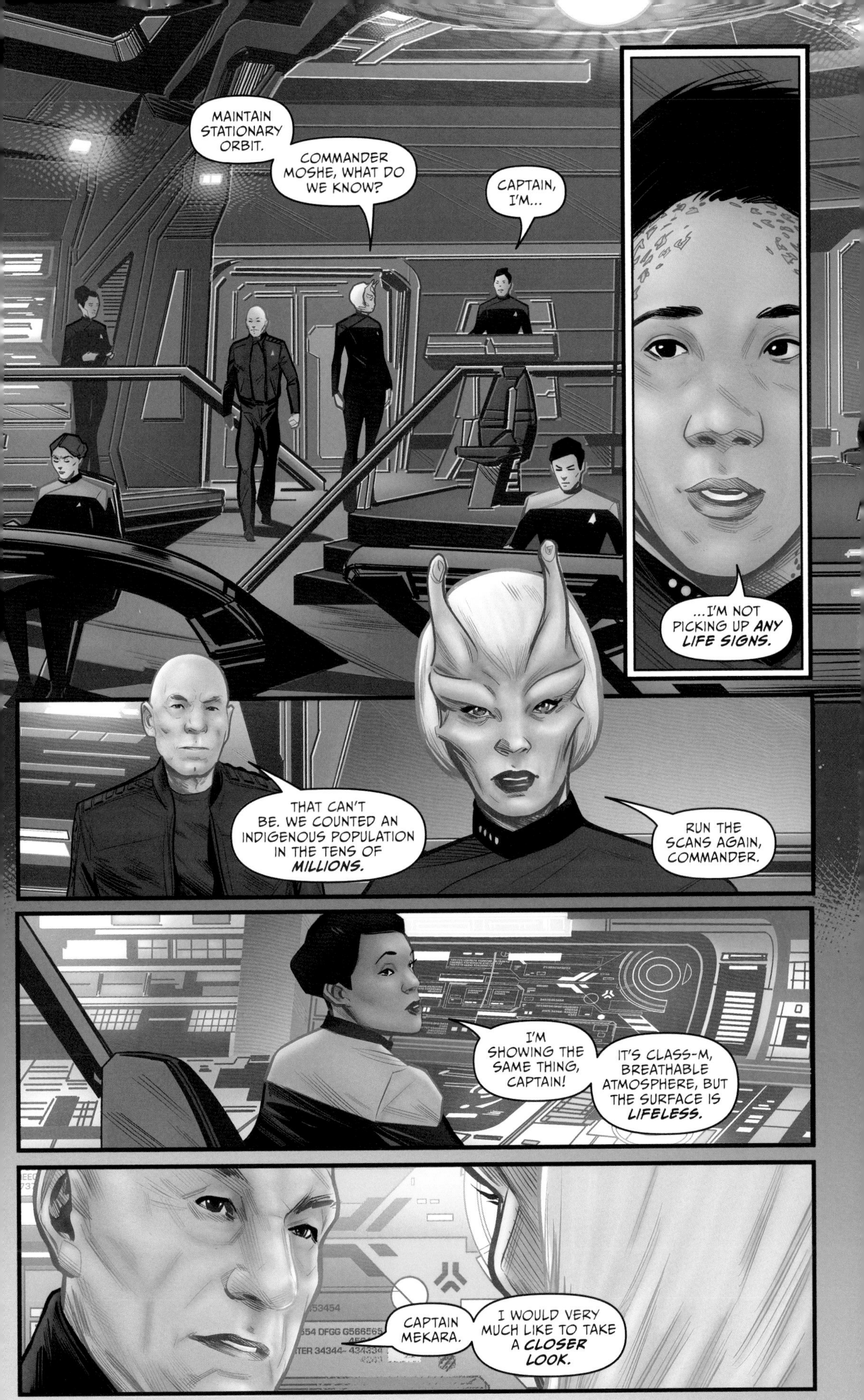
MAINTAIN STATIONARY ORBIT.
COMMANDER MOSHE, WHAT DO WE KNOW?
CAPTAIN, I'M...
...I'M NOT PICKING UP ANY LIFE SIGNS.
THAT CAN'T BE. WE COUNTED AN INDIGENOUS POPULATION IN THE TENS OF MILLIONS.
RUN THE SCANS AGAIN, COMMANDER.
I'M SHOWING THE SAME THING, CAPTAIN!
IT'S CLASS-M, BREATHABLE ATMOSPHERE, BUT THE SURFACE IS LIFELESS.
CAPTAIN MEKARA.
I WOULD VERY MUCH LIKE TO TAKE A CLOSER LOOK.

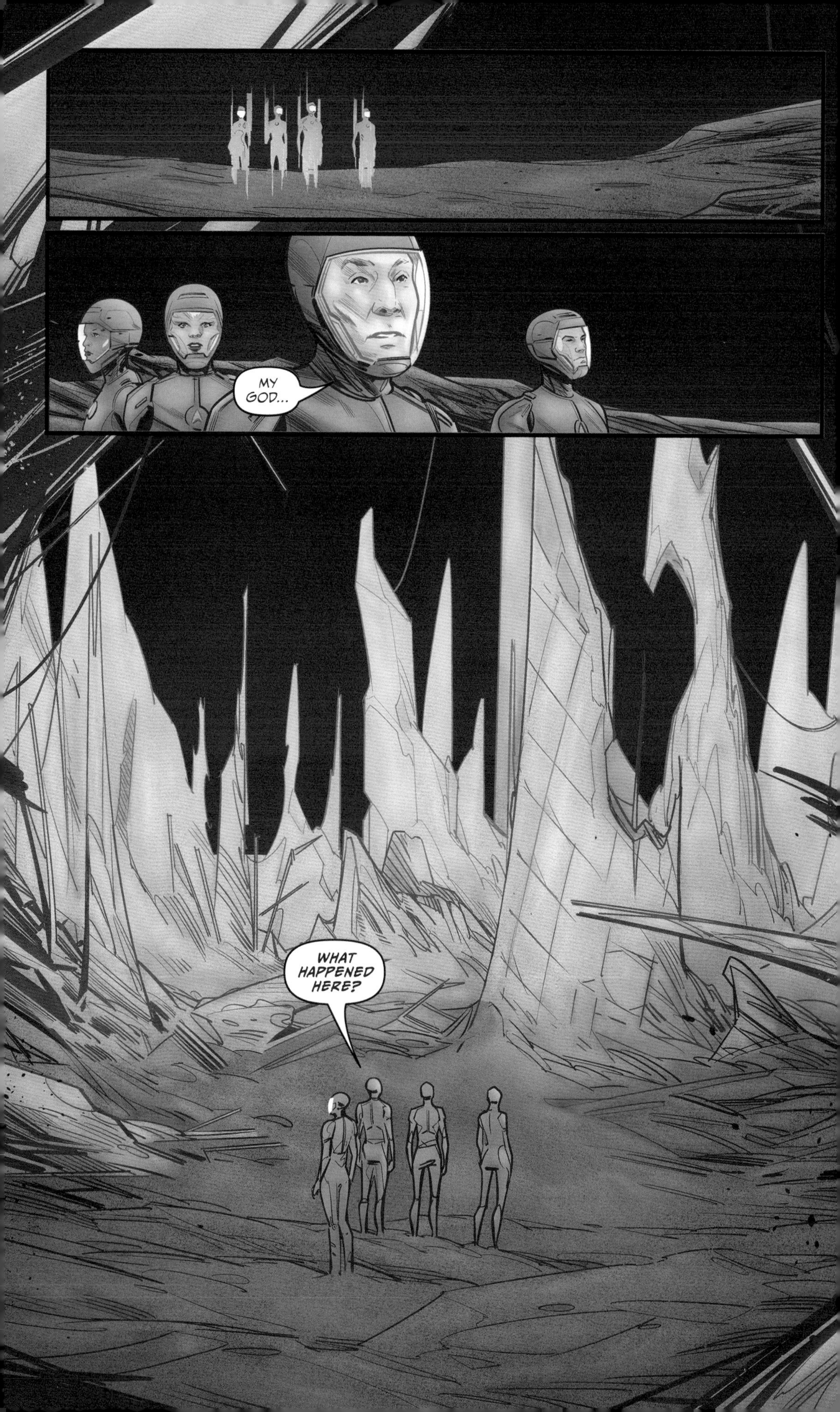
MY GOD...
WHAT HAPPENED HERE?

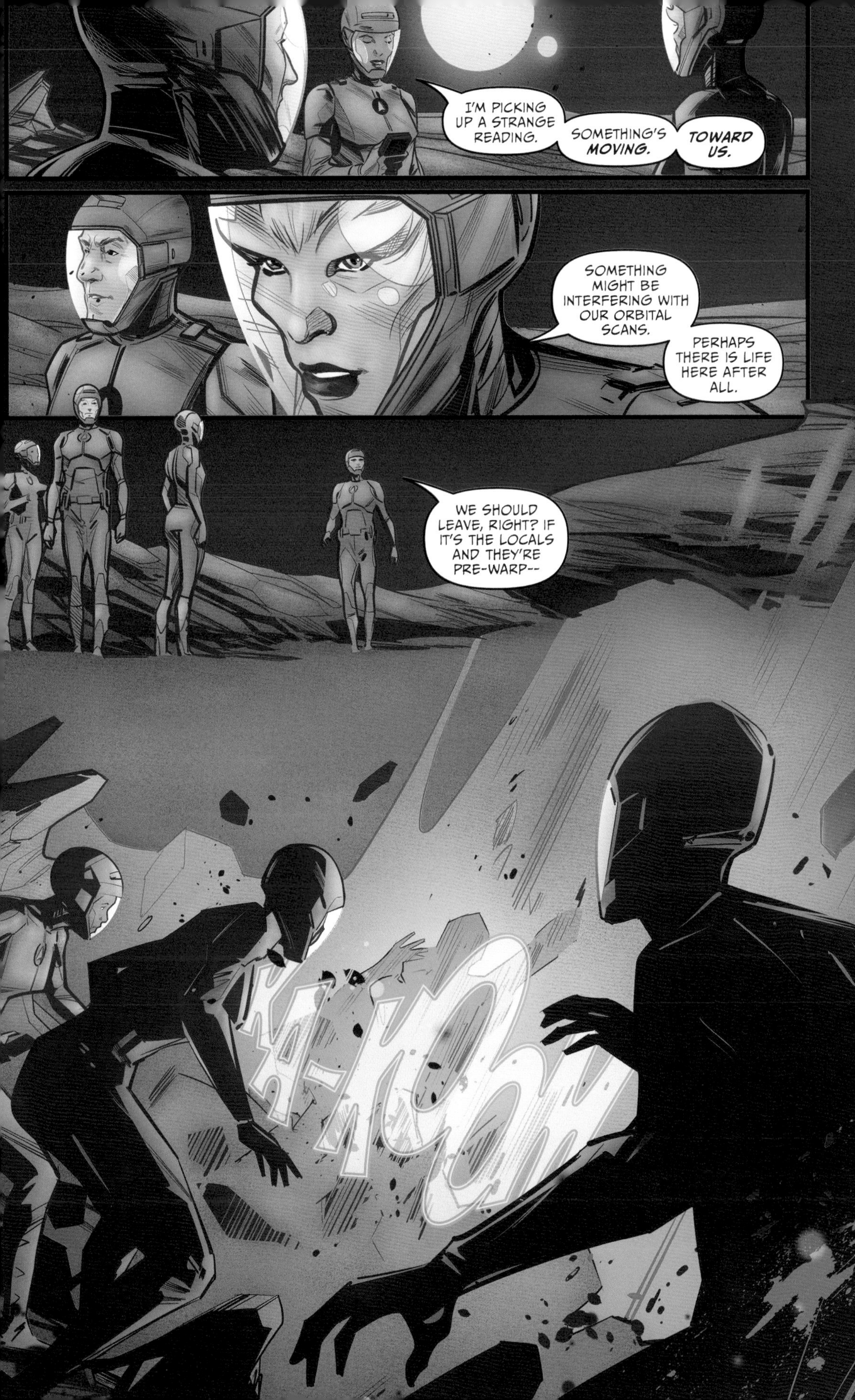

I'M PICKING UP A STRANGE READING.
SOMETHING'S MOVING.
TOWARD US.
SOMETHING MIGHT BE INTERFERING WITH OUR ORBITAL SCANS.
PERHAPS THERE IS LIFE HERE AFTER ALL.
WE SHOULD LEAVE, RIGHT? IF IT'S THE LOCALS AND THEY'RE PRE-WARP--
KA-BOOM

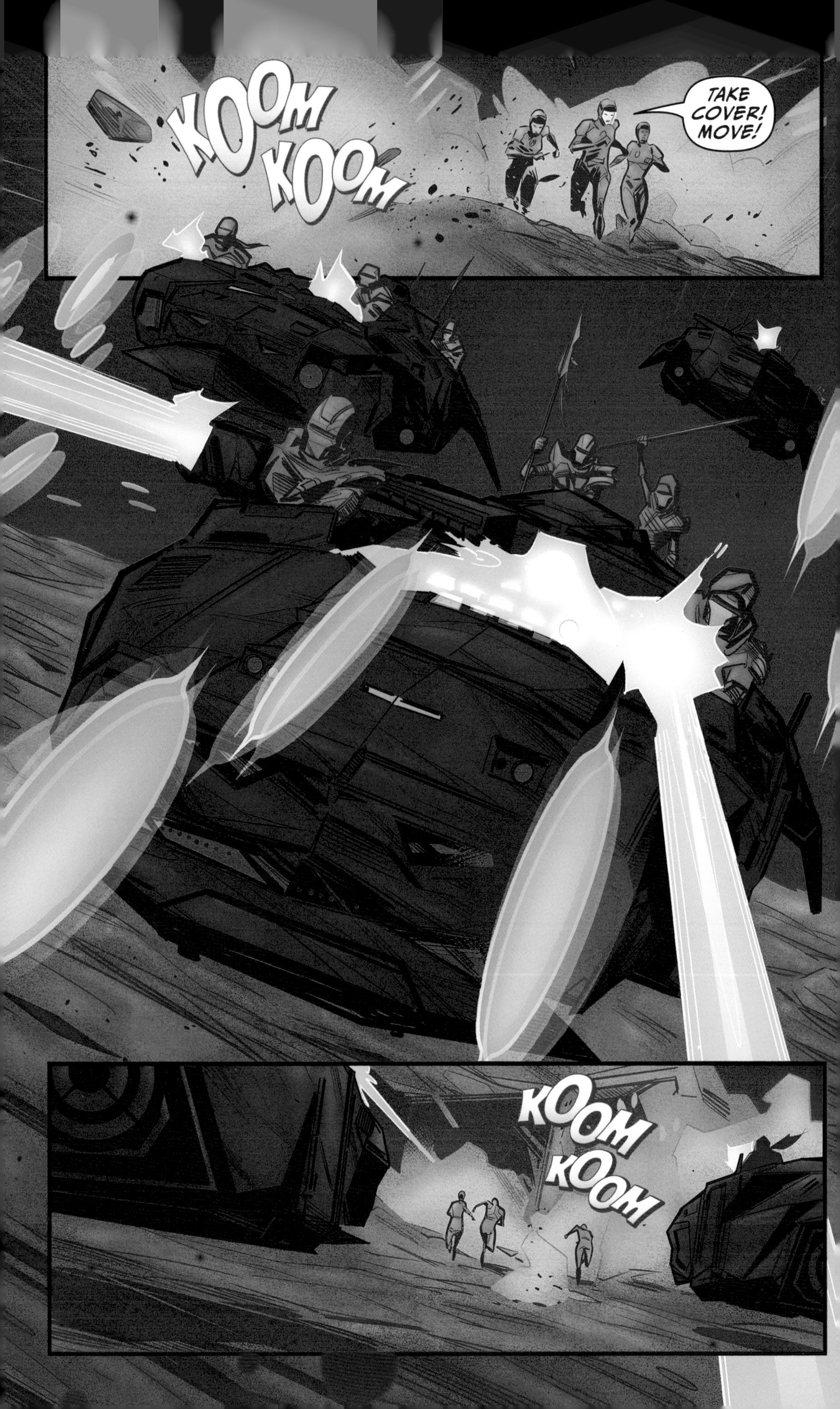
KOOM
KOOM
TAKE COVER! MOVE!
KOOM
KOOM

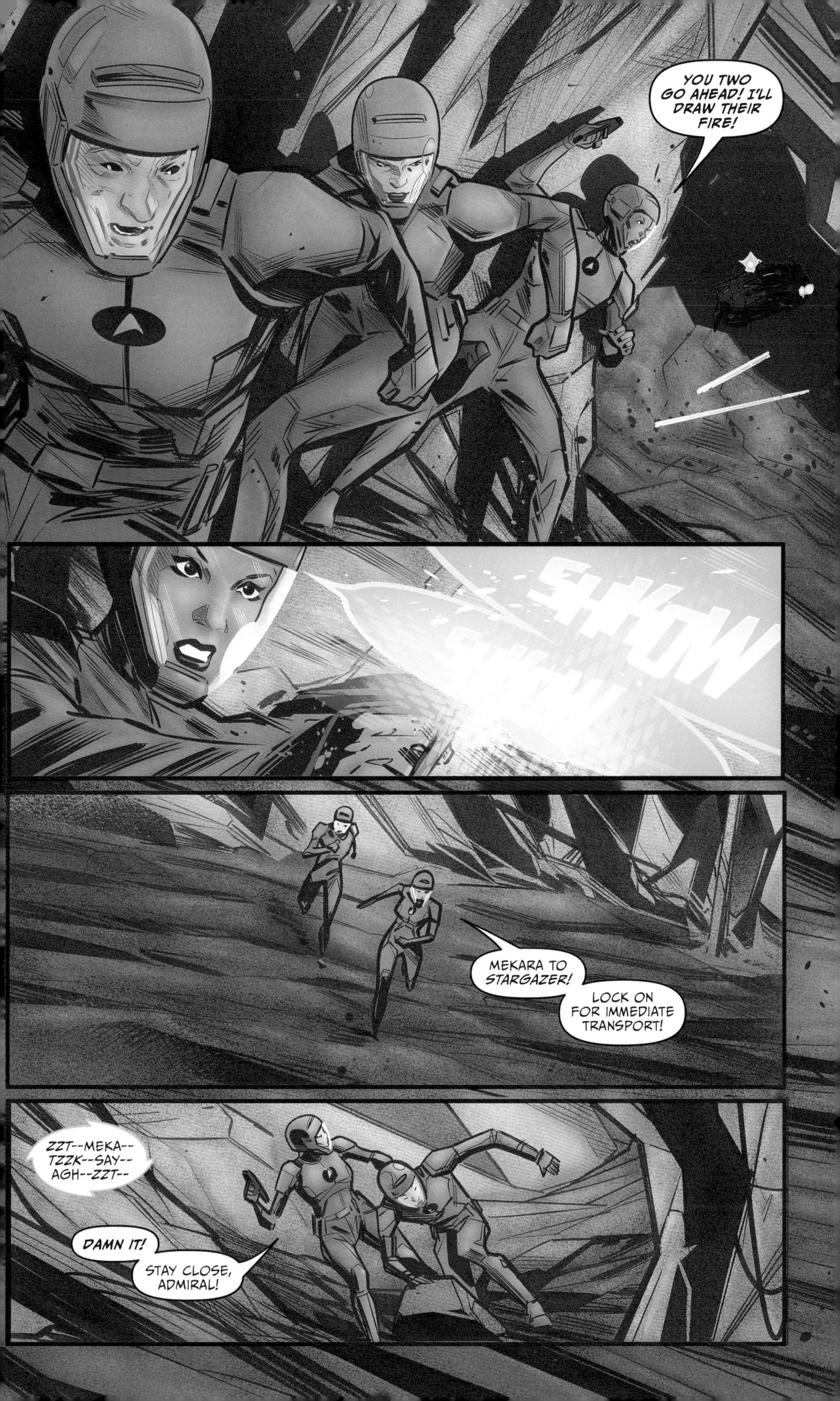
YOU TWO GO AHEAD! I'LL DRAW THEIR FIRE!
SHOW
MEKARA TO STARGAZER!
LOCK ON FOR IMMEDIATE TRANSPORT!
ZZT--MEKA-- TZZK--SAY-- AGH--ZZT--
DAMN IT!
STAY CLOSE, ADMIRAL!

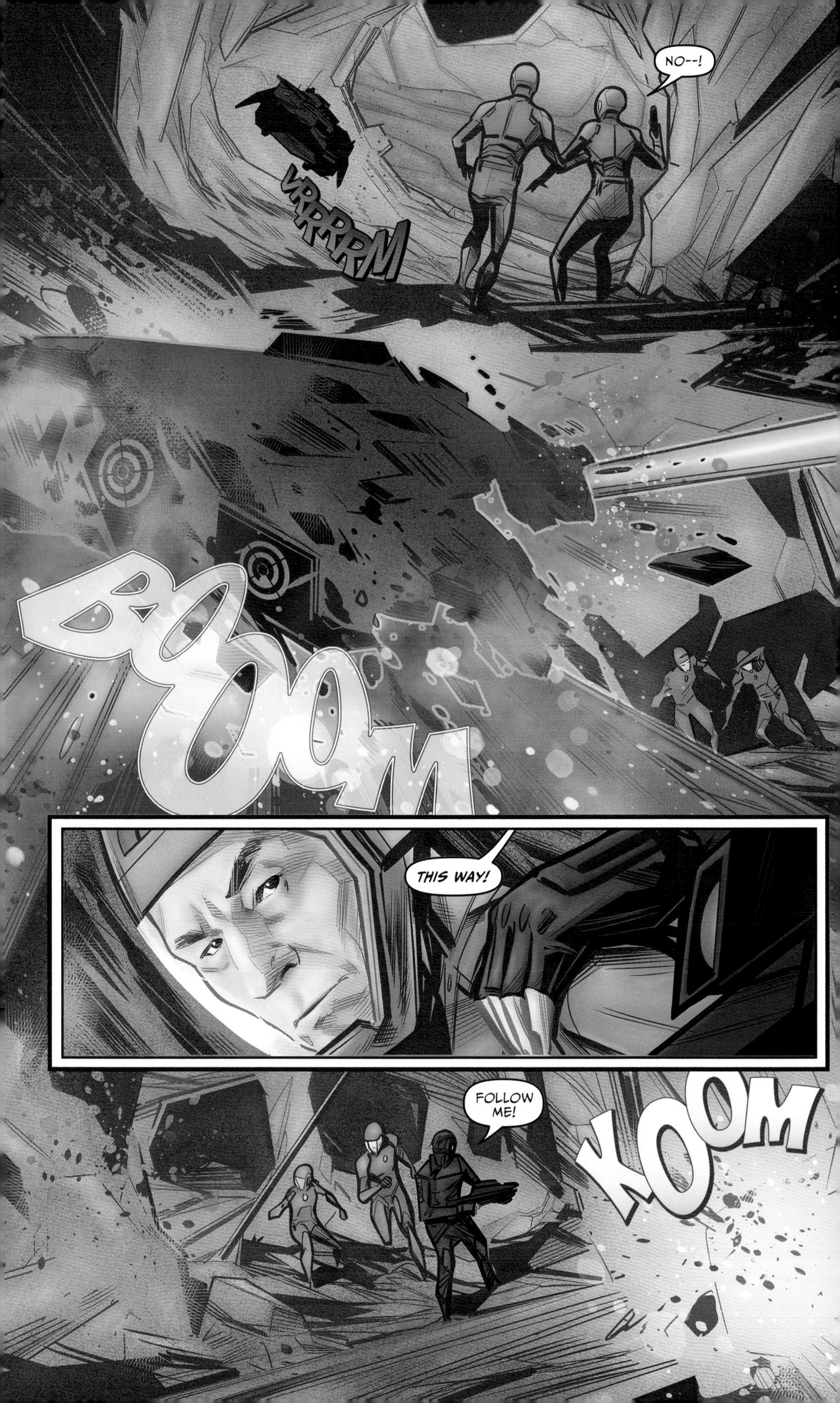
NO--!
VRRRRM
BOOM
THIS WAY!
FOLLOW ME!
KOOOM

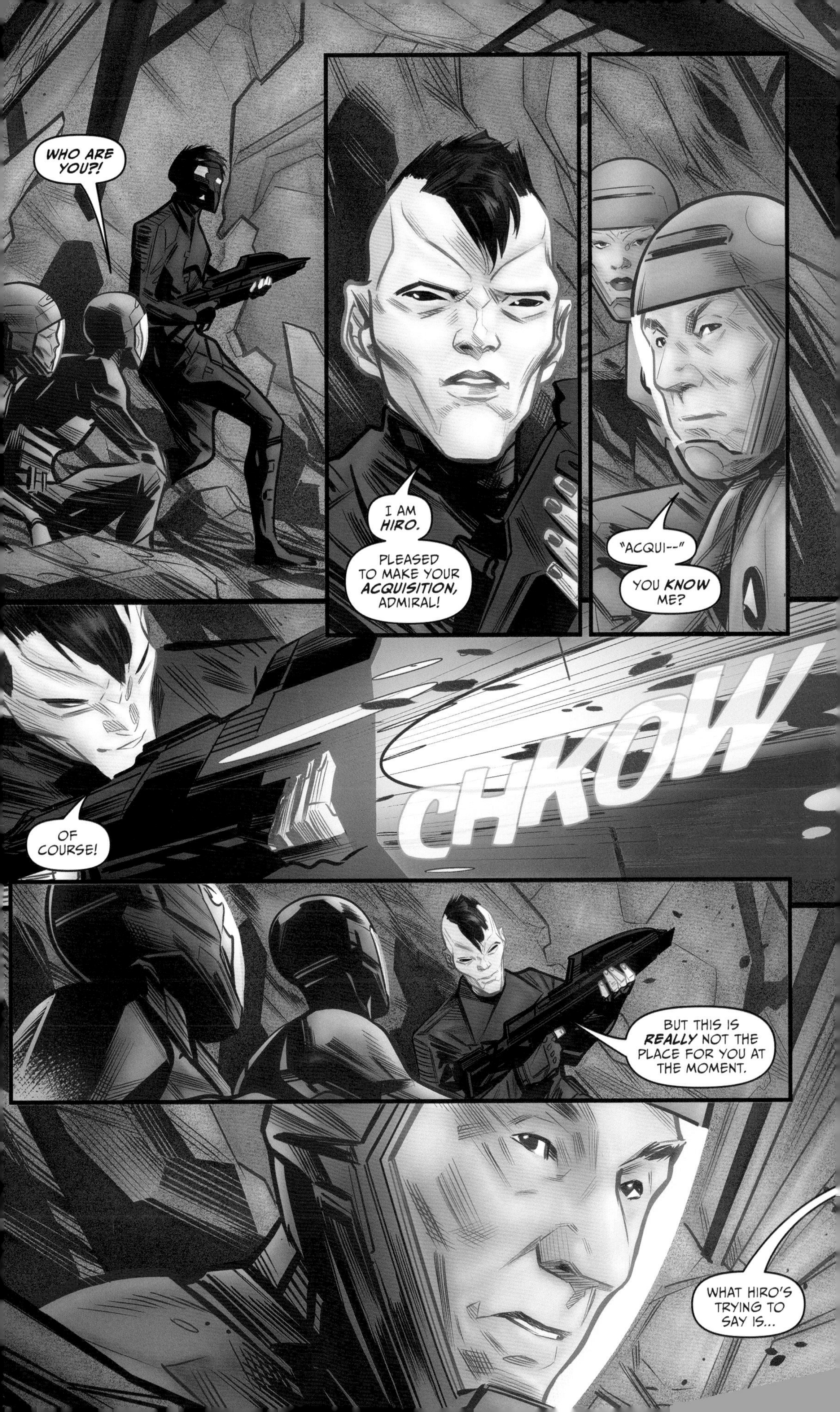
WHO ARE YOU?!
I AM HIRO.
PLEASED TO MAKE YOUR ACQUISITION, ADMIRAL!
"ACQUI--"
YOU KNOW ME?
OF COURSE!
CHKOW
BUT THIS IS REALLY NOT THE PLACE FOR YOU AT THE MOMENT.
WHAT HIRO'S TRYING TO SAY IS...

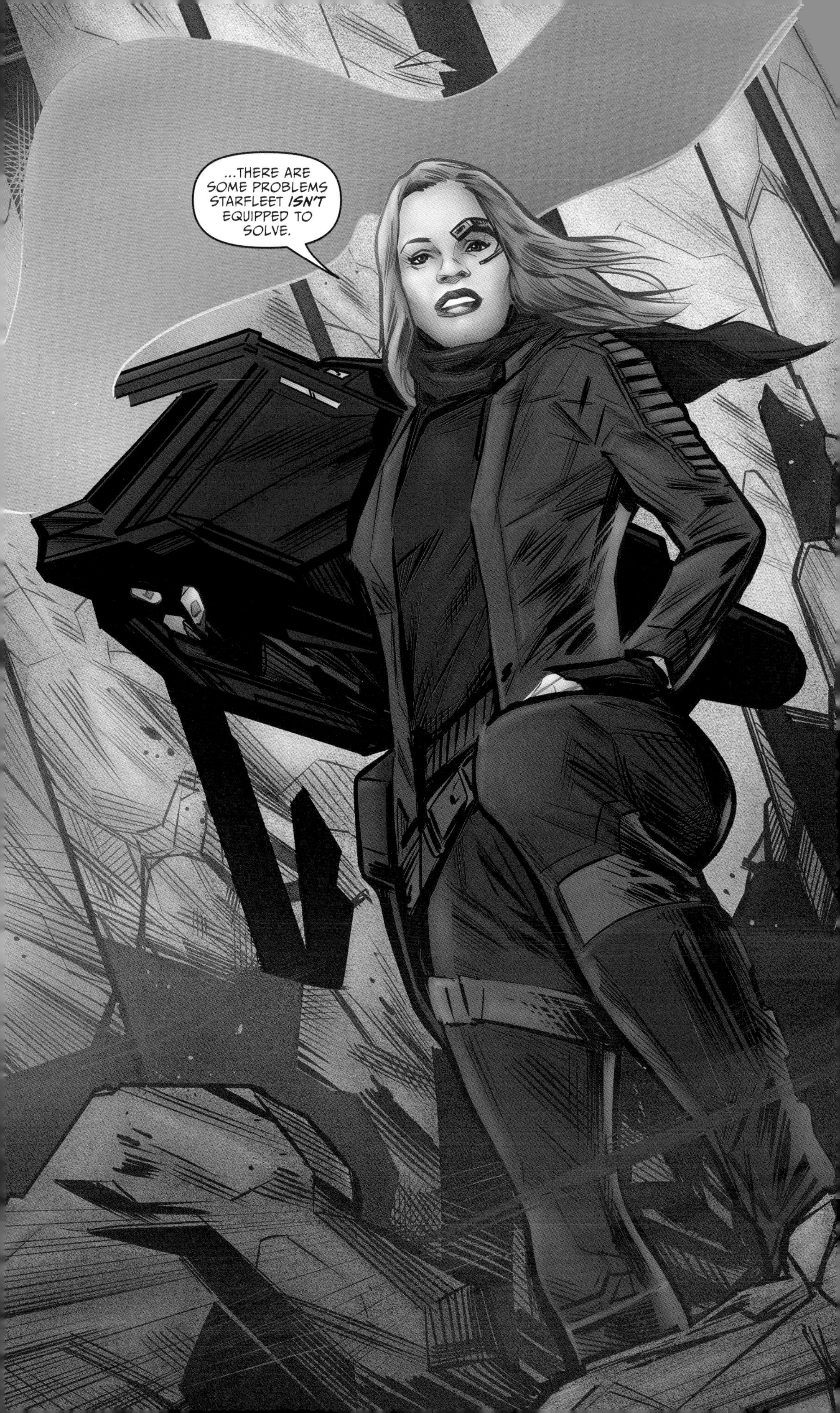
...THERE ARE SOME PROBLEMS STARFLEET ISN'T EQUIPPED TO SOLVE.

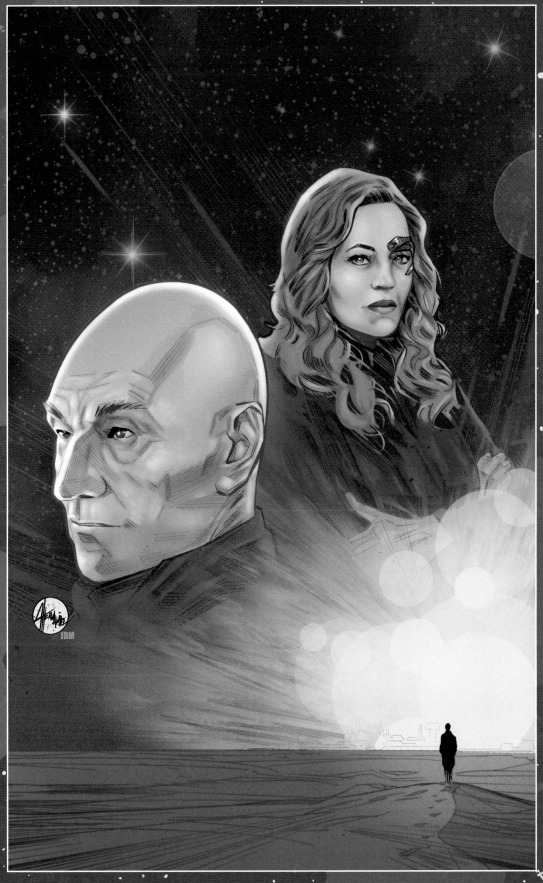

art by ANGEL HERNANDEZ | colors by J.D. METTLER

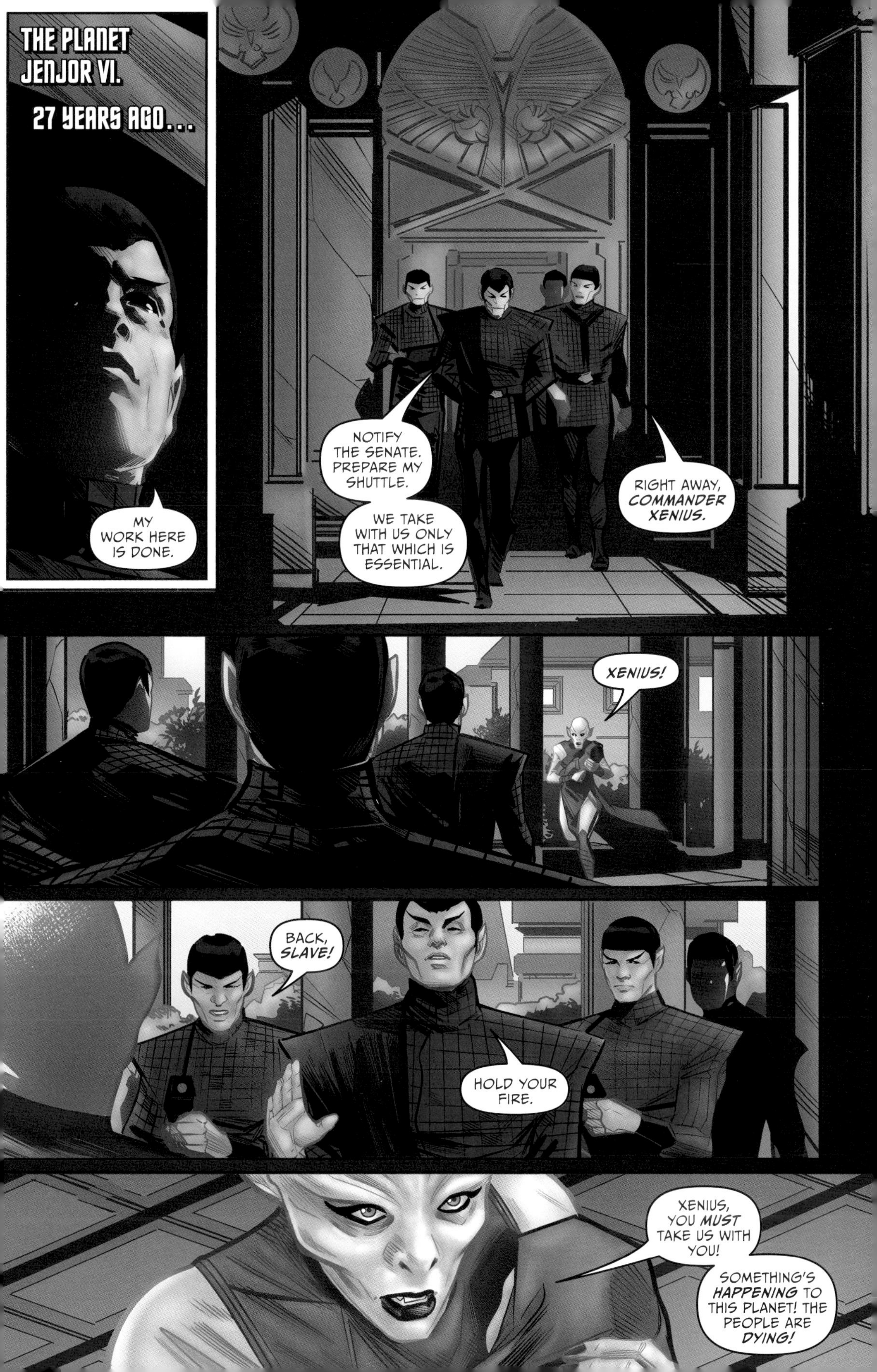
THE PLANET JENJOR VI.
27 YEARS AGO...
MY WORK HERE IS DONE.
NOTIFY THE SENATE. PREPARE MY SHUTTLE.
WE TAKE WITH US ONLY THAT WHICH IS ESSENTIAL.
RIGHT AWAY, COMMANDER XENIUS.
XENIUS!
BACK, SLAVE!
HOLD YOUR FIRE.
XENIUS, YOU MUST TAKE US WITH YOU!
SOMETHING'S HAPPENING TO THIS PLANET! THE PEOPLE ARE DYING!

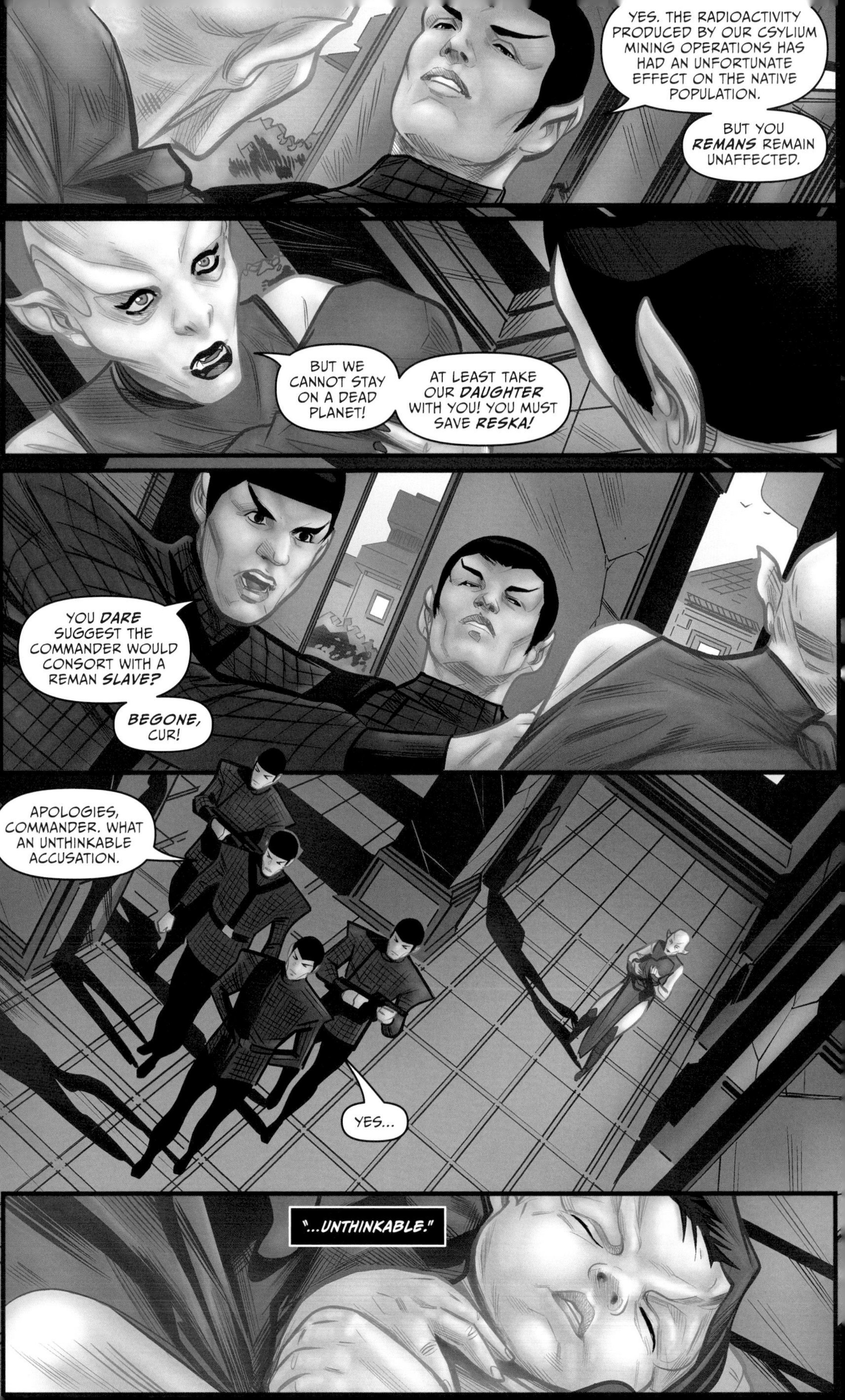
YES. THE RADIOACTIVITY PRODUCED BY OUR CSYLIUM MINING OPERATIONS HAS HAD AN UNFORTUNATE EFFECT ON THE NATIVE POPULATION.
BUT YOU REMANS REMAIN UNAFFECTED.
BUT WE CANNOT STAY ON A DEAD PLANET!
AT LEAST TAKE OUR DAUGHTER WITH YOU! YOU MUST SAVE RESKA!
YOU DARE SUGGEST THE COMMANDER WOULD CONSORT WITH A REMAN SLAVE?
BEGONE, CUR!
APOLOGIES, COMMANDER. WHAT AN UNTHINKABLE ACCUSATION.
YES...
"...UNTHINKABLE."

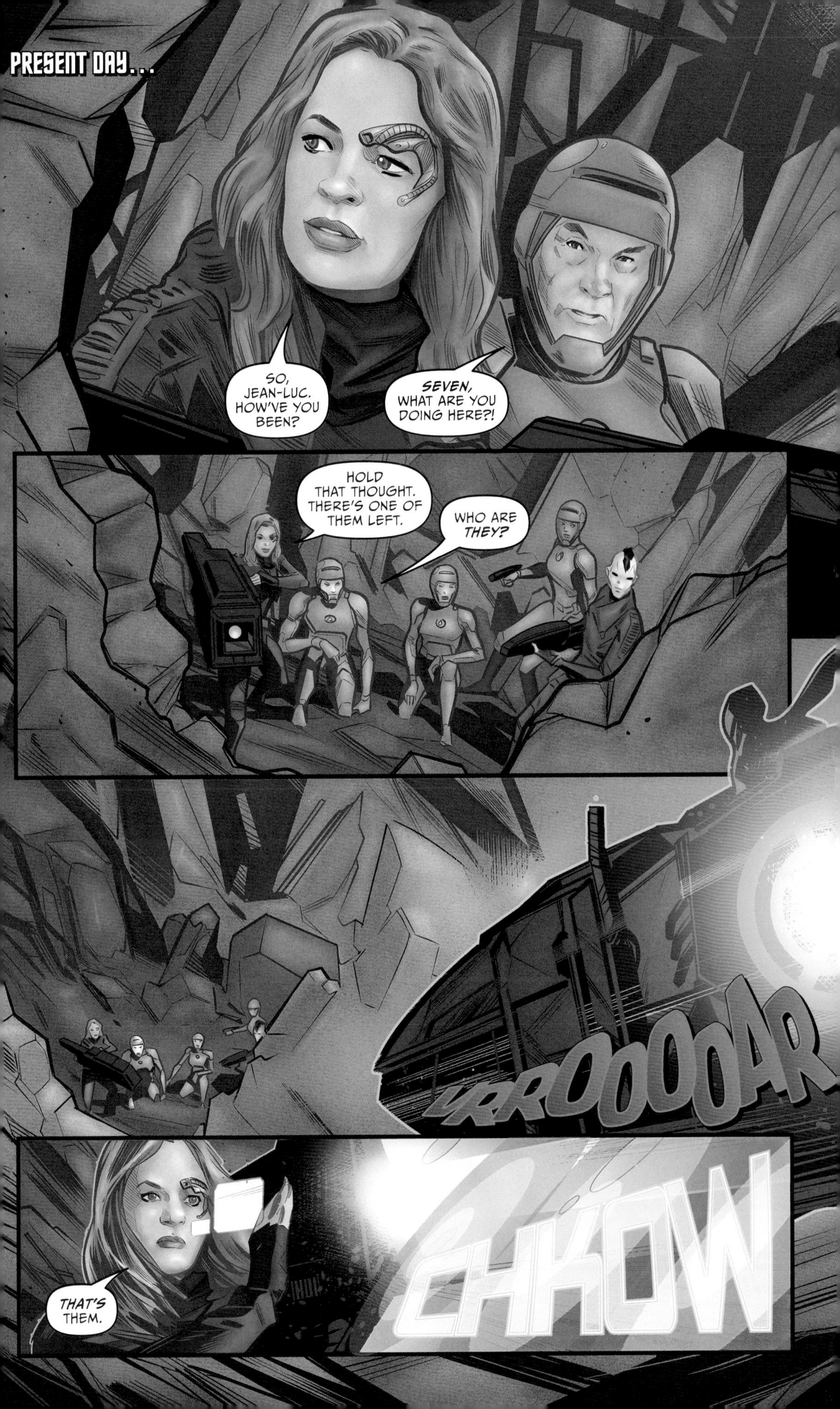
PRESENT DAY...
SO, JEAN-LUC. HOW'VE YOU BEEN?
SEVEN, WHAT ARE YOU DOING HERE?!
HOLD THAT THOUGHT. THERE'S ONE OF THEM LEFT.
WHO ARE THEY?
VRROOOOOAR
CHKOW
THAT'S THEM.

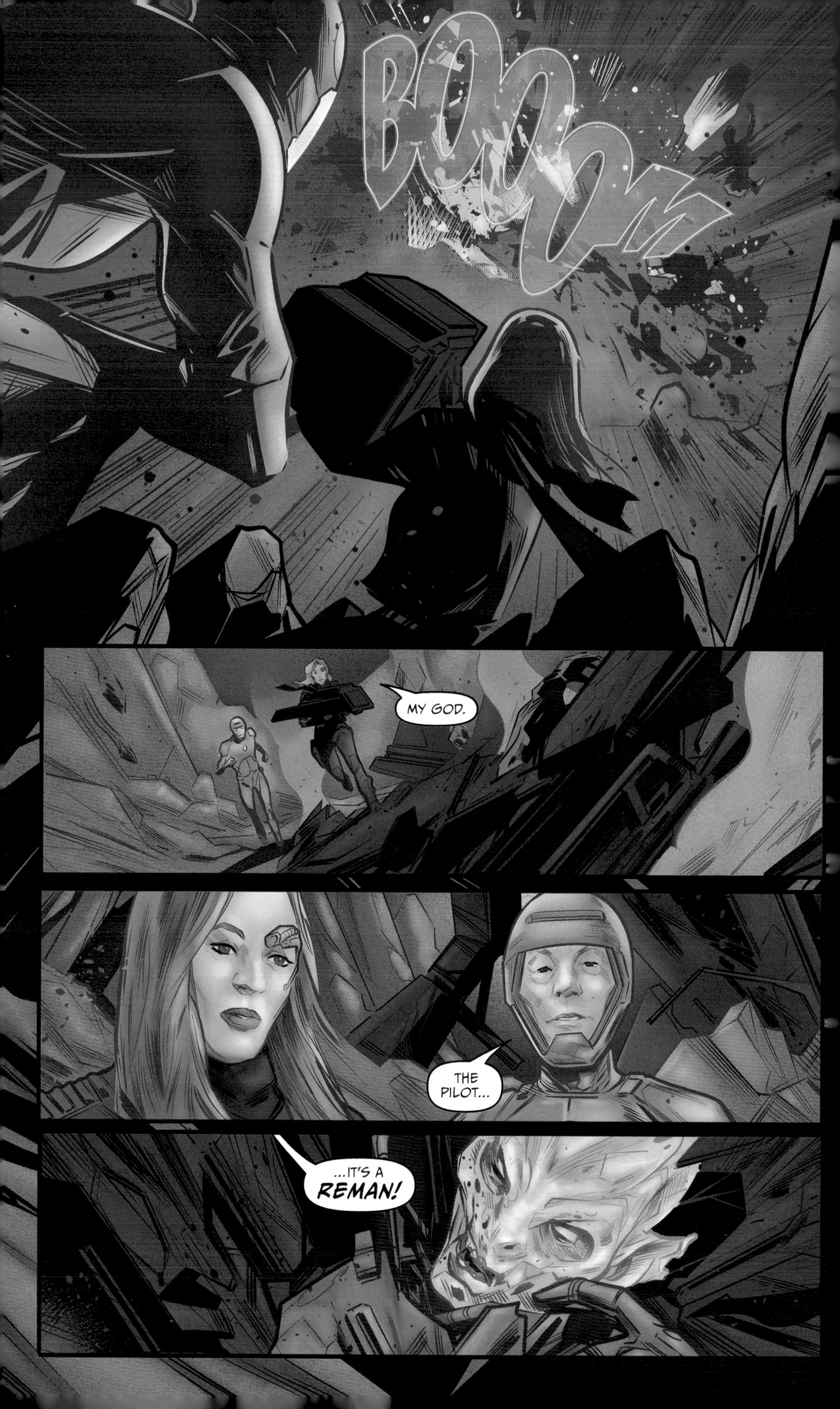
BOOOM
MY GOD.
THE PILOT...
...IT'S A REMAN!

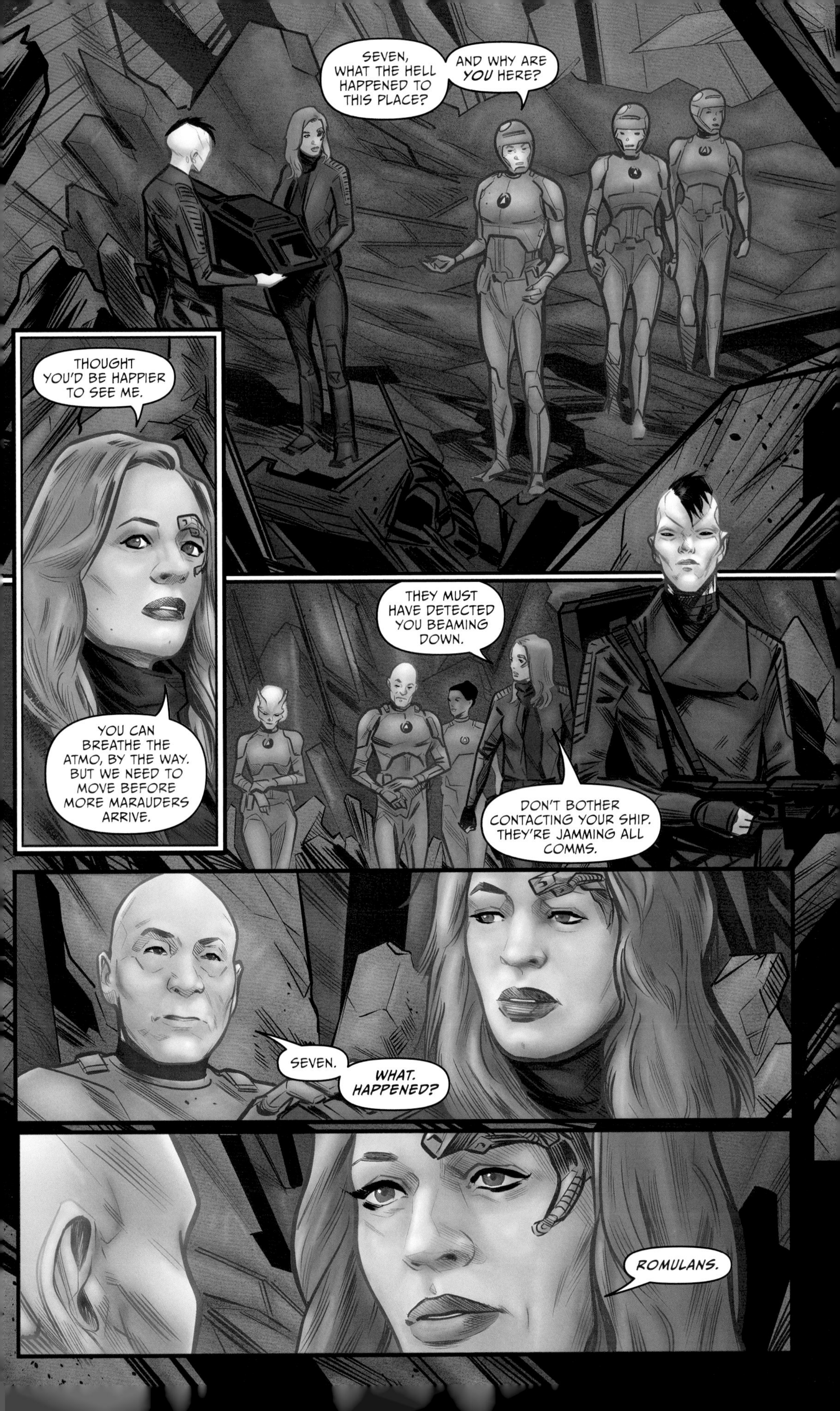
SEVEN, WHAT THE HELL HAPPENED TO THIS PLACE?
AND WHY ARE *YOU* HERE?
THOUGHT YOU'D BE HAPPIER TO SEE ME.
YOU CAN BREATHE THE ATMO, BY THE WAY. BUT WE NEED TO MOVE BEFORE MORE MARAUDERS ARRIVE.
THEY MUST HAVE DETECTED YOU BEAMING DOWN.
DON'T BOTHER CONTACTING YOUR SHIP. THEY'RE JAMMING ALL COMMS.
SEVEN.
WHAT. HAPPENED?
ROMULANS.

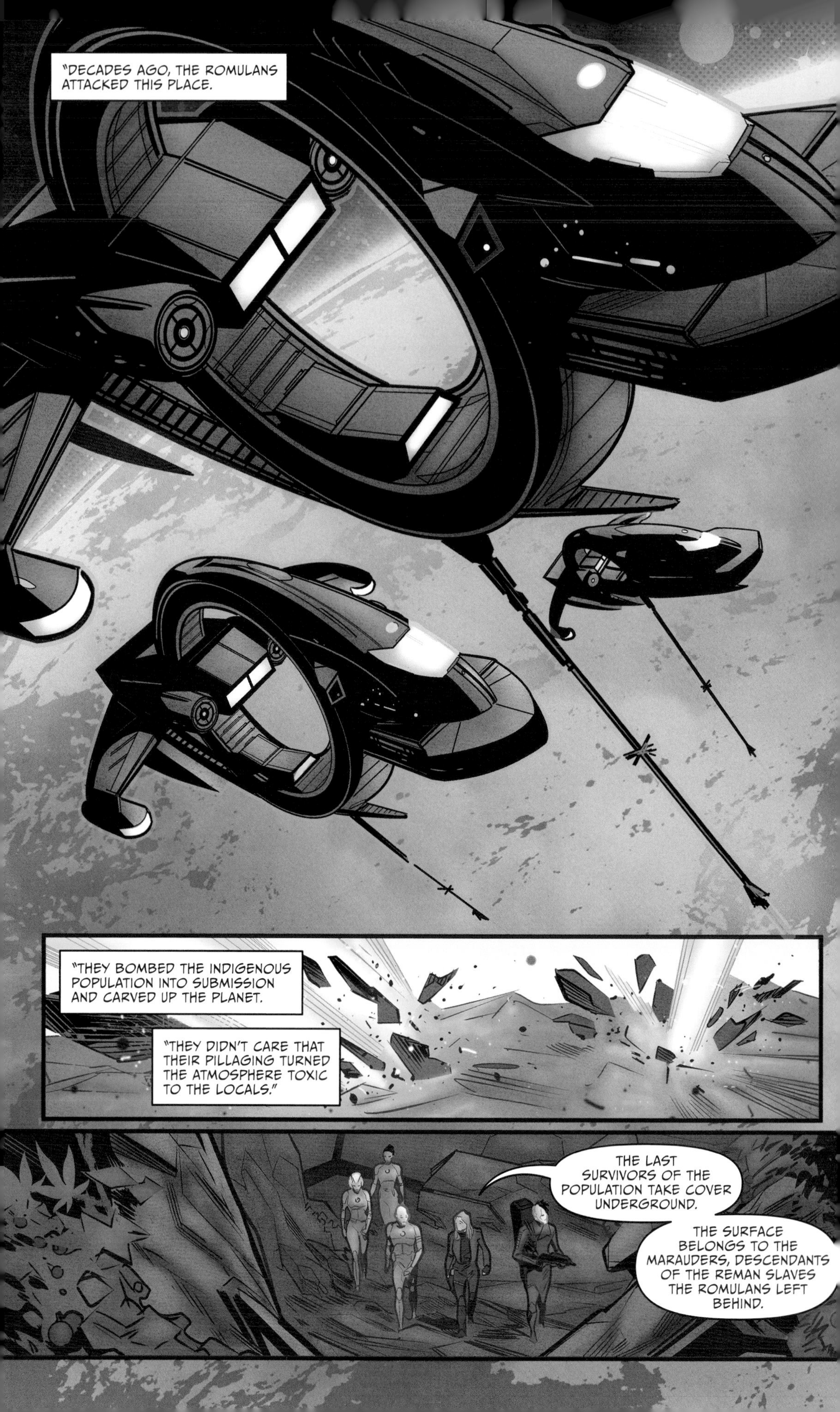
"DECADES AGO, THE ROMULANS ATTACKED THIS PLACE.
"THEY BOMBED THE INDIGENOUS POPULATION INTO SUBMISSION AND CARVED UP THE PLANET.
"THEY DIDN'T CARE THAT THEIR PILLAGING TURNED THE ATMOSPHERE TOXIC TO THE LOCALS."
THE LAST SURVIVORS OF THE POPULATION TAKE COVER UNDERGROUND.
THE SURFACE BELONGS TO THE MARAUDERS, DESCENDANTS OF THE REMAN SLAVES THE ROMULANS LEFT BEHIND.

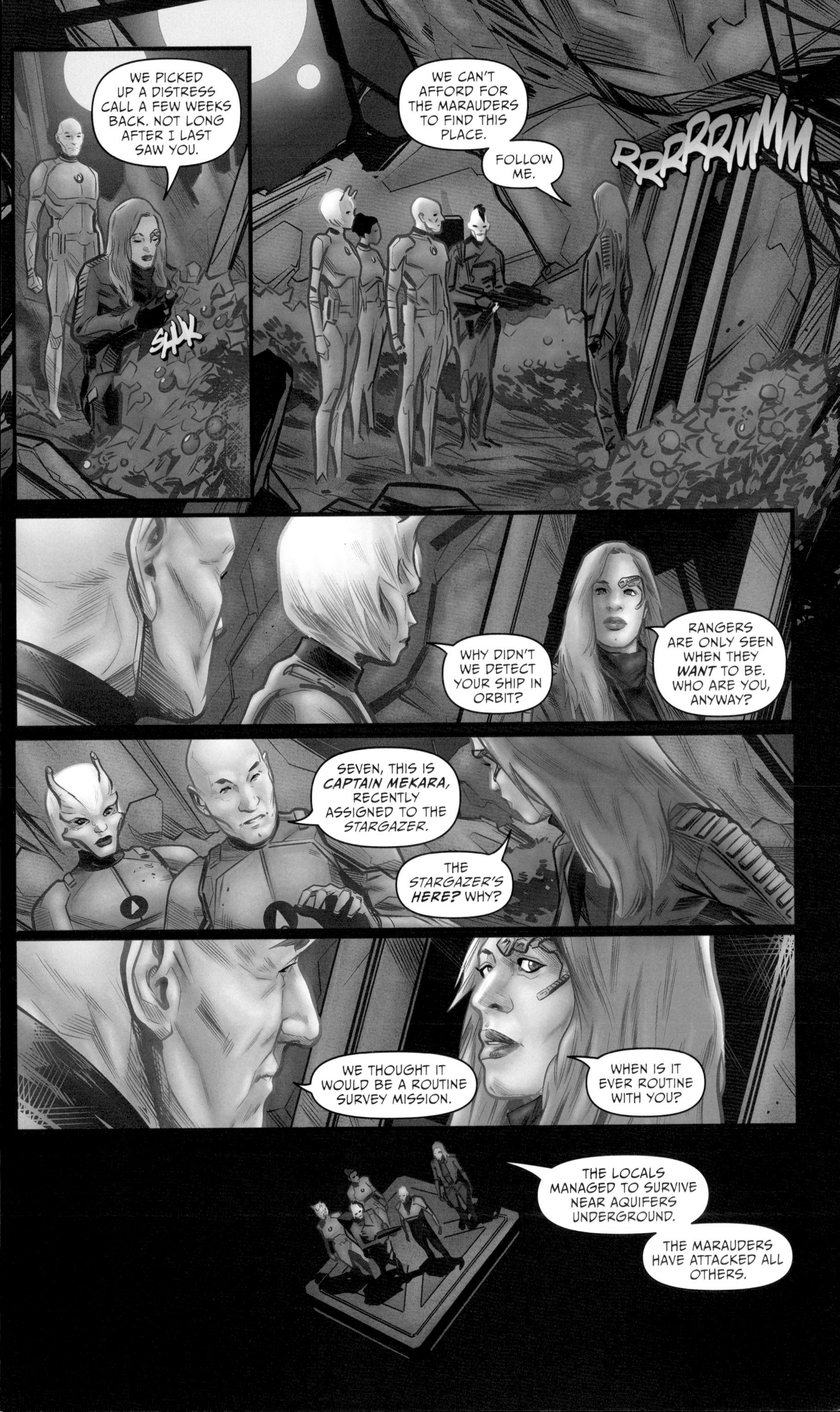
WE PICKED UP A DISTRESS CALL A FEW WEEKS BACK. NOT LONG AFTER I LAST SAW YOU.
SHK
WE CAN'T AFFORD FOR THE MARAUDERS TO FIND THIS PLACE.
FOLLOW ME.
RRRRRMMM
WHY DIDN'T WE DETECT YOUR SHIP IN ORBIT?
RANGERS ARE ONLY SEEN WHEN THEY WANT TO BE. WHO ARE YOU, ANYWAY?
SEVEN, THIS IS CAPTAIN MEKARA, RECENTLY ASSIGNED TO THE STARGAZER.
THE STARGAZER'S HERE? WHY?
WE THOUGHT IT WOULD BE A ROUTINE SURVEY MISSION.
WHEN IS IT EVER ROUTINE WITH YOU?
THE LOCALS MANAGED TO SURVIVE NEAR AQUIFERS UNDERGROUND.
THE MARAUDERS HAVE ATTACKED ALL OTHERS.

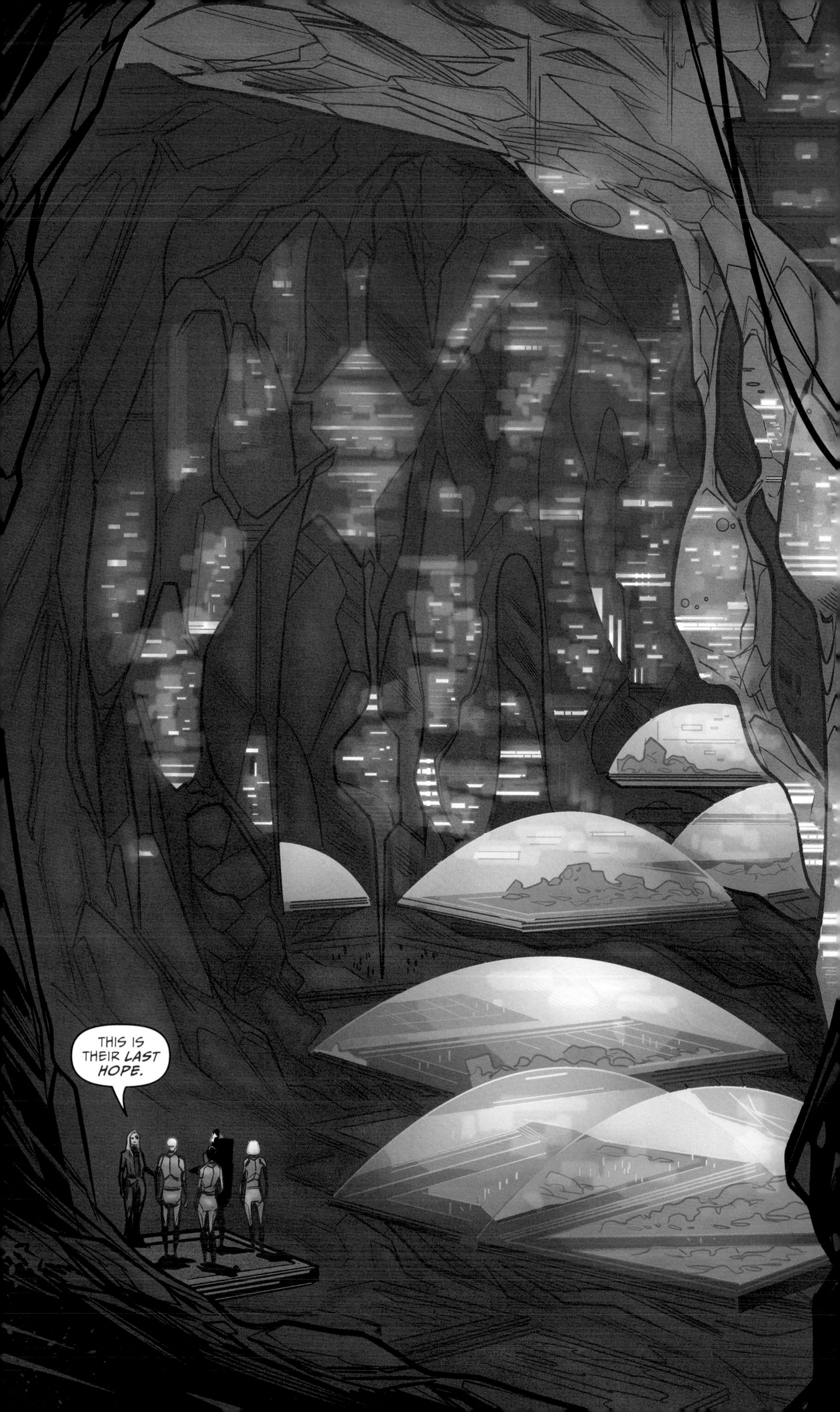
THIS IS THEIR LAST HOPE.

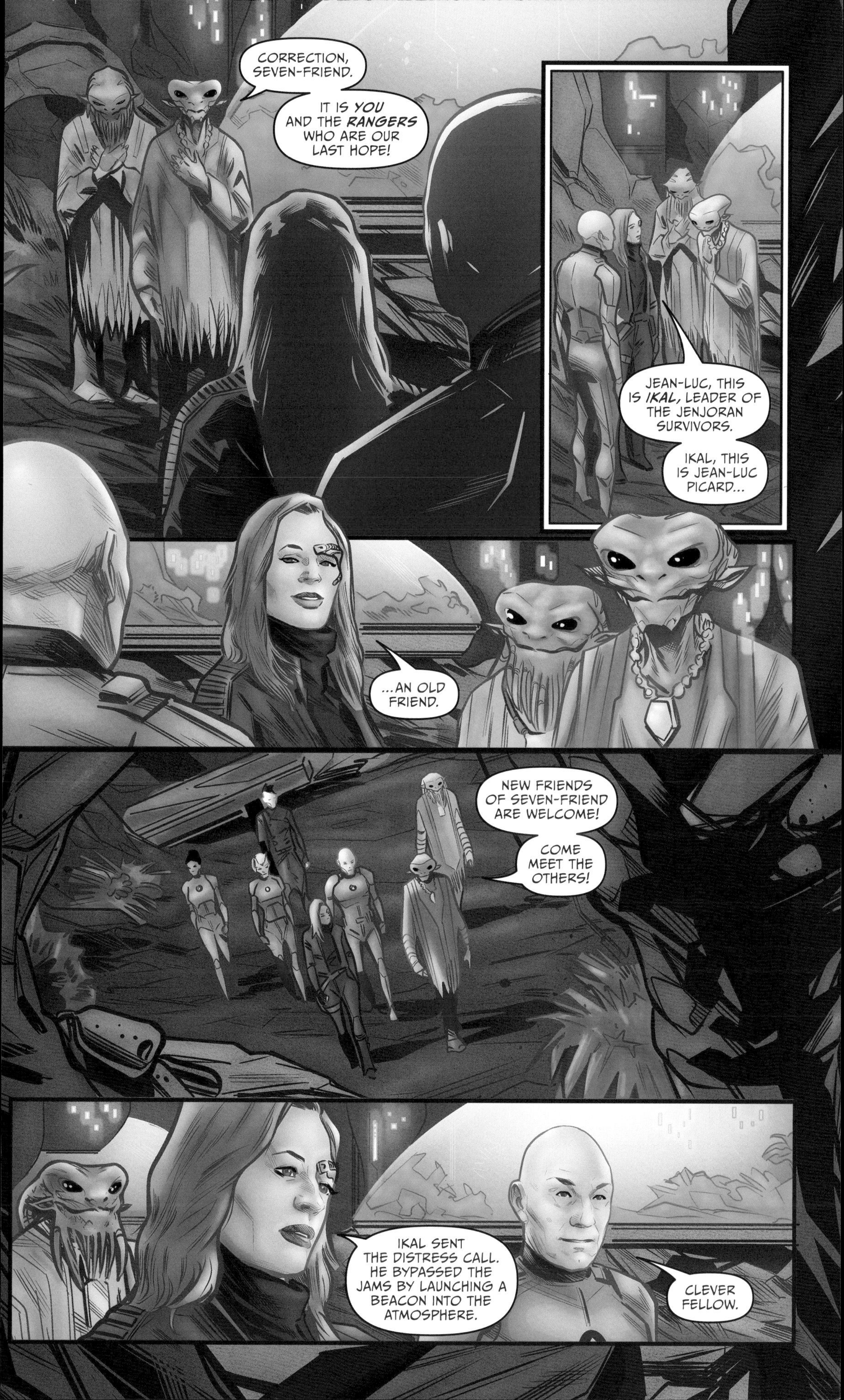
CORRECTION, SEVEN-FRIEND.
IT IS *YOU* AND THE ***RANGERS*** WHO ARE OUR LAST HOPE!
JEAN-LUC, THIS IS ***IKAL,*** LEADER OF THE JENJORAN SURVIVORS.
IKAL, THIS IS JEAN-LUC PICARD...
...AN OLD FRIEND.
NEW FRIENDS OF SEVEN-FRIEND ARE WELCOME!
COME MEET THE OTHERS!
IKAL SENT THE DISTRESS CALL. HE BYPASSED THE JAMS BY LAUNCHING A BEACON INTO THE ATMOSPHERE.
CLEVER FELLOW.

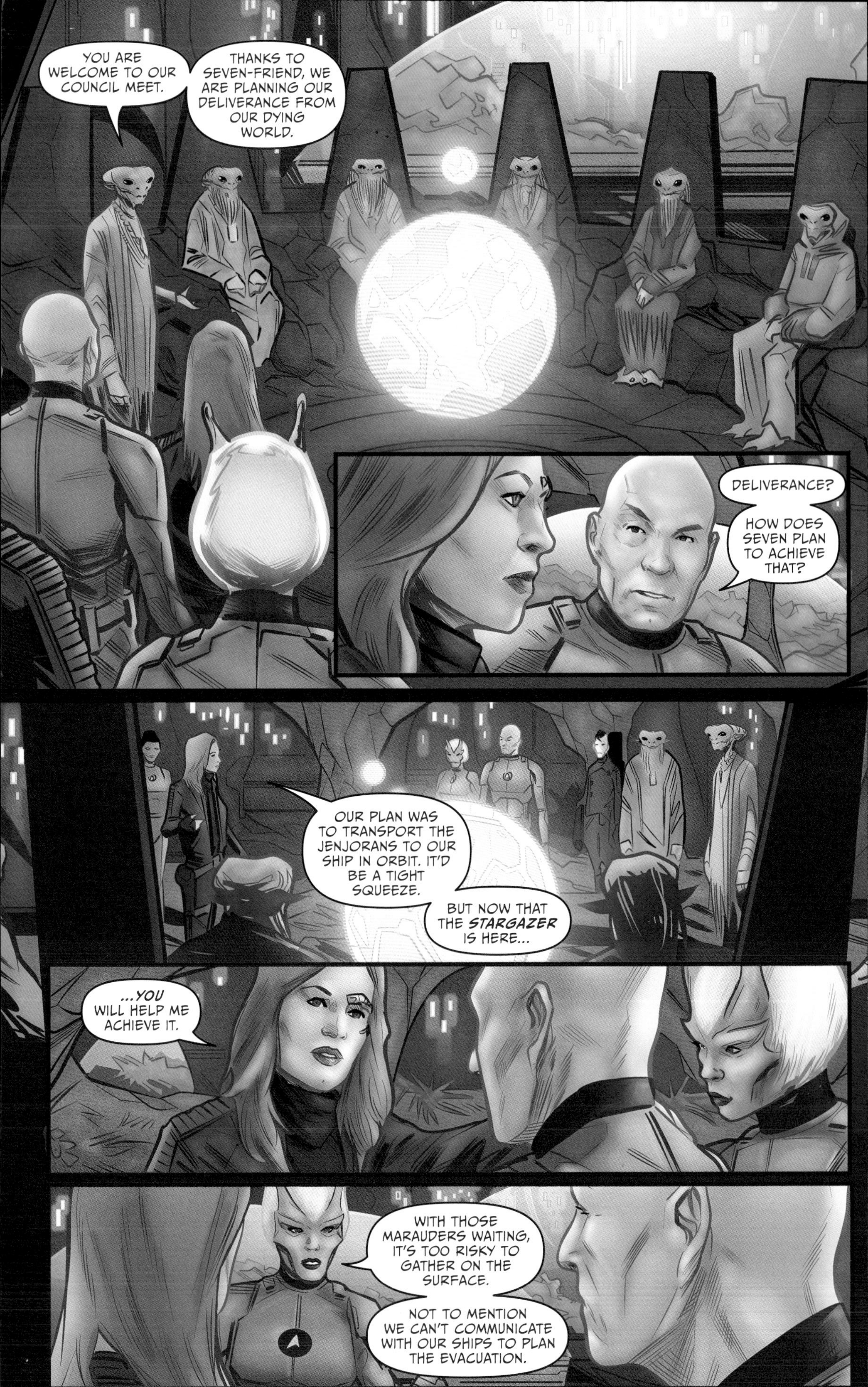
YOU ARE WELCOME TO OUR COUNCIL MEET.
THANKS TO SEVEN-FRIEND, WE ARE PLANNING OUR DELIVERANCE FROM OUR DYING WORLD.
DELIVERANCE?
HOW DOES SEVEN PLAN TO ACHIEVE THAT?
OUR PLAN WAS TO TRANSPORT THE JENJORANS TO OUR SHIP IN ORBIT. IT'D BE A TIGHT SQUEEZE.
BUT NOW THAT THE *STARGAZER* IS HERE...
...YOU WILL HELP ME ACHIEVE IT.
WITH THOSE MARAUDERS WAITING, IT'S TOO RISKY TO GATHER ON THE SURFACE.
NOT TO MENTION WE CAN'T COMMUNICATE WITH OUR SHIPS TO PLAN THE EVACUATION.

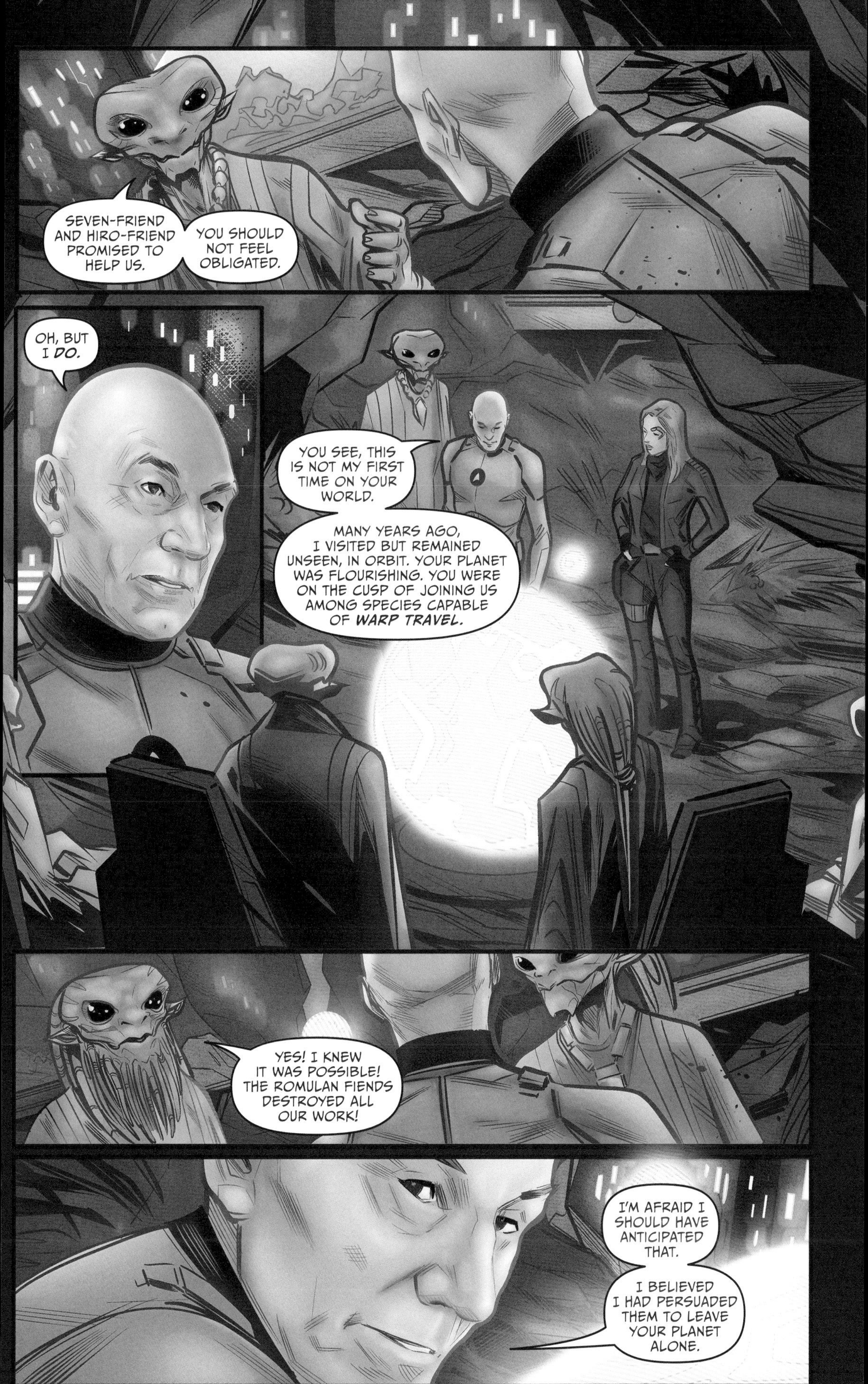
SEVEN-FRIEND AND HIRO-FRIEND PROMISED TO HELP US.
YOU SHOULD NOT FEEL OBLIGATED.
OH, BUT I *DO.*
YOU SEE, THIS IS NOT MY FIRST TIME ON YOUR WORLD.
MANY YEARS AGO, I VISITED BUT REMAINED UNSEEN, IN ORBIT. YOUR PLANET WAS FLOURISHING. YOU WERE ON THE CUSP OF JOINING US AMONG SPECIES CAPABLE OF ***WARP TRAVEL.***
YES! I KNEW IT WAS POSSIBLE! THE ROMULAN FIENDS DESTROYED ALL OUR WORK!
I'M AFRAID I SHOULD HAVE ANTICIPATED THAT.
I BELIEVED I HAD PERSUADED THEM TO LEAVE YOUR PLANET ALONE.

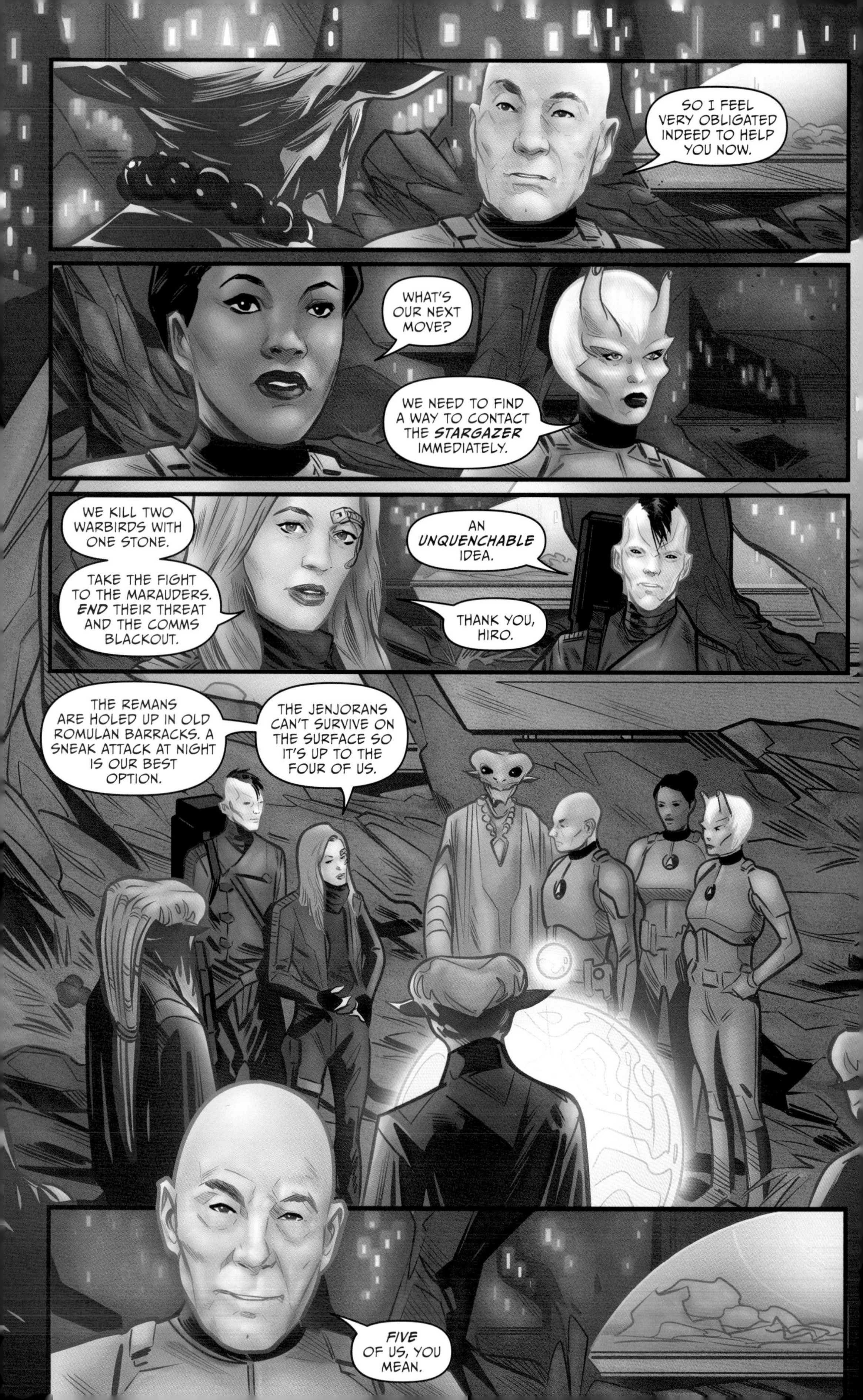
SO I FEEL VERY OBLIGATED INDEED TO HELP YOU NOW.
WHAT'S OUR NEXT MOVE?
WE NEED TO FIND A WAY TO CONTACT THE STARGAZER IMMEDIATELY.
WE KILL TWO WARBIRDS WITH ONE STONE.
TAKE THE FIGHT TO THE MARAUDERS. END THEIR THREAT AND THE COMMS BLACKOUT.
AN UNQUENCHABLE IDEA.
THANK YOU, HIRO.
THE REMANS ARE HOLED UP IN OLD ROMULAN BARRACKS. A SNEAK ATTACK AT NIGHT IS OUR BEST OPTION.
THE JENJORANS CAN'T SURVIVE ON THE SURFACE SO IT'S UP TO THE FOUR OF US.
FIVE OF US, YOU MEAN.

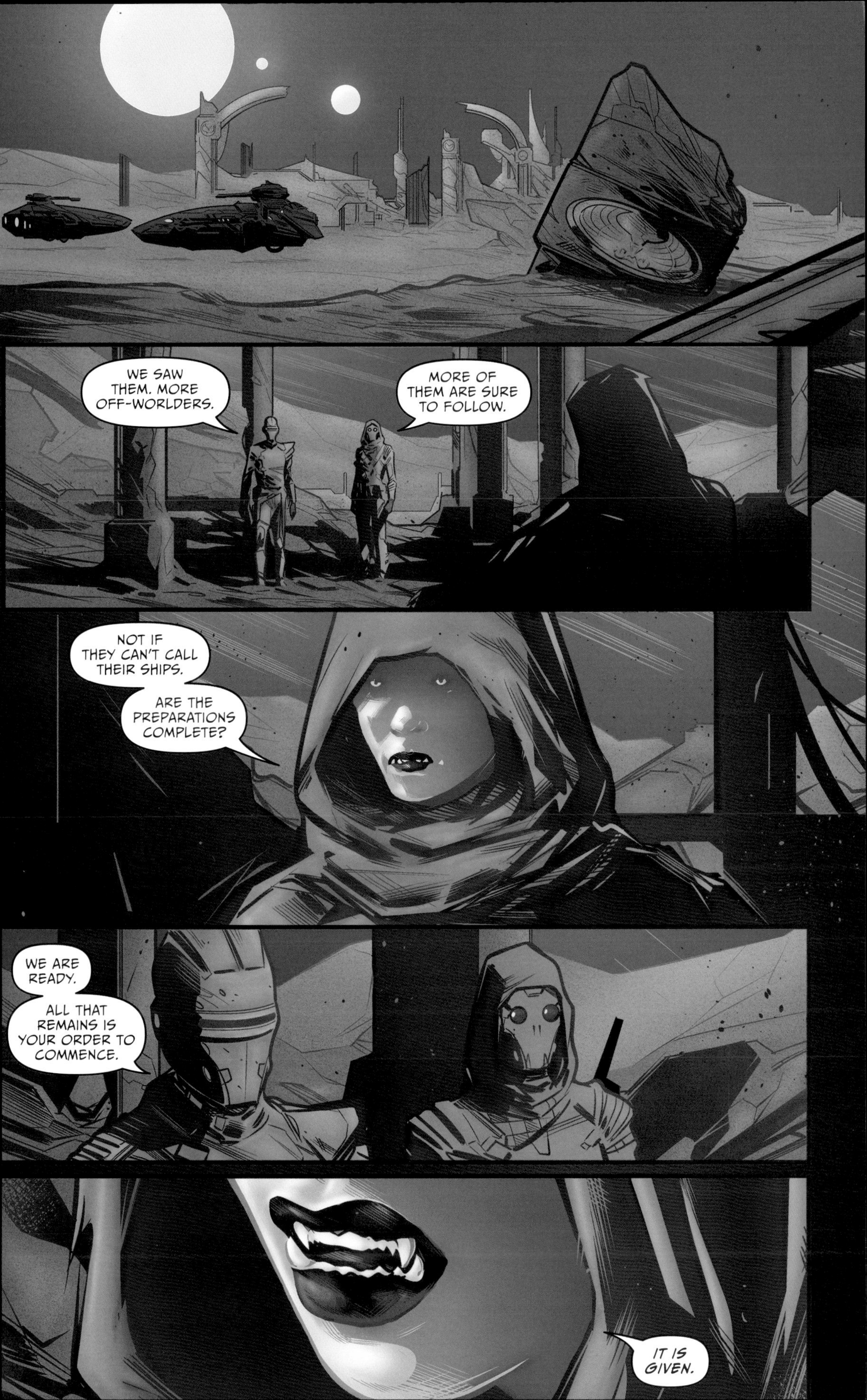
WE SAW THEM. MORE OFF-WORLDERS.
MORE OF THEM ARE SURE TO FOLLOW.
NOT IF THEY CAN'T CALL THEIR SHIPS.
ARE THE PREPARATIONS COMPLETE?
WE ARE READY.
ALL THAT REMAINS IS YOUR ORDER TO COMMENCE.
IT IS GIVEN.

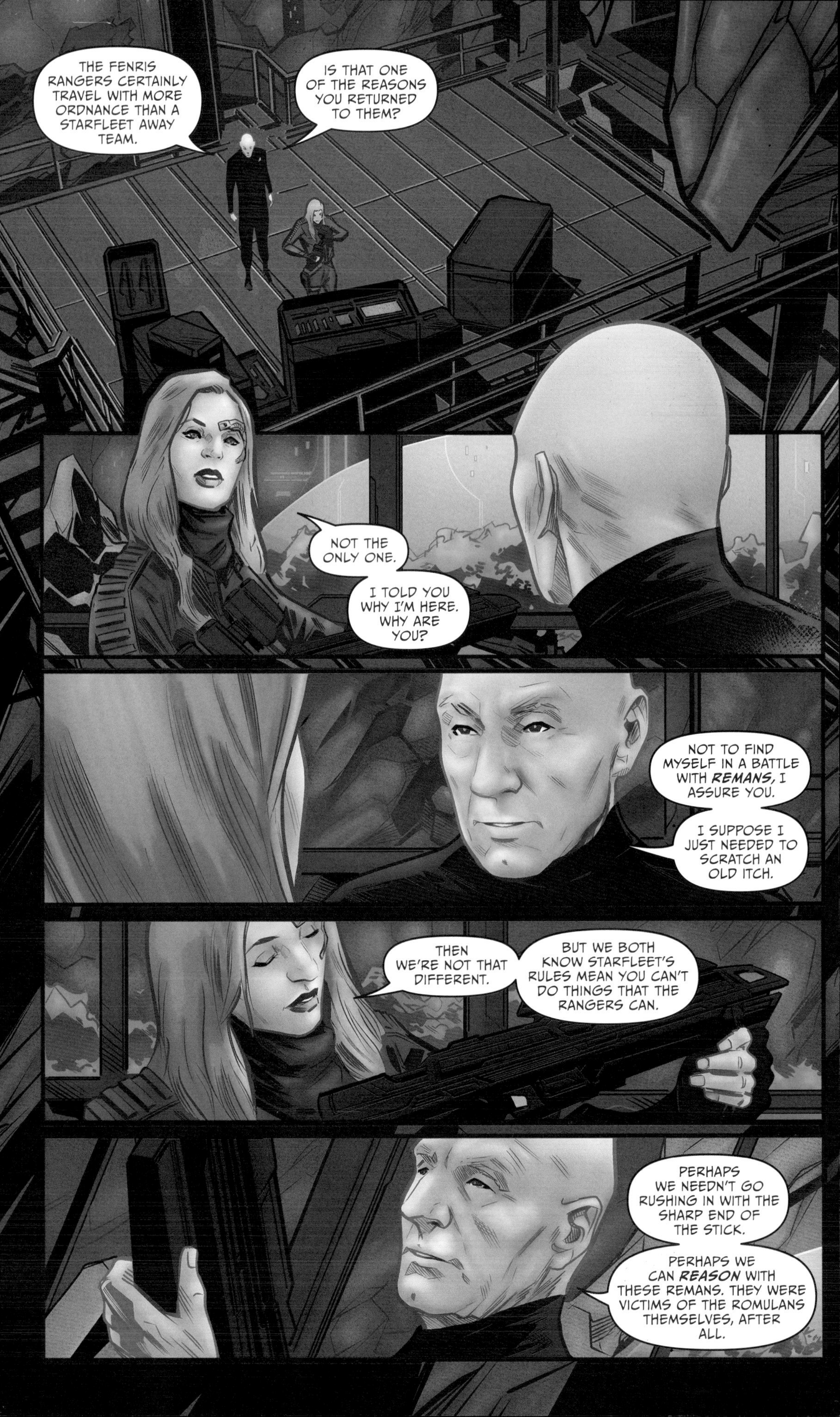
THE FENRIS RANGERS CERTAINLY TRAVEL WITH MORE ORDNANCE THAN A STARFLEET AWAY TEAM.
IS THAT ONE OF THE REASONS YOU RETURNED TO THEM?
NOT THE ONLY ONE.
I TOLD YOU WHY I'M HERE. WHY ARE YOU?
NOT TO FIND MYSELF IN A BATTLE WITH *REMANS,* I ASSURE YOU.
I SUPPOSE I JUST NEEDED TO SCRATCH AN OLD ITCH.
THEN WE'RE NOT THAT DIFFERENT.
BUT WE BOTH KNOW STARFLEET'S RULES MEAN YOU CAN'T DO THINGS THAT THE RANGERS CAN.
PERHAPS WE NEEDN'T GO RUSHING IN WITH THE SHARP END OF THE STICK.
PERHAPS WE CAN *REASON* WITH THESE REMANS. THEY WERE VICTIMS OF THE ROMULANS THEMSELVES, AFTER ALL.

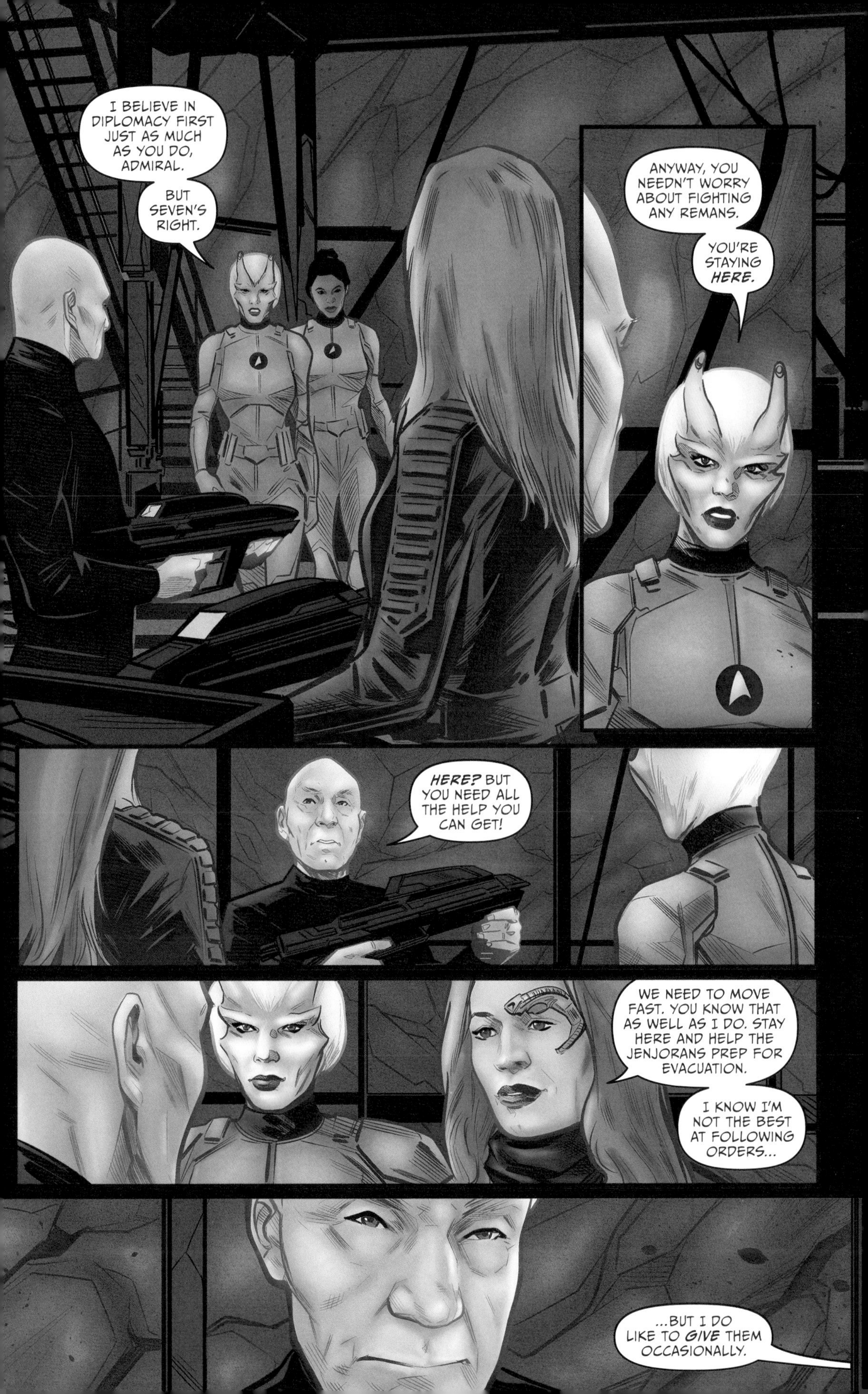

I BELIEVE IN DIPLOMACY FIRST JUST AS MUCH AS YOU DO, ADMIRAL.
BUT SEVEN'S RIGHT.
ANYWAY, YOU NEEDN'T WORRY ABOUT FIGHTING ANY REMANS.
YOU'RE STAYING *HERE.*
HERE? BUT YOU NEED ALL THE HELP YOU CAN GET!
WE NEED TO MOVE FAST. YOU KNOW THAT AS WELL AS I DO. STAY HERE AND HELP THE JENJORANS PREP FOR EVACUATION.
I KNOW I'M NOT THE BEST AT FOLLOWING ORDERS...
...BUT I DO LIKE TO *GIVE* THEM OCCASIONALLY.

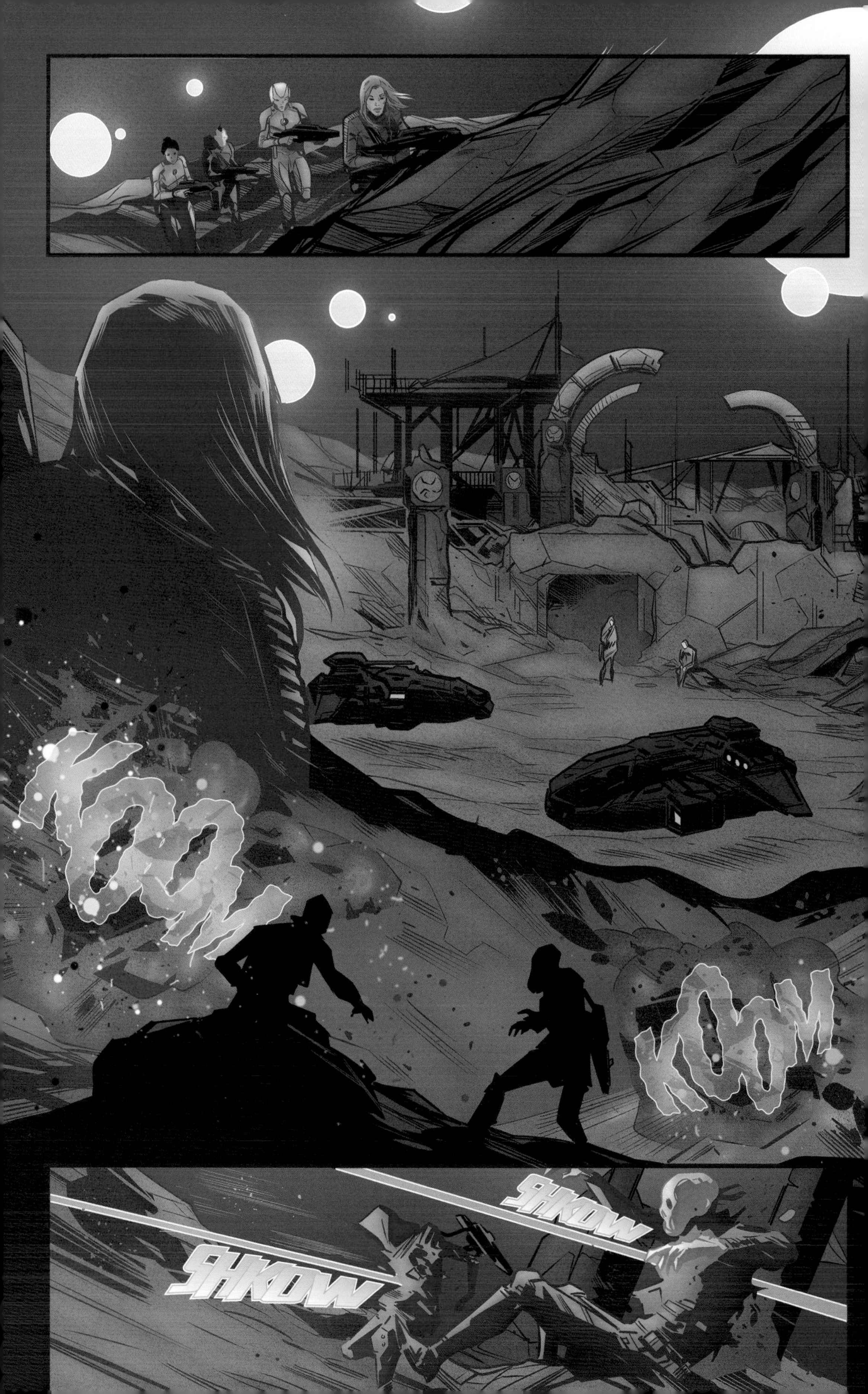
KOOM
KOOM
SHKOW
SHKOW

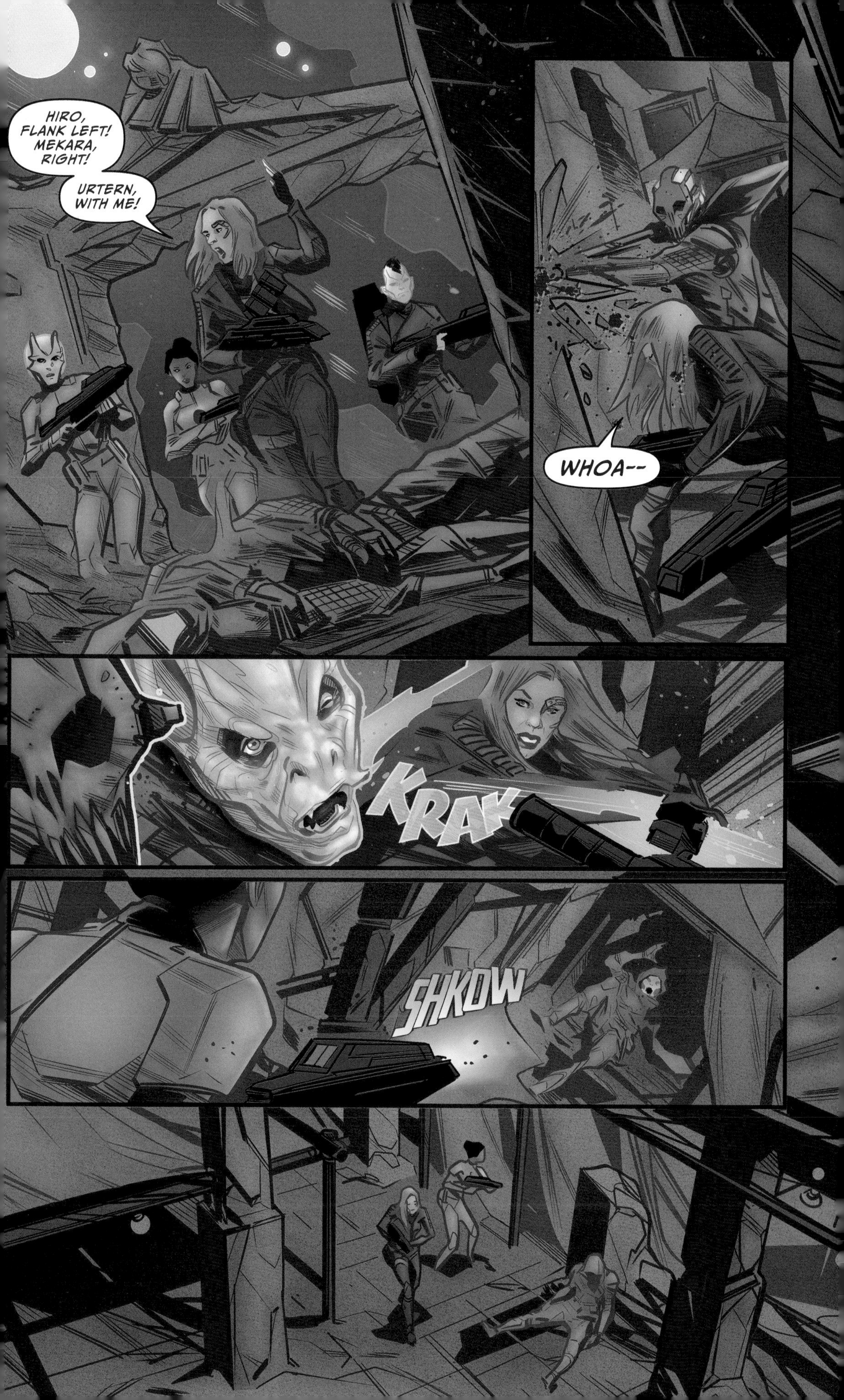
HIRO, FLANK LEFT! MEKARA, RIGHT!
URTERN, WITH ME!
WHOA--
KRAK
SHKOW

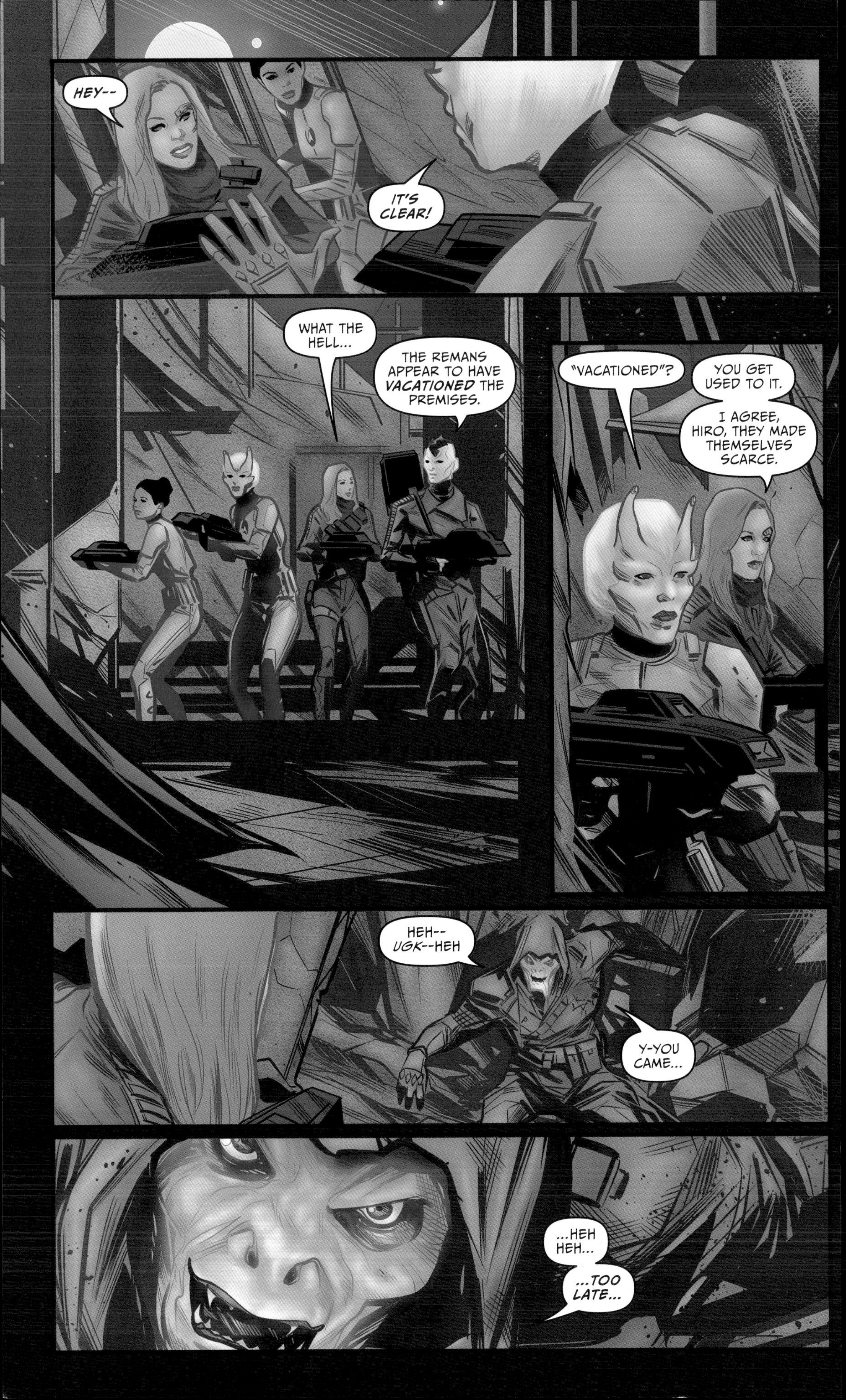
HEY--
IT'S CLEAR!
WHAT THE HELL...
THE REMANS APPEAR TO HAVE VACATIONED THE PREMISES.
"VACATIONED"?
YOU GET USED TO IT.
I AGREE, HIRO, THEY MADE THEMSELVES SCARCE.
HEH-- UGK--HEH
Y-YOU CAME...
...HEH HEH...
...TOO LATE...

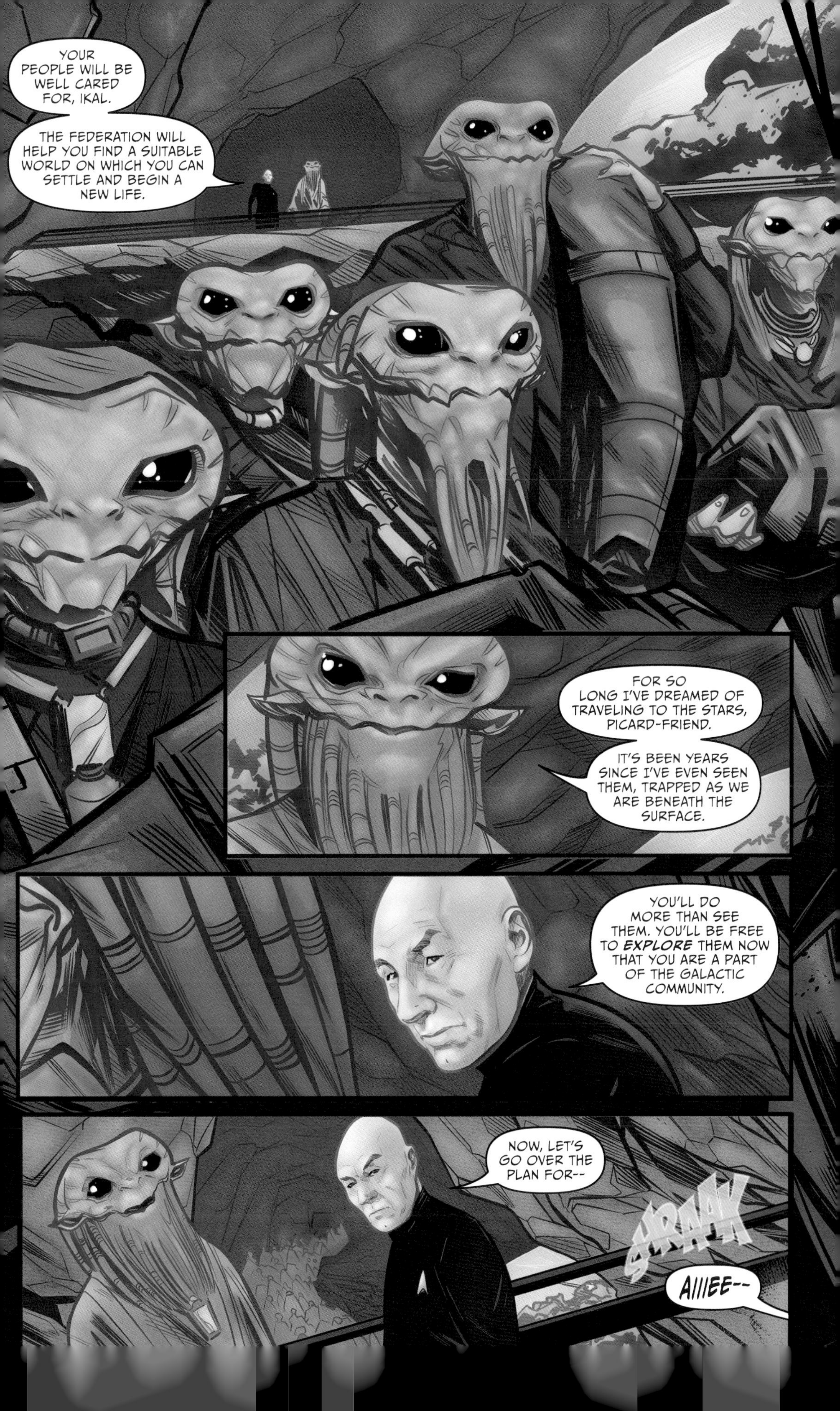
YOUR PEOPLE WILL BE WELL CARED FOR, IKAL.
THE FEDERATION WILL HELP YOU FIND A SUITABLE WORLD ON WHICH YOU CAN SETTLE AND BEGIN A NEW LIFE.
FOR SO LONG I'VE DREAMED OF TRAVELING TO THE STARS, PICARD-FRIEND.
IT'S BEEN YEARS SINCE I'VE EVEN SEEN THEM, TRAPPED AS WE ARE BENEATH THE SURFACE.
YOU'LL DO MORE THAN SEE THEM. YOU'LL BE FREE TO *EXPLORE* THEM NOW THAT YOU ARE A PART OF THE GALACTIC COMMUNITY.
NOW, LET'S GO OVER THE PLAN FOR--
SHRAAK
AIIIEE--

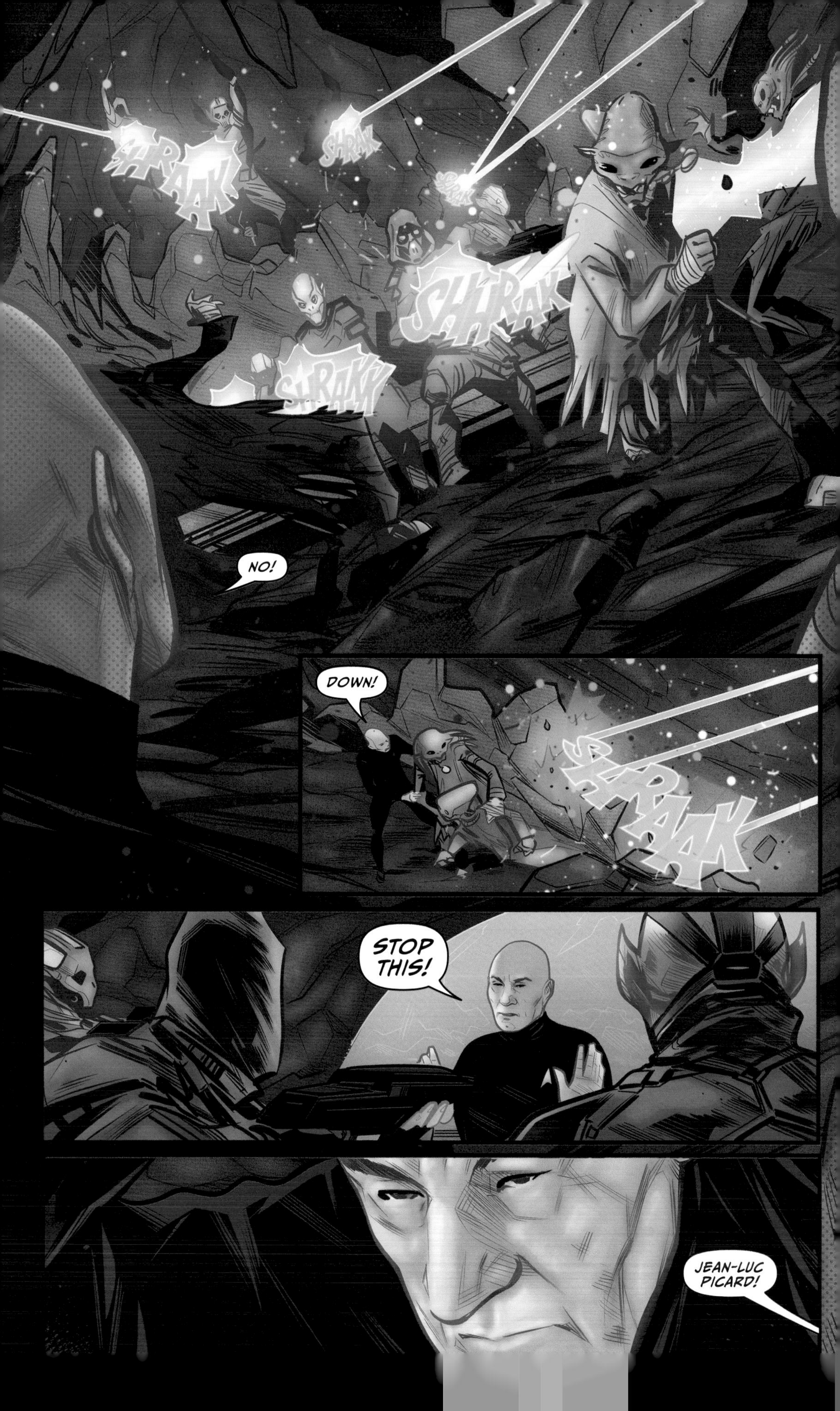
SHRAAK
SHRAK
SHRAK
SHRAK
SHRAAK
NO!
DOWN!
SHRAAK
STOP THIS!
JEAN-LUC PICARD!

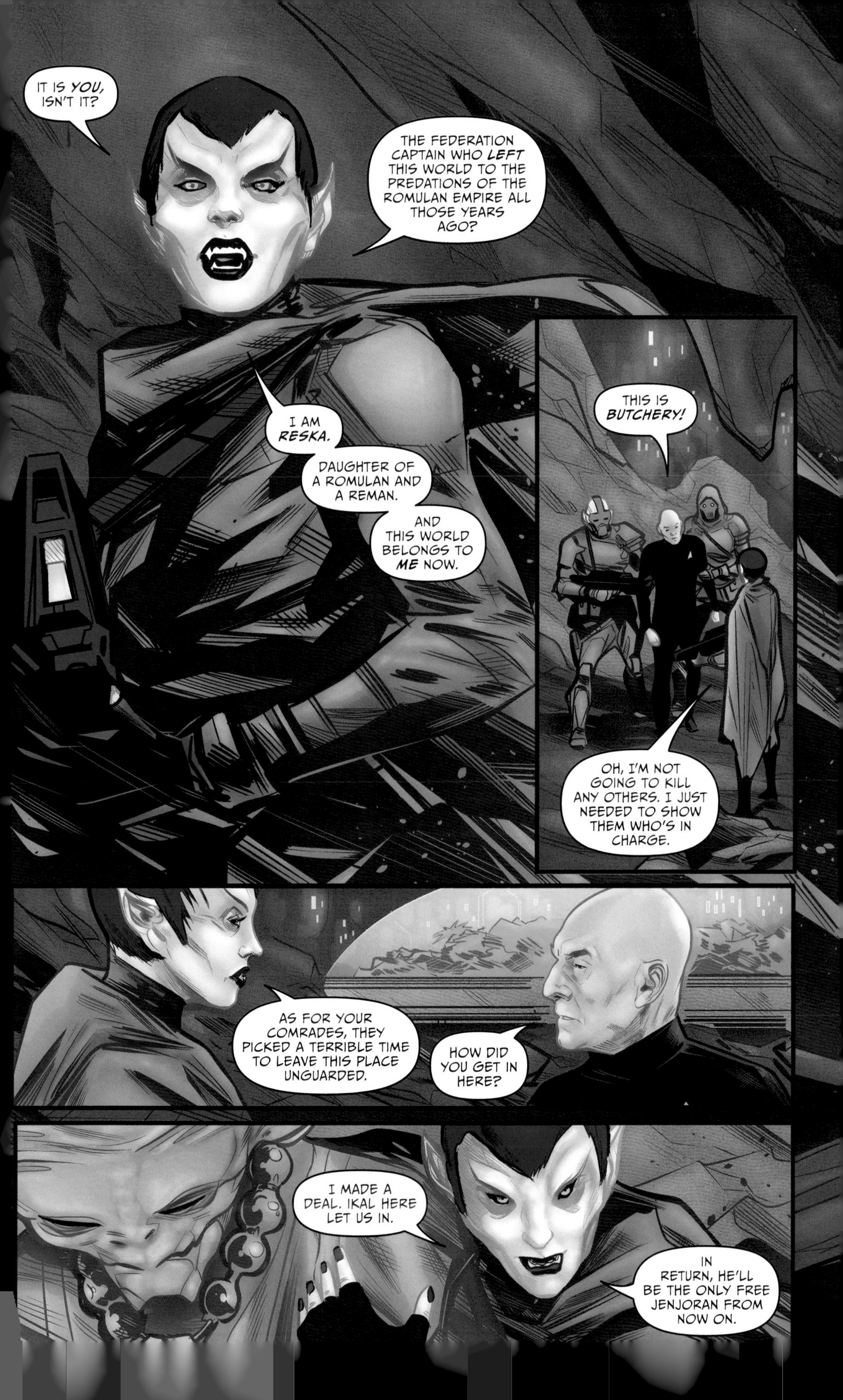
IT IS YOU, ISN'T IT?
THE FEDERATION CAPTAIN WHO LEFT THIS WORLD TO THE PREDATIONS OF THE ROMULAN EMPIRE ALL THOSE YEARS AGO?
I AM RESKA.
DAUGHTER OF A ROMULAN AND A REMAN.
AND THIS WORLD BELONGS TO ME NOW.
THIS IS BUTCHERY!
OH, I'M NOT GOING TO KILL ANY OTHERS. I JUST NEEDED TO SHOW THEM WHO'S IN CHARGE.
AS FOR YOUR COMRADES, THEY PICKED A TERRIBLE TIME TO LEAVE THIS PLACE UNGUARDED.
HOW DID YOU GET IN HERE?
I MADE A DEAL. IKAL HERE LET US IN.
IN RETURN, HE'LL BE THE ONLY FREE JENJORAN FROM NOW ON.

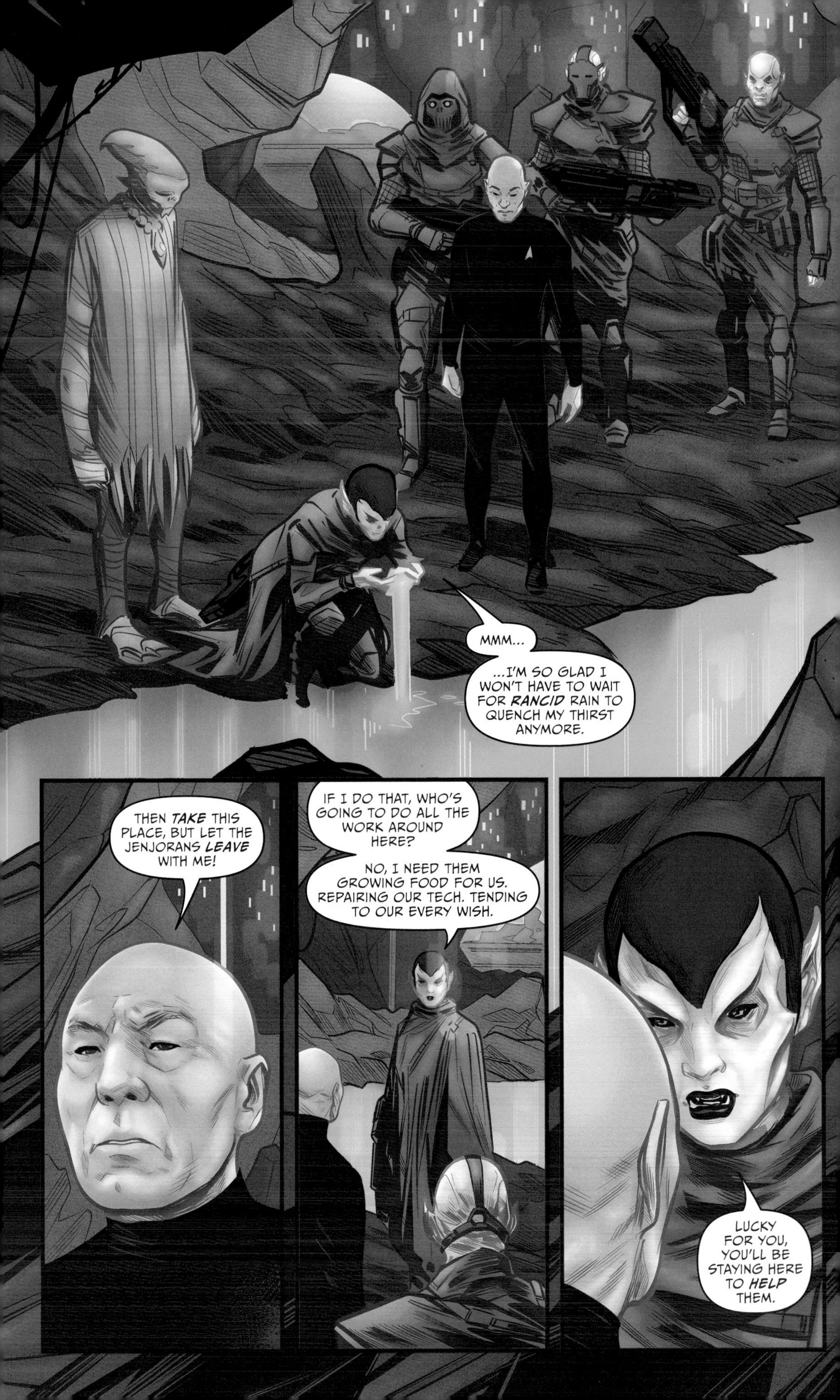
MMM...
...I'M SO GLAD I WON'T HAVE TO WAIT FOR RANCID RAIN TO QUENCH MY THIRST ANYMORE.
THEN TAKE THIS PLACE, BUT LET THE JENJORANS LEAVE WITH ME!
IF I DO THAT, WHO'S GOING TO DO ALL THE WORK AROUND HERE?
NO, I NEED THEM GROWING FOOD FOR US. REPAIRING OUR TECH. TENDING TO OUR EVERY WISH.
LUCKY FOR YOU, YOU'LL BE STAYING HERE TO HELP THEM.

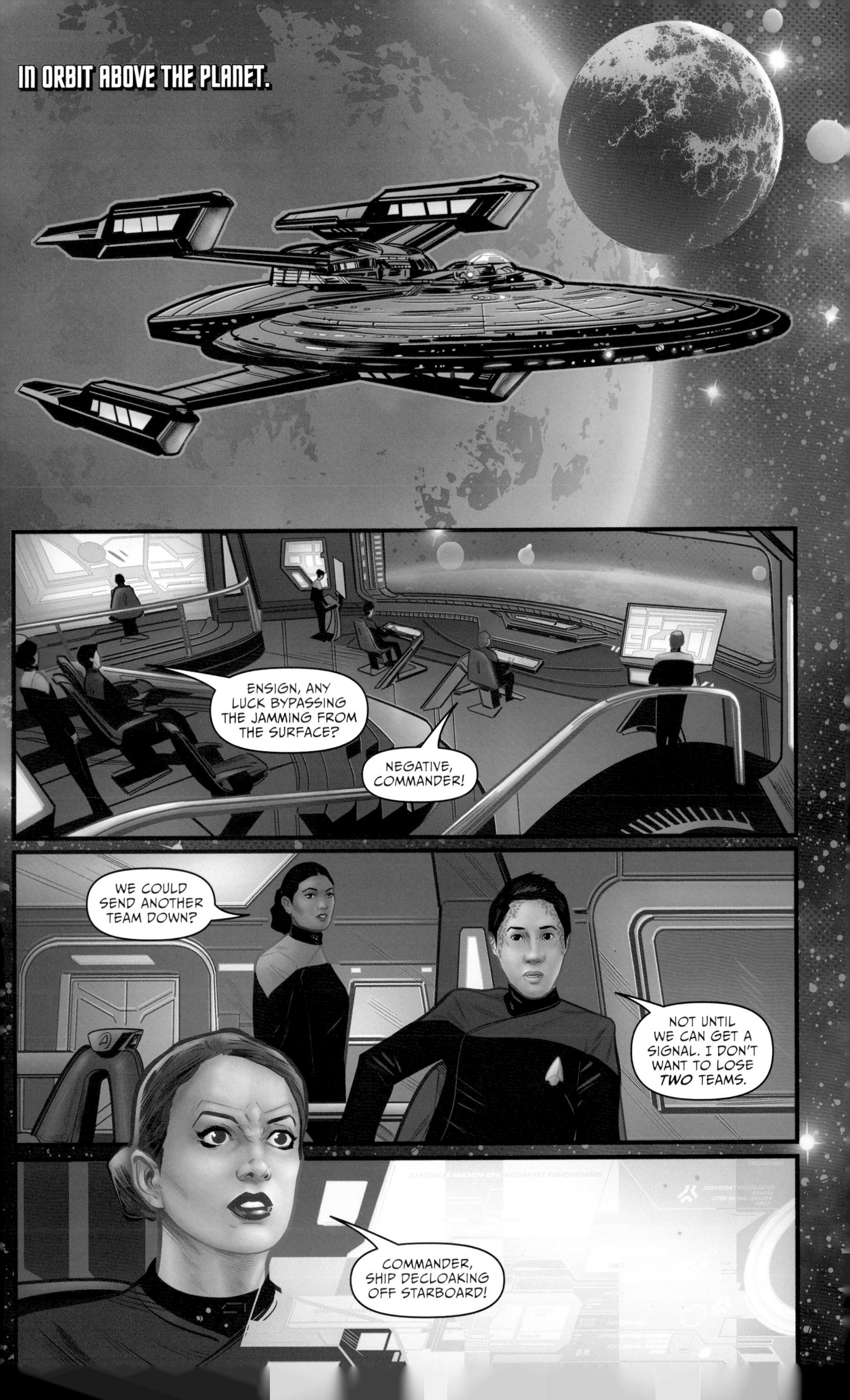
IN ORBIT ABOVE THE PLANET.
ENSIGN, ANY LUCK BYPASSING THE JAMMING FROM THE SURFACE?
NEGATIVE, COMMANDER!
WE COULD SEND ANOTHER TEAM DOWN?
NOT UNTIL WE CAN GET A SIGNAL. I DON'T WANT TO LOSE *TWO* TEAMS.
COMMANDER, SHIP DECLOAKING OFF STARBOARD!

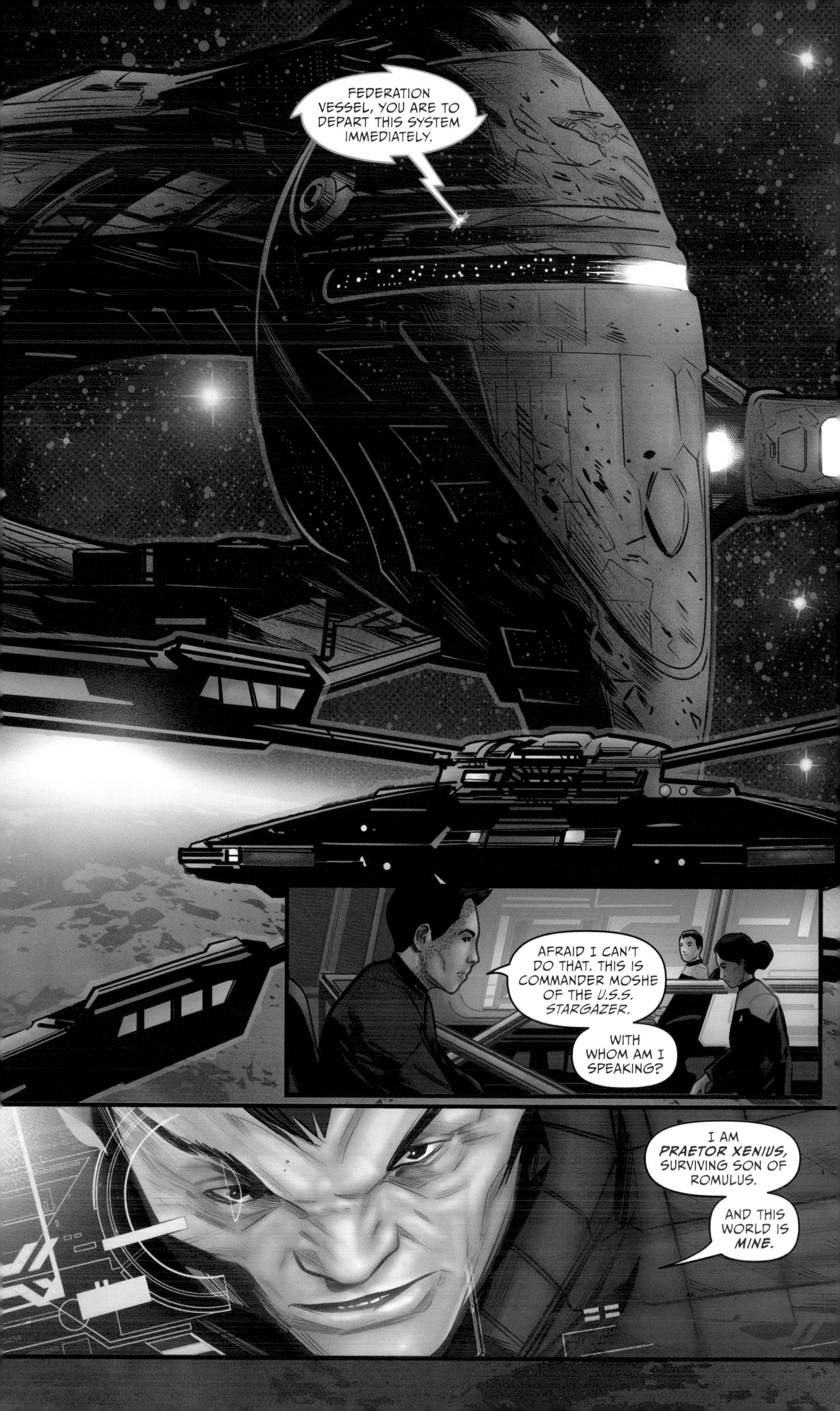
FEDERATION VESSEL, YOU ARE TO DEPART THIS SYSTEM IMMEDIATELY.
AFRAID I CAN'T DO THAT. THIS IS COMMANDER MOSHE OF THE *U.S.S. STARGAZER.*
WITH WHOM AM I SPEAKING?
I AM ***PRAETOR XENIUS,*** SURVIVING SON OF ROMULUS.
AND THIS WORLD IS ***MINE.***

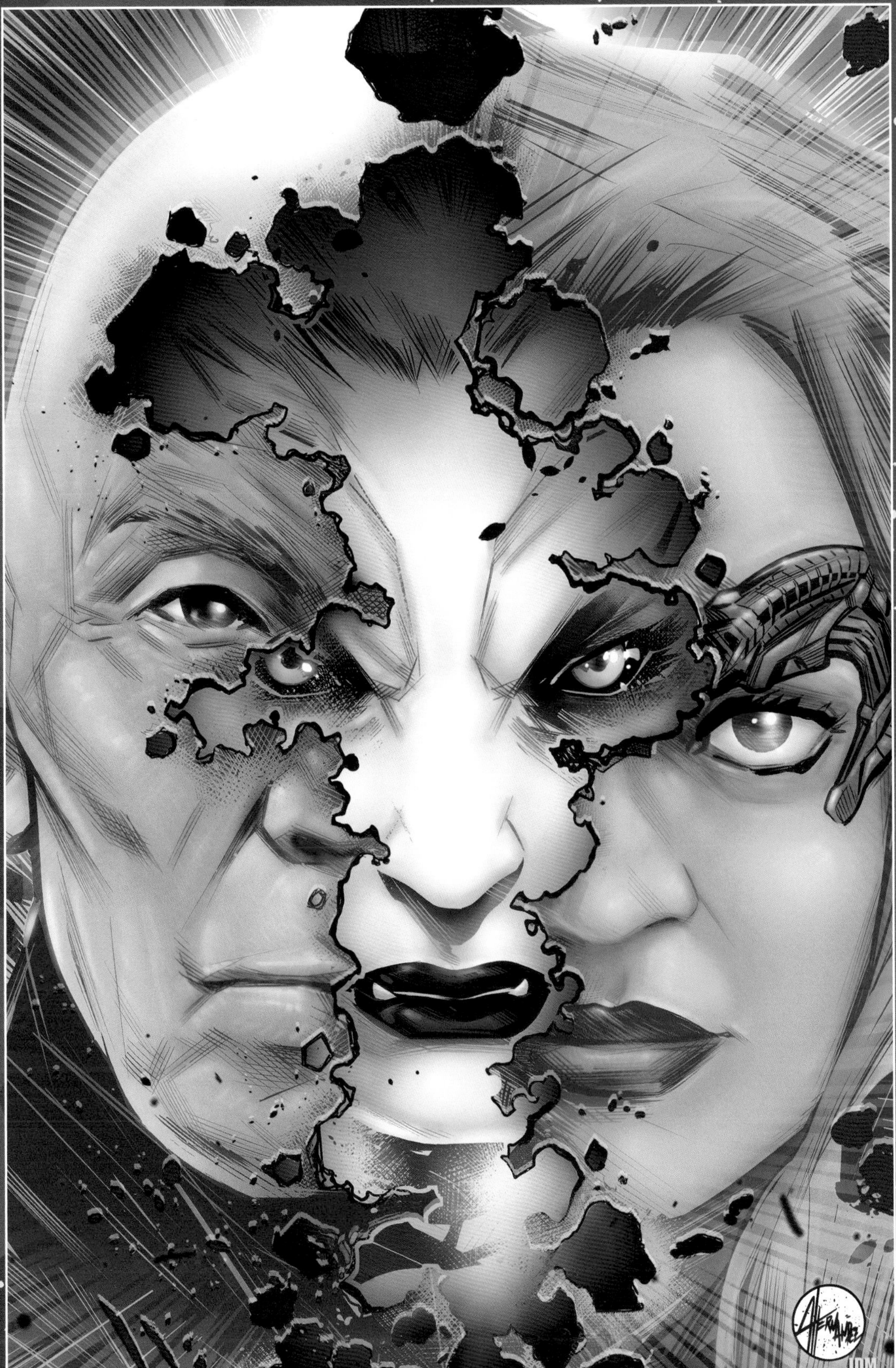

HERNANDEZ
JDM

art by ANGEL HERNANDEZ | colors by J.D. METTLER

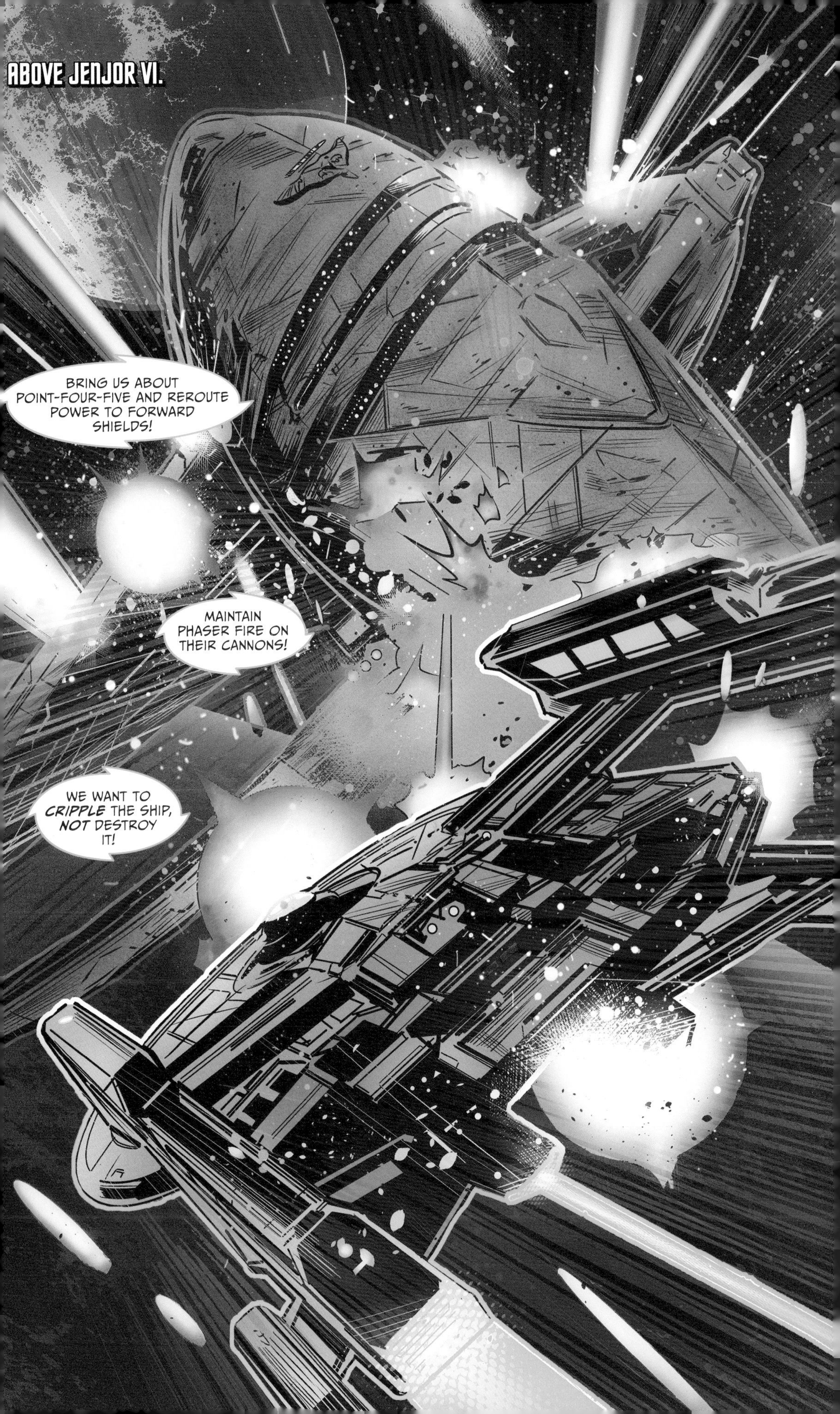
ABOVE JENJOR VI.
BRING US ABOUT POINT-FOUR-FIVE AND REROUTE POWER TO FORWARD SHIELDS!
MAINTAIN PHASER FIRE ON THEIR CANNONS!
WE WANT TO *CRIPPLE* THE SHIP, ***NOT*** DESTROY IT!

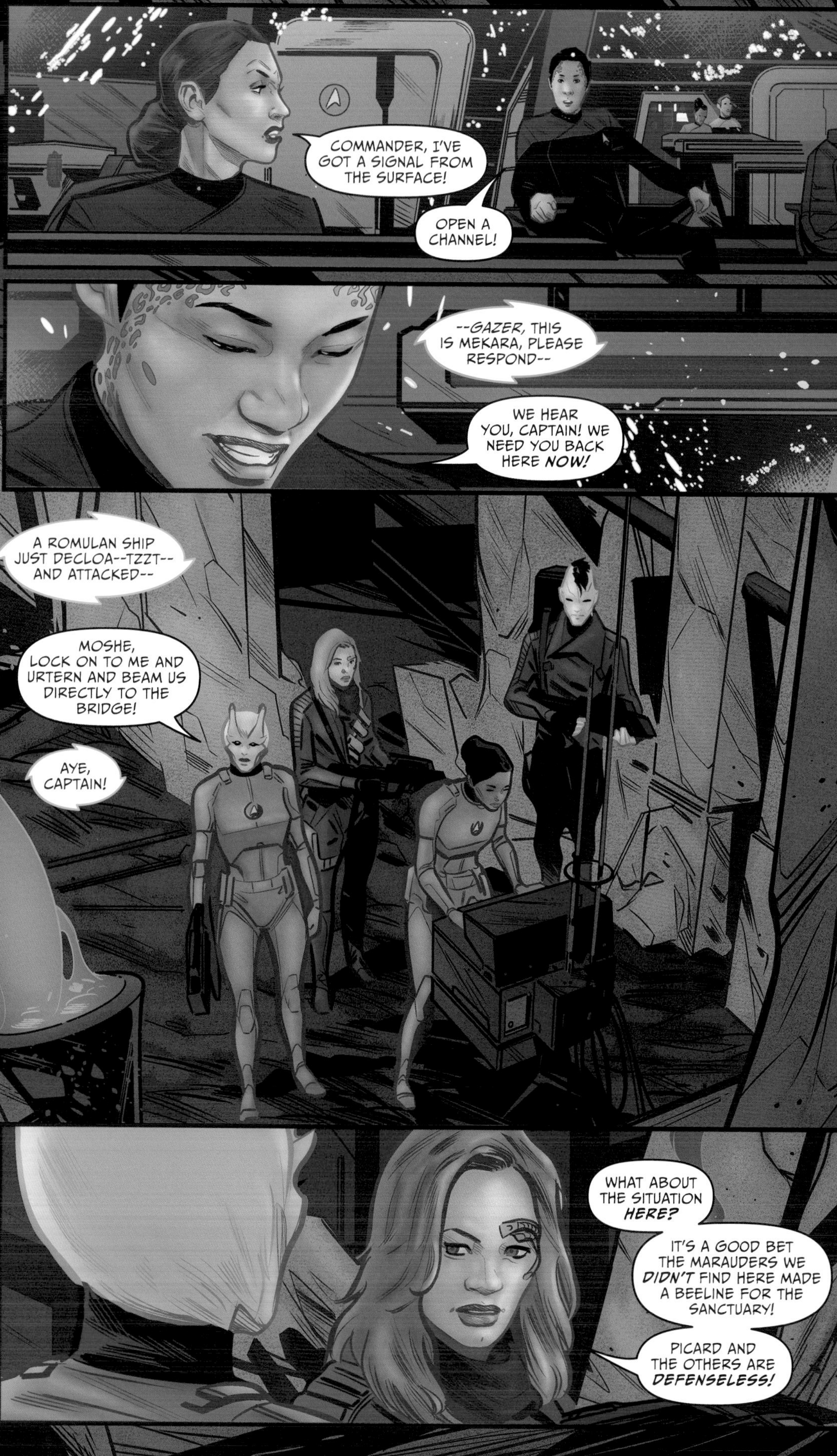

COMMANDER, I'VE GOT A SIGNAL FROM THE SURFACE!
OPEN A CHANNEL!
--GAZER, THIS IS MEKARA, PLEASE RESPOND--
WE HEAR YOU, CAPTAIN! WE NEED YOU BACK HERE *NOW!*
A ROMULAN SHIP JUST DECLOA--TZZT-- AND ATTACKED--
MOSHE, LOCK ON TO ME AND URTERN AND BEAM US DIRECTLY TO THE BRIDGE!
AYE, CAPTAIN!
WHAT ABOUT THE SITUATION *HERE?*
IT'S A GOOD BET THE MARAUDERS WE *DIDN'T* FIND HERE MADE A BEELINE FOR THE SANCTUARY!
PICARD AND THE OTHERS ARE *DEFENSELESS!*

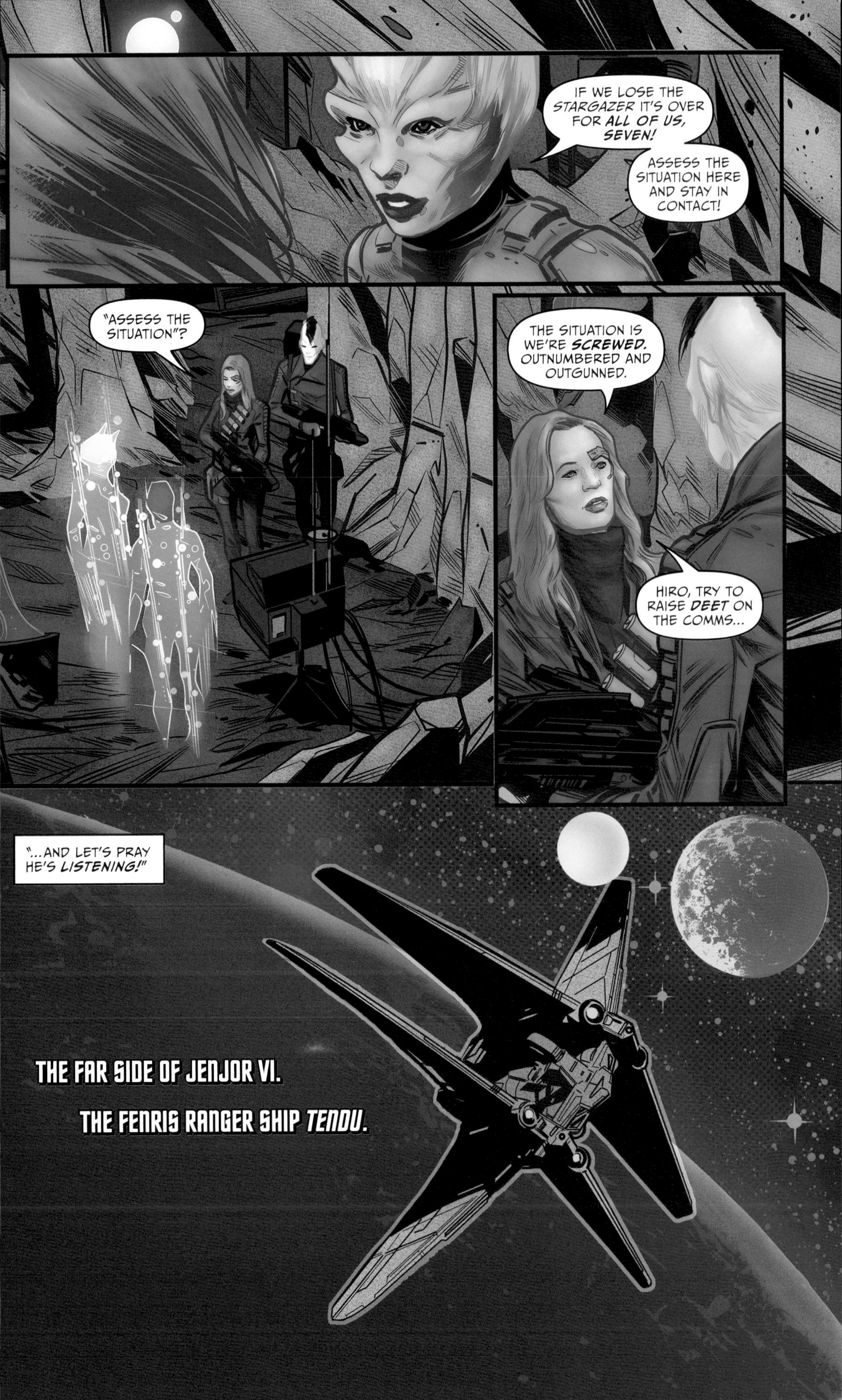

IF WE LOSE THE STARGAZER IT'S OVER FOR ALL OF US, SEVEN!
ASSESS THE SITUATION HERE AND STAY IN CONTACT!
"ASSESS THE SITUATION"?
THE SITUATION IS WE'RE SCREWED. OUTNUMBERED AND OUTGUNNED.
HIRO, TRY TO RAISE DEET ON THE COMMS...
"...AND LET'S PRAY HE'S LISTENING!"
THE FAR SIDE OF JENJOR VI.
THE FENRIS RANGER SHIP TENDU.

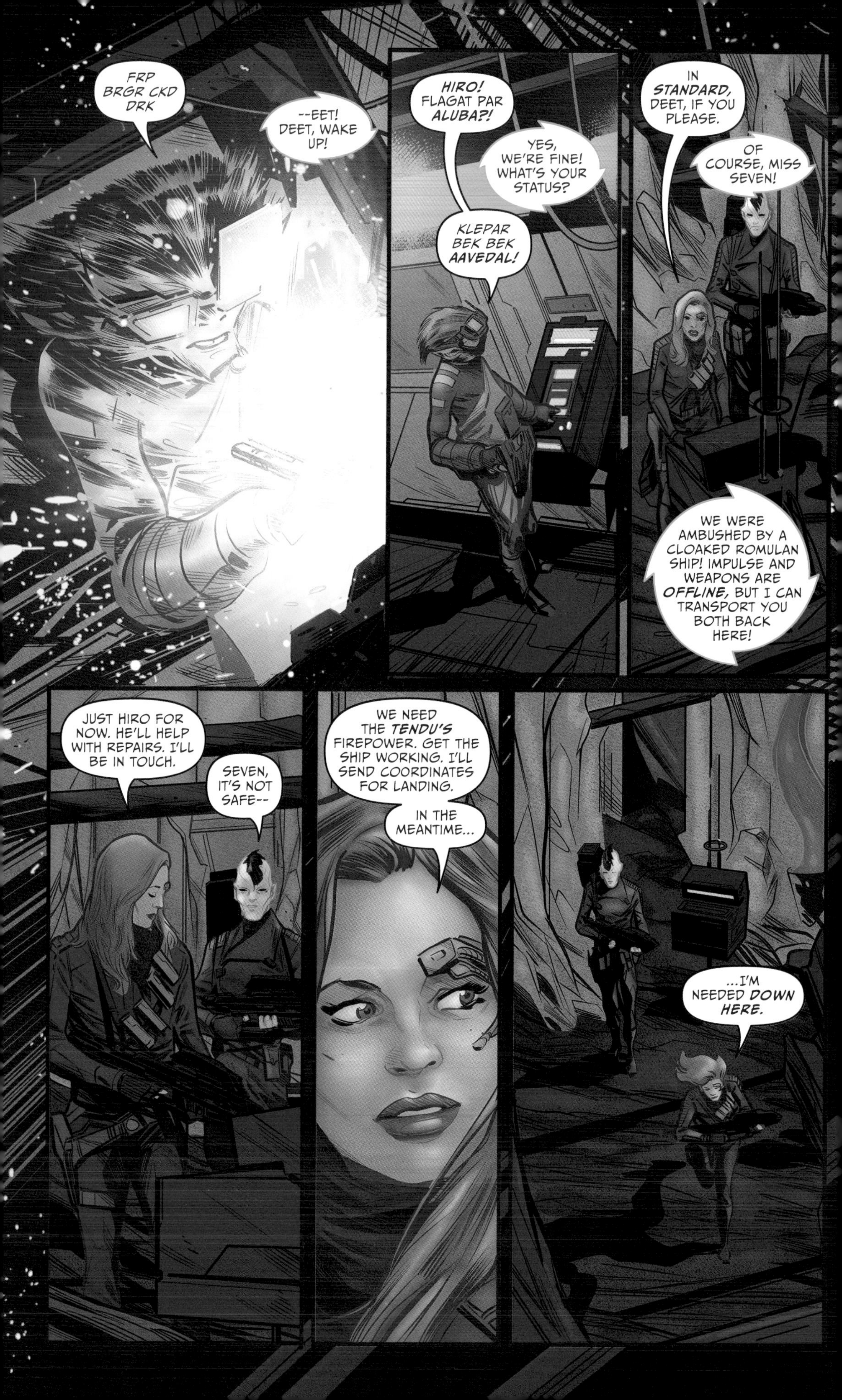
FRP BRGR CKD DRK
--EET! DEET, WAKE UP!
HIRO! FLAGAT PAR ALUBA?!
YES, WE'RE FINE! WHAT'S YOUR STATUS?
KLEPAR BEK BEK AAVEDAL!
IN STANDARD, DEET, IF YOU PLEASE.
OF COURSE, MISS SEVEN!
WE WERE AMBUSHED BY A CLOAKED ROMULAN SHIP! IMPULSE AND WEAPONS ARE OFFLINE, BUT I CAN TRANSPORT YOU BOTH BACK HERE!
JUST HIRO FOR NOW. HE'LL HELP WITH REPAIRS. I'LL BE IN TOUCH.
SEVEN, IT'S NOT SAFE--
WE NEED THE TENDU'S FIREPOWER. GET THE SHIP WORKING. I'LL SEND COORDINATES FOR LANDING.
IN THE MEANTIME...
...I'M NEEDED DOWN HERE.

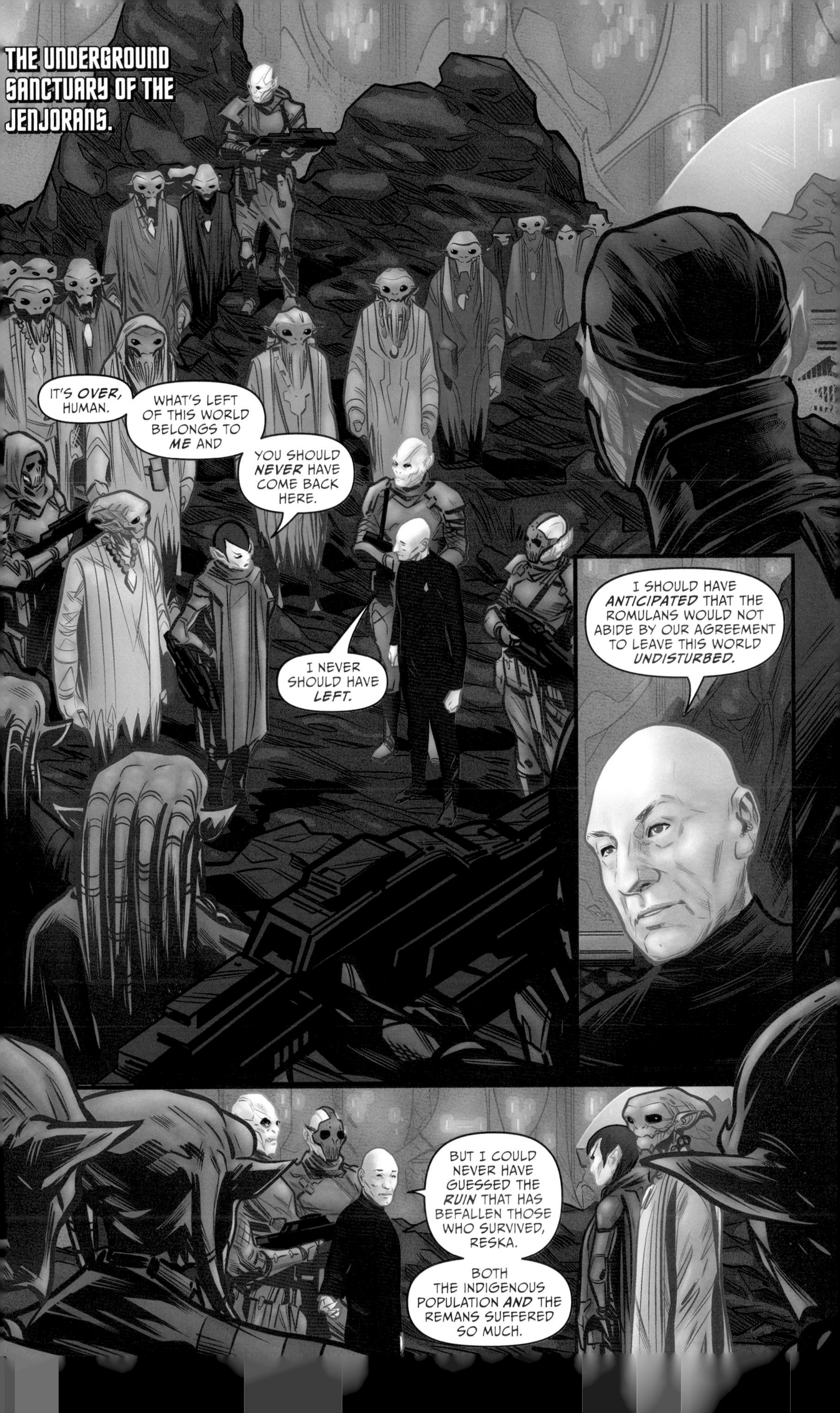
THE UNDERGROUND SANCTUARY OF THE JENJORANS.
IT'S OVER, HUMAN.
WHAT'S LEFT OF THIS WORLD BELONGS TO ME AND
YOU SHOULD NEVER HAVE COME BACK HERE.
I NEVER SHOULD HAVE LEFT.
I SHOULD HAVE ANTICIPATED THAT THE ROMULANS WOULD NOT ABIDE BY OUR AGREEMENT TO LEAVE THIS WORLD UNDISTURBED.
BUT I COULD NEVER HAVE GUESSED THE RUIN THAT HAS BEFALLEN THOSE WHO SURVIVED, RESKA.
BOTH THE INDIGENOUS POPULATION AND THE REMANS SUFFERED SO MUCH.

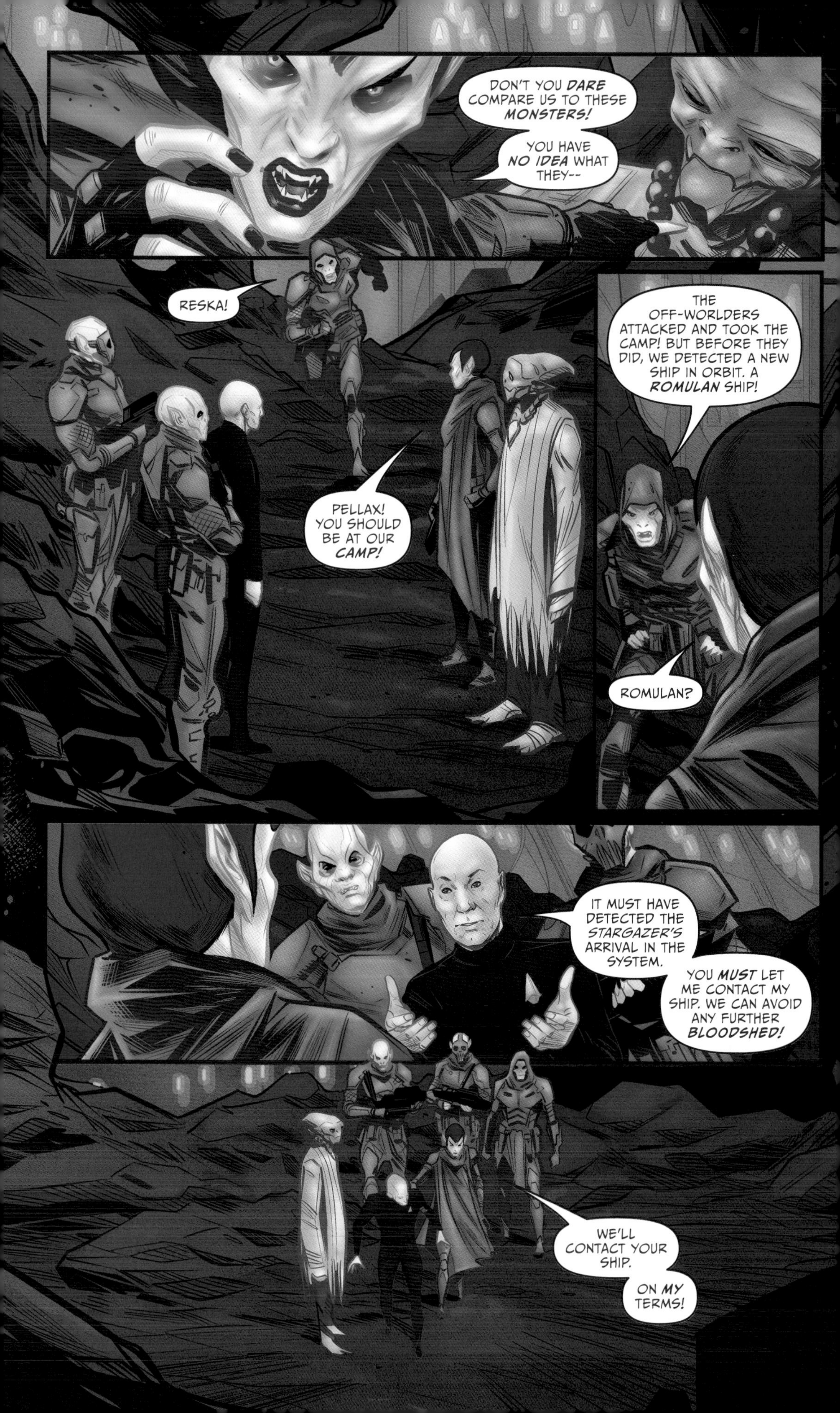
DON'T YOU DARE COMPARE US TO THESE MONSTERS!
YOU HAVE NO IDEA WHAT THEY--
RESKA!
PELLAX! YOU SHOULD BE AT OUR CAMP!
THE OFF-WORLDERS ATTACKED AND TOOK THE CAMP! BUT BEFORE THEY DID, WE DETECTED A NEW SHIP IN ORBIT. A ROMULAN SHIP!
ROMULAN?
IT MUST HAVE DETECTED THE STARGAZER'S ARRIVAL IN THE SYSTEM.
YOU MUST LET ME CONTACT MY SHIP. WE CAN AVOID ANY FURTHER BLOODSHED!
WE'LL CONTACT YOUR SHIP.
ON MY TERMS!

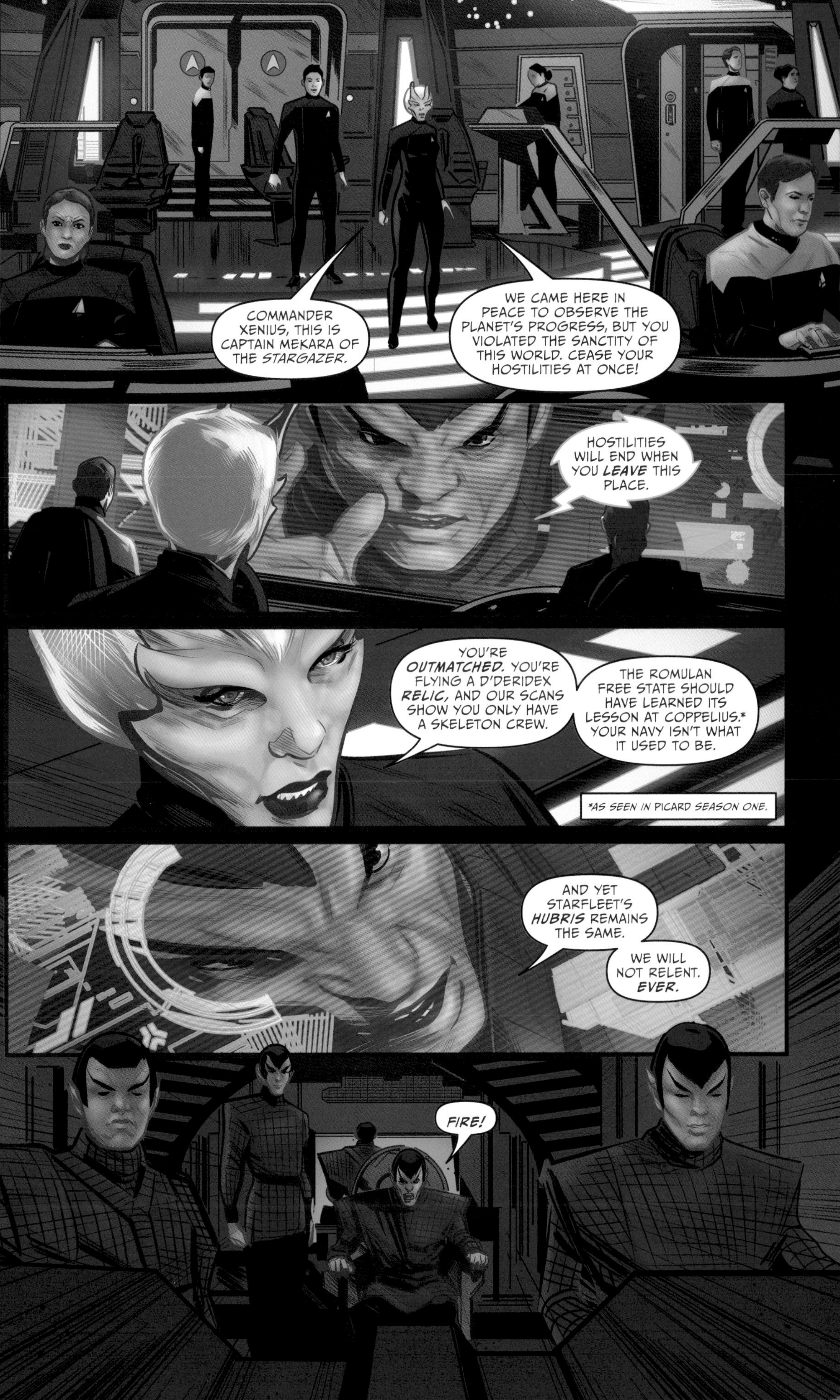
COMMANDER XENIUS, THIS IS CAPTAIN MEKARA OF THE STARGAZER.
WE CAME HERE IN PEACE TO OBSERVE THE PLANET'S PROGRESS, BUT YOU VIOLATED THE SANCTITY OF THIS WORLD. CEASE YOUR HOSTILITIES AT ONCE!
HOSTILITIES WILL END WHEN YOU LEAVE THIS PLACE.
YOU'RE OUTMATCHED. YOU'RE FLYING A D'DERIDEX RELIC, AND OUR SCANS SHOW YOU ONLY HAVE A SKELETON CREW.
THE ROMULAN FREE STATE SHOULD HAVE LEARNED ITS LESSON AT COPPELIUS.* YOUR NAVY ISN'T WHAT IT USED TO BE.
*AS SEEN IN PICARD SEASON ONE.
AND YET STARFLEET'S HUBRIS REMAINS THE SAME.
WE WILL NOT RELENT. EVER.
FIRE!

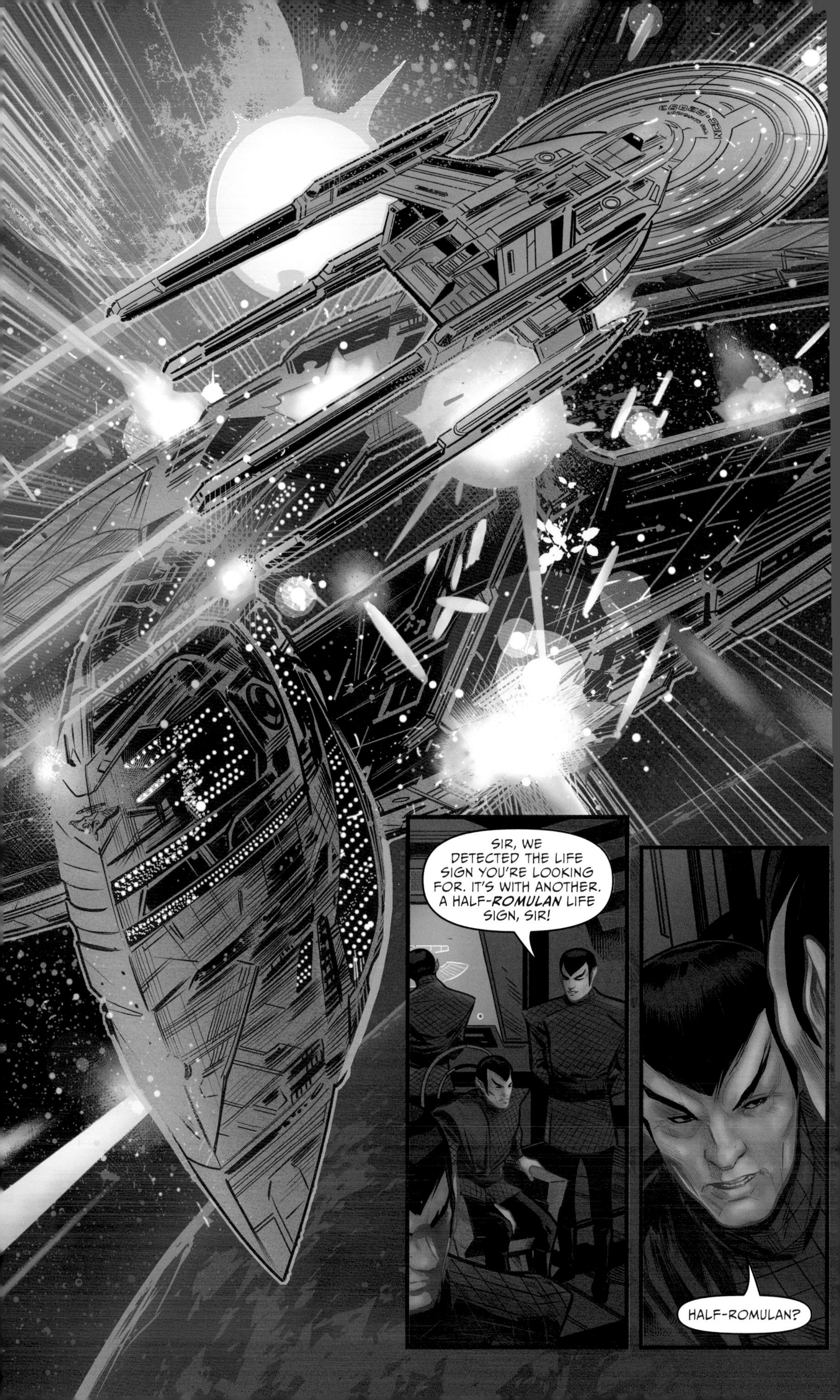
SIR, WE DETECTED THE LIFE SIGN YOU'RE LOOKING FOR. IT'S WITH ANOTHER. A HALF-ROMULAN LIFE SIGN, SIR!
HALF-ROMULAN?

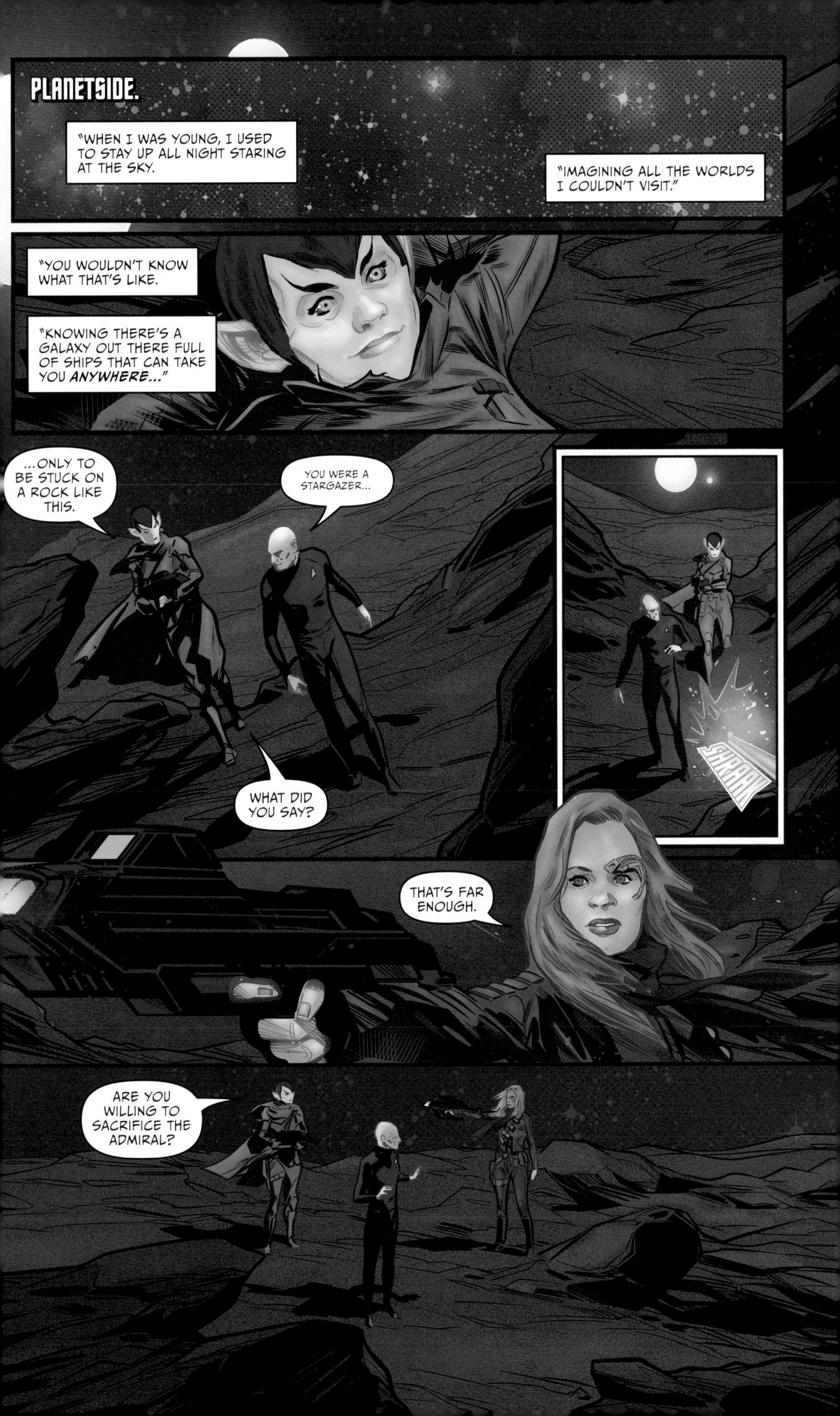
PLANETSIDE.
"WHEN I WAS YOUNG, I USED TO STAY UP ALL NIGHT STARING AT THE SKY.
"IMAGINING ALL THE WORLDS I COULDN'T VISIT."
"YOU WOULDN'T KNOW WHAT THAT'S LIKE.
"KNOWING THERE'S A GALAXY OUT THERE FULL OF SHIPS THAT CAN TAKE YOU ***ANYWHERE...***"
...ONLY TO BE STUCK ON A ROCK LIKE THIS.
YOU WERE A STARGAZER...
WHAT DID YOU SAY?
SHRAK
THAT'S FAR ENOUGH.
ARE YOU WILLING TO SACRIFICE THE ADMIRAL?

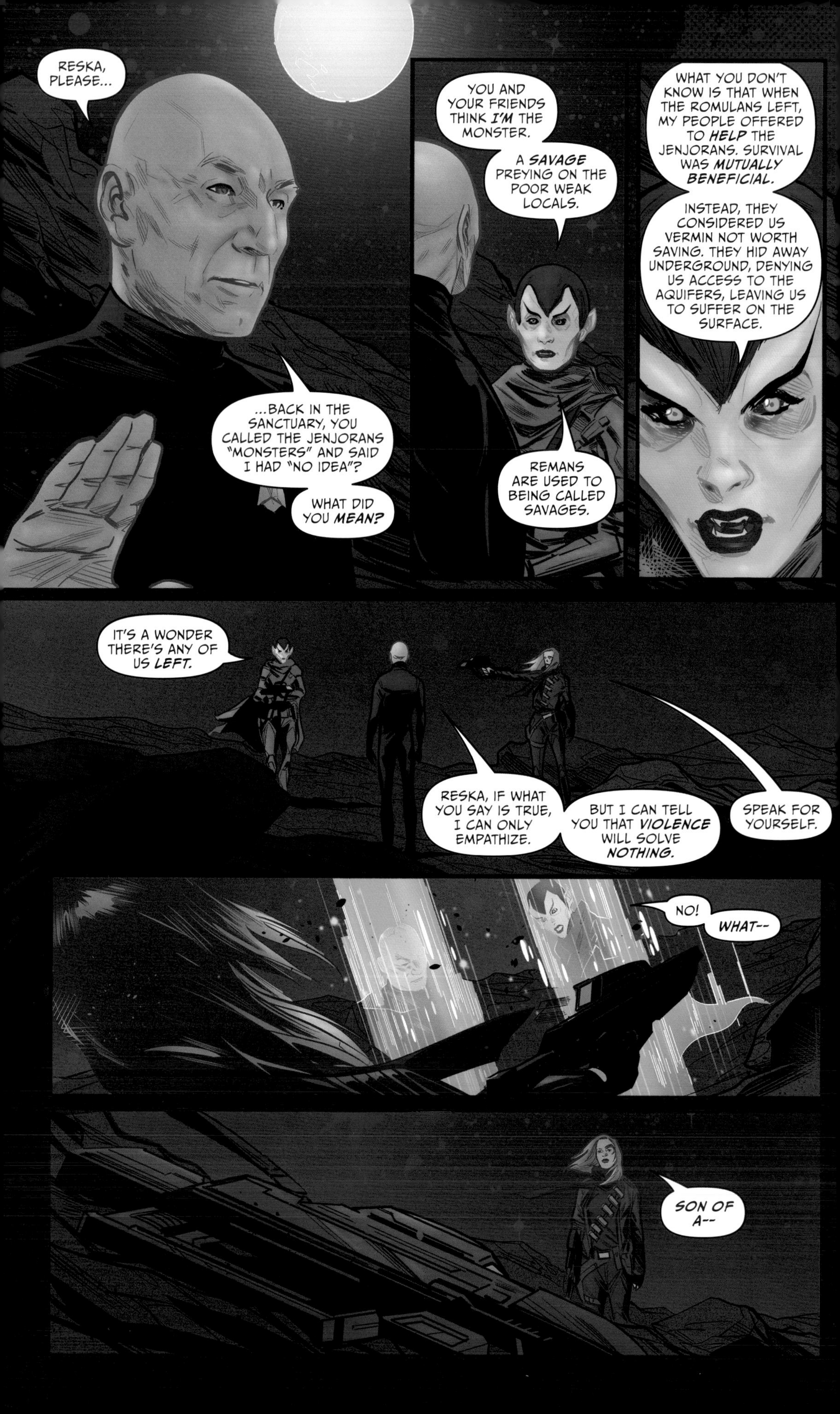
RESKA, PLEASE...
...BACK IN THE SANCTUARY, YOU CALLED THE JENJORANS "MONSTERS" AND SAID I HAD "NO IDEA"?
WHAT DID YOU *MEAN?*
YOU AND YOUR FRIENDS THINK *I'M* THE MONSTER.
A *SAVAGE* PREYING ON THE POOR WEAK LOCALS.
REMANS ARE USED TO BEING CALLED SAVAGES.
WHAT YOU DON'T KNOW IS THAT WHEN THE ROMULANS LEFT, MY PEOPLE OFFERED TO *HELP* THE JENJORANS. SURVIVAL WAS *MUTUALLY BENEFICIAL.*
INSTEAD, THEY CONSIDERED US VERMIN NOT WORTH SAVING. THEY HID AWAY UNDERGROUND, DENYING US ACCESS TO THE AQUIFERS, LEAVING US TO SUFFER ON THE SURFACE.
IT'S A WONDER THERE'S ANY OF US *LEFT.*
RESKA, IF WHAT YOU SAY IS TRUE, I CAN ONLY EMPATHIZE.
BUT I CAN TELL YOU THAT *VIOLENCE* WILL SOLVE *NOTHING.*
SPEAK FOR YOURSELF.
NO!
WHAT--
SON OF A--

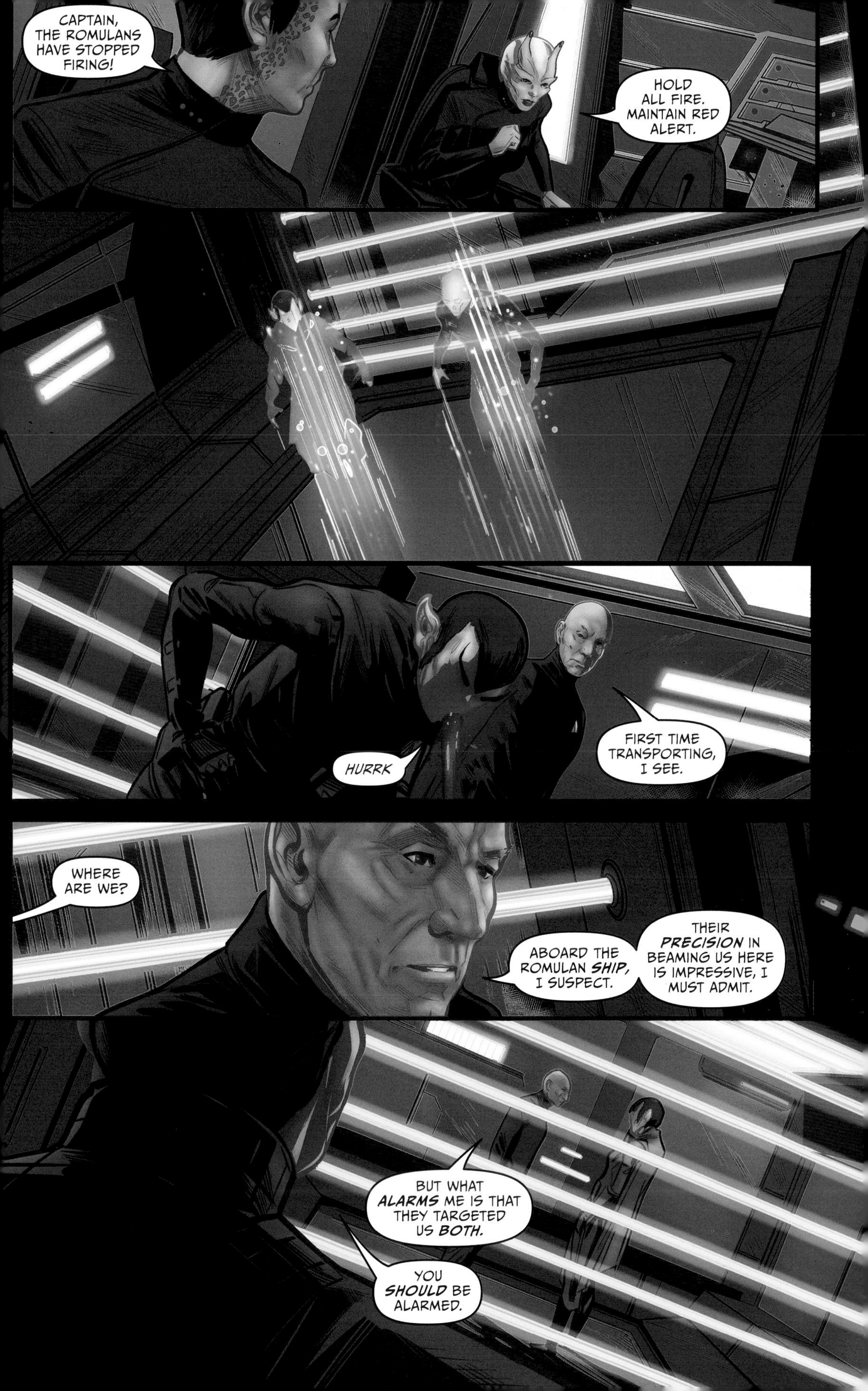
CAPTAIN, THE ROMULANS HAVE STOPPED FIRING!
HOLD ALL FIRE. MAINTAIN RED ALERT.
HURRK
FIRST TIME TRANSPORTING, I SEE.
WHERE ARE WE?
ABOARD THE ROMULAN *SHIP,* I SUSPECT.
THEIR *PRECISION* IN BEAMING US HERE IS IMPRESSIVE, I MUST ADMIT.
BUT WHAT *ALARMS* ME IS THAT THEY TARGETED US *BOTH.*
YOU *SHOULD* BE ALARMED.

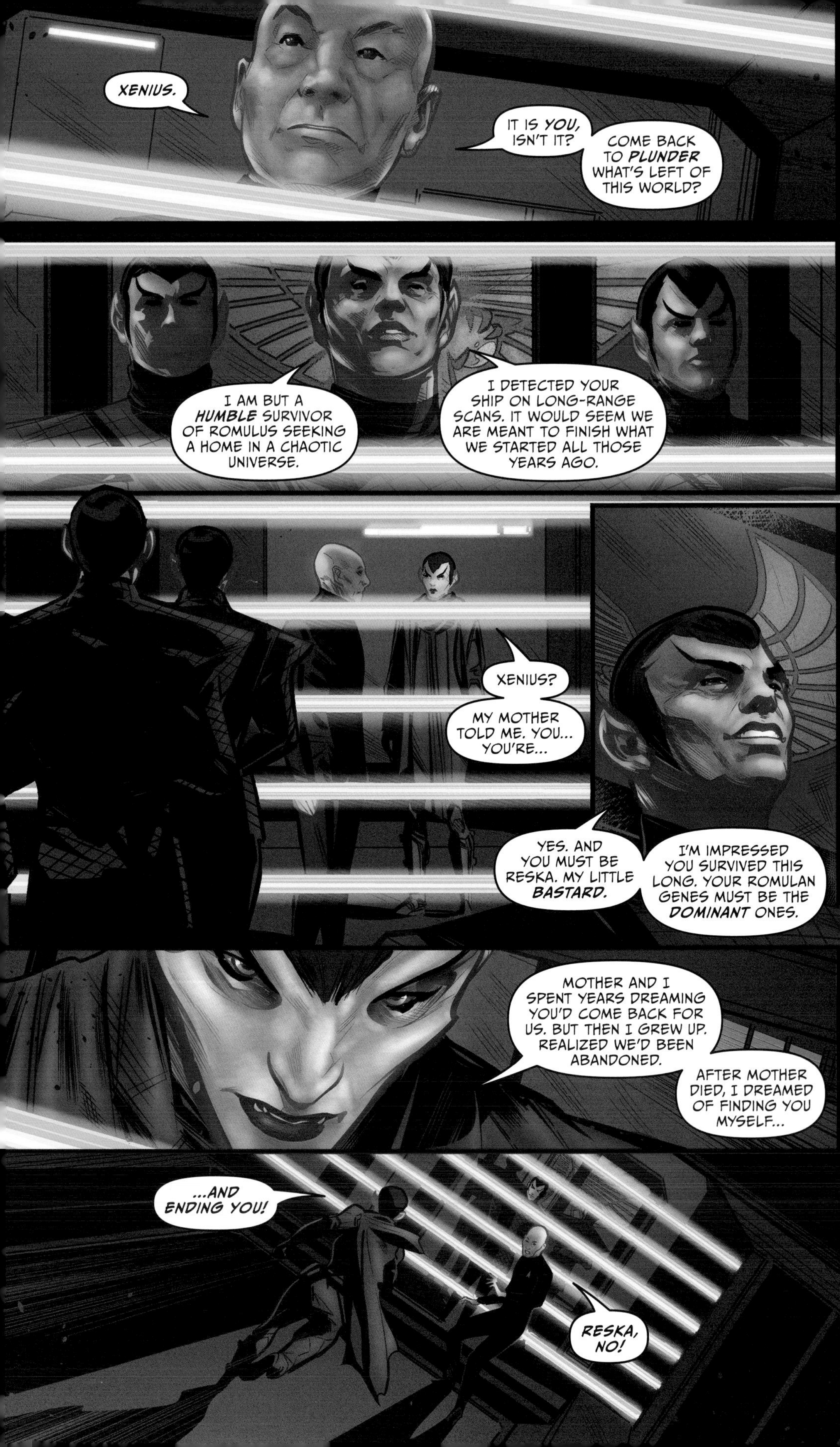
XENIUS.
IT IS YOU, ISN'T IT?
COME BACK TO PLUNDER WHAT'S LEFT OF THIS WORLD?
I AM BUT A HUMBLE SURVIVOR OF ROMULUS SEEKING A HOME IN A CHAOTIC UNIVERSE.
I DETECTED YOUR SHIP ON LONG-RANGE SCANS. IT WOULD SEEM WE ARE MEANT TO FINISH WHAT WE STARTED ALL THOSE YEARS AGO.
XENIUS?
MY MOTHER TOLD ME. YOU... YOU'RE...
YES. AND YOU MUST BE RESKA. MY LITTLE BASTARD.
I'M IMPRESSED YOU SURVIVED THIS LONG. YOUR ROMULAN GENES MUST BE THE DOMINANT ONES.
MOTHER AND I SPENT YEARS DREAMING YOU'D COME BACK FOR US. BUT THEN I GREW UP. REALIZED WE'D BEEN ABANDONED.
AFTER MOTHER DIED, I DREAMED OF FINDING YOU MYSELF...
...AND ENDING YOU!
RESKA, NO!

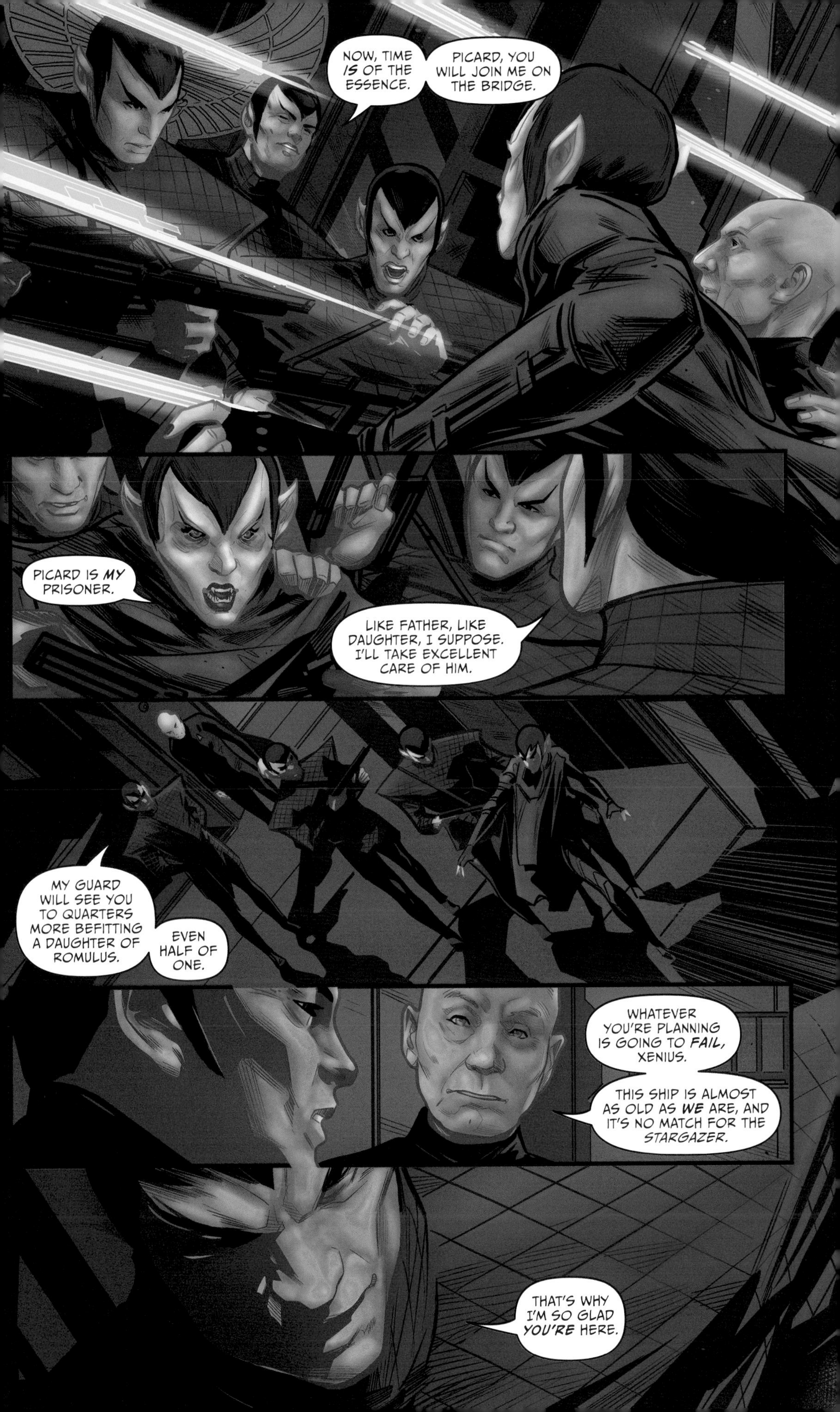
NOW, TIME *IS* OF THE ESSENCE.
PICARD, YOU WILL JOIN ME ON THE BRIDGE.
PICARD IS **MY** PRISONER.
LIKE FATHER, LIKE DAUGHTER, I SUPPOSE. I'LL TAKE EXCELLENT CARE OF HIM.
MY GUARD WILL SEE YOU TO QUARTERS MORE BEFITTING A DAUGHTER OF ROMULUS.
EVEN HALF OF ONE.
WHATEVER YOU'RE PLANNING IS GOING TO *FAIL*, XENIUS.
THIS SHIP IS ALMOST AS OLD AS **WE** ARE, AND IT'S NO MATCH FOR THE *STARGAZER*.
THAT'S WHY I'M SO GLAD ***YOU'RE*** HERE.

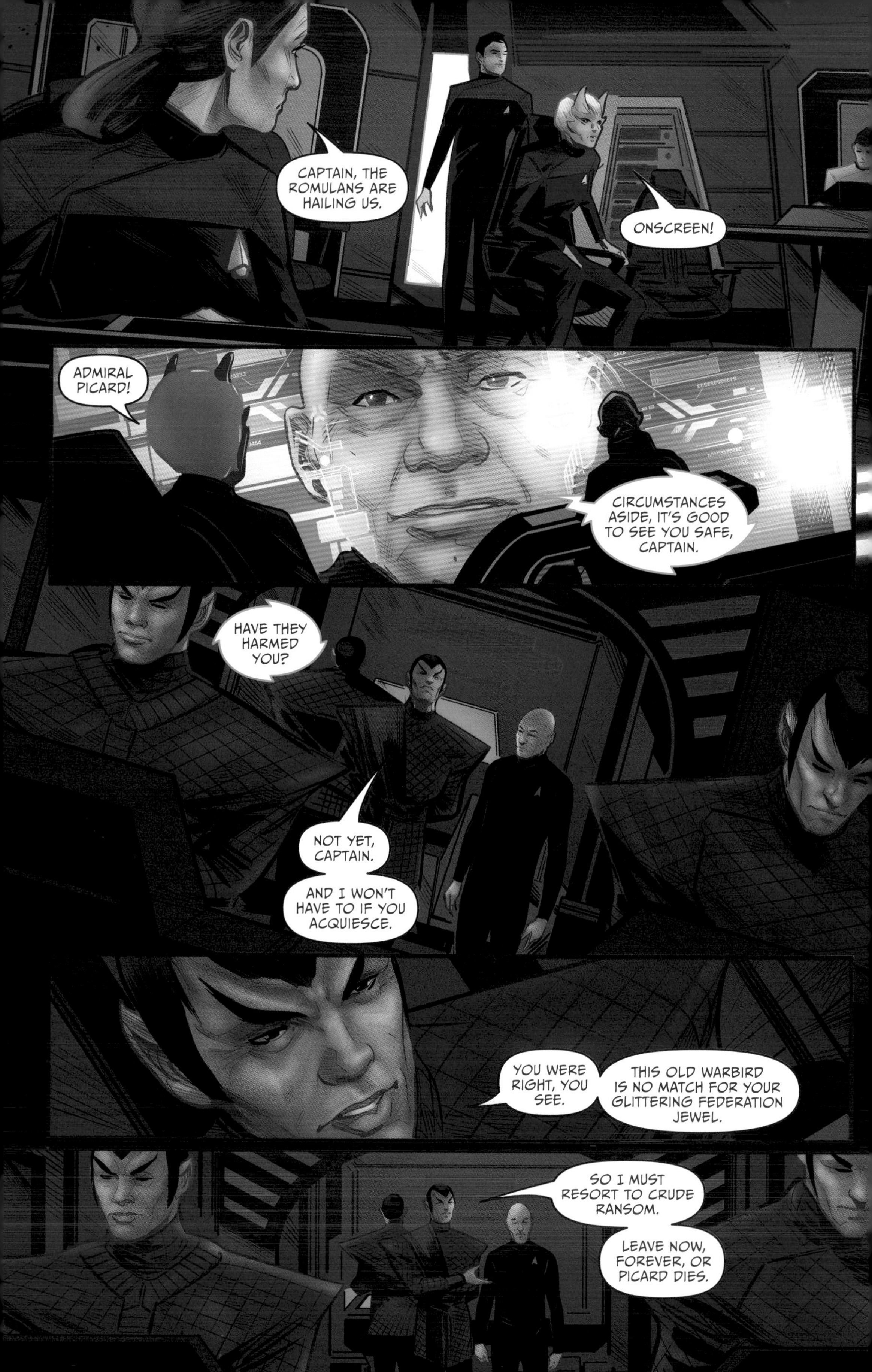
CAPTAIN, THE ROMULANS ARE HAILING US.
ONSCREEN!
ADMIRAL PICARD!
CIRCUMSTANCES ASIDE, IT'S GOOD TO SEE YOU SAFE, CAPTAIN.
HAVE THEY HARMED YOU?
NOT YET, CAPTAIN.
AND I WON'T HAVE TO IF YOU ACQUIESCE.
YOU WERE RIGHT, YOU SEE.
THIS OLD WARBIRD IS NO MATCH FOR YOUR GLITTERING FEDERATION JEWEL.
SO I MUST RESORT TO CRUDE RANSOM.
LEAVE NOW, FOREVER, OR PICARD DIES.

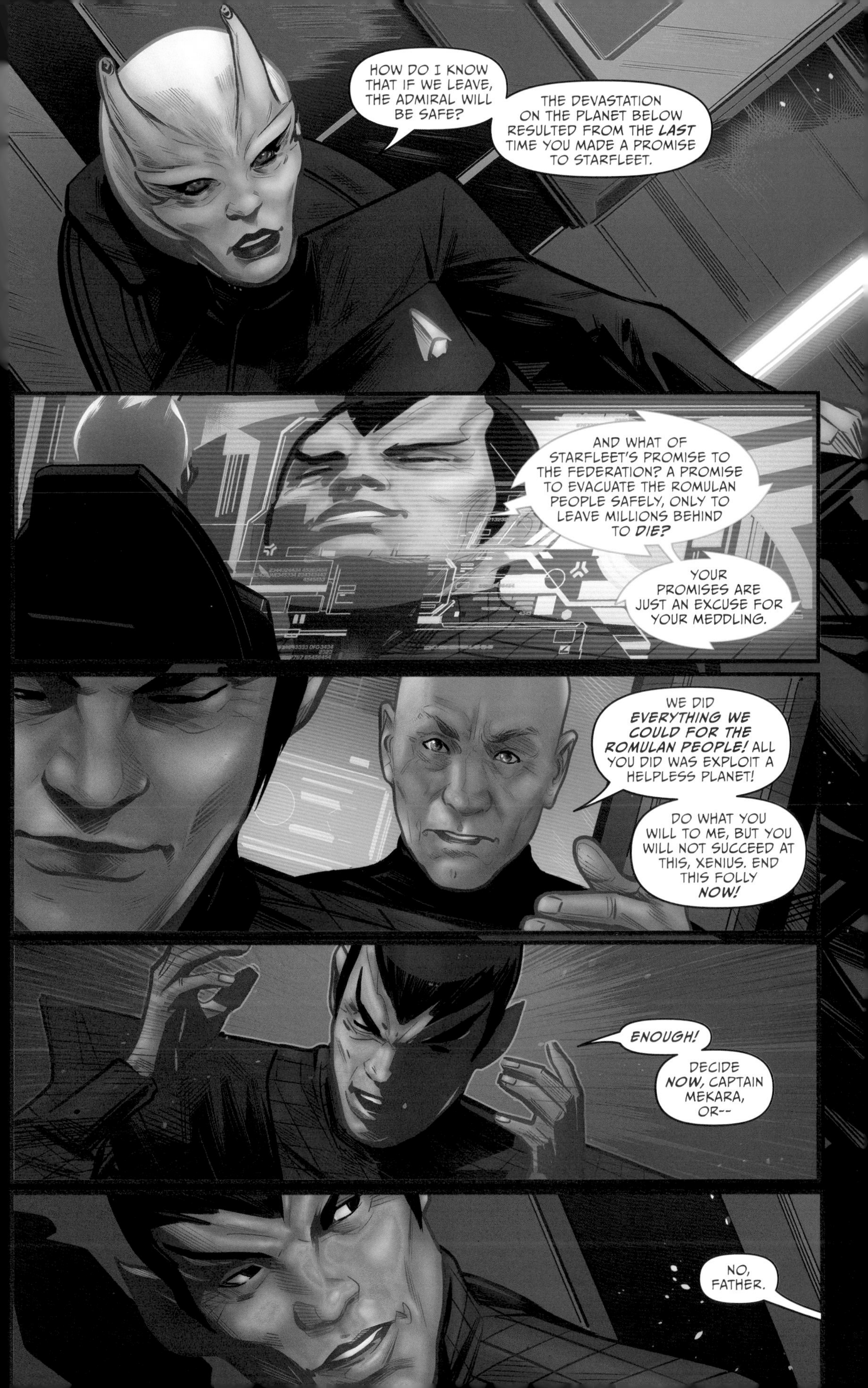
HOW DO I KNOW THAT IF WE LEAVE, THE ADMIRAL WILL BE SAFE?
THE DEVASTATION ON THE PLANET BELOW RESULTED FROM THE *LAST* TIME YOU MADE A PROMISE TO STARFLEET.
AND WHAT OF STARFLEET'S PROMISE TO THE FEDERATION? A PROMISE TO EVACUATE THE ROMULAN PEOPLE SAFELY, ONLY TO LEAVE MILLIONS BEHIND TO *DIE?*
YOUR PROMISES ARE JUST AN EXCUSE FOR YOUR MEDDLING.
WE DID ***EVERYTHING WE COULD FOR THE ROMULAN PEOPLE!*** ALL YOU DID WAS EXPLOIT A HELPLESS PLANET!
DO WHAT YOU WILL TO ME, BUT YOU WILL NOT SUCCEED AT THIS, XENIUS. END THIS FOLLY ***NOW!***
ENOUGH!
DECIDE *NOW,* CAPTAIN MEKARA, OR--
NO, FATHER.

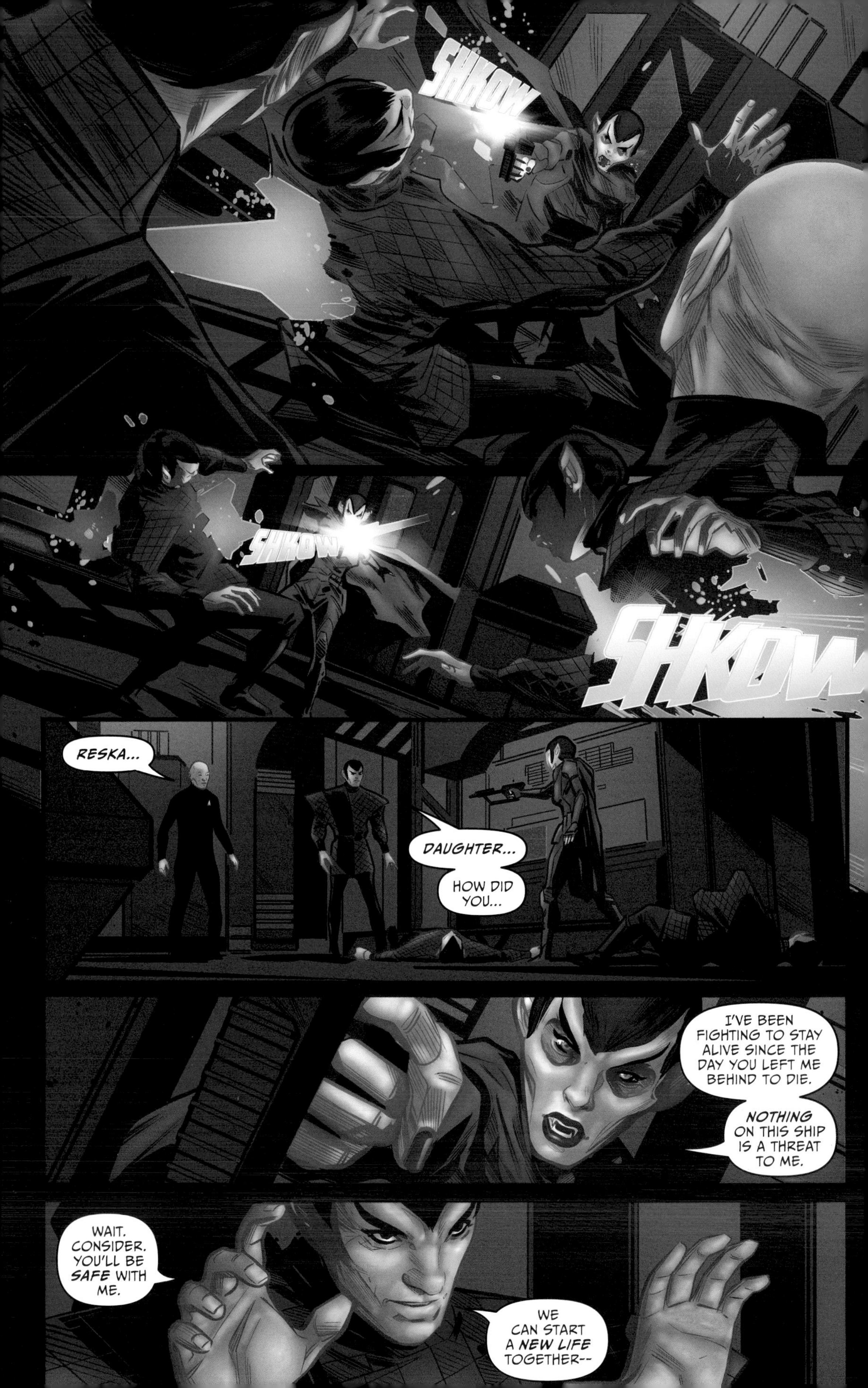
SHKOW
SHKOW
SHKOW
RESKA...
DAUGHTER...
HOW DID YOU...
I'VE BEEN FIGHTING TO STAY ALIVE SINCE THE DAY YOU LEFT ME BEHIND TO DIE.
NOTHING ON THIS SHIP IS A THREAT TO ME.
WAIT. CONSIDER. YOU'LL BE SAFE WITH ME.
WE CAN START A NEW LIFE TOGETHER--

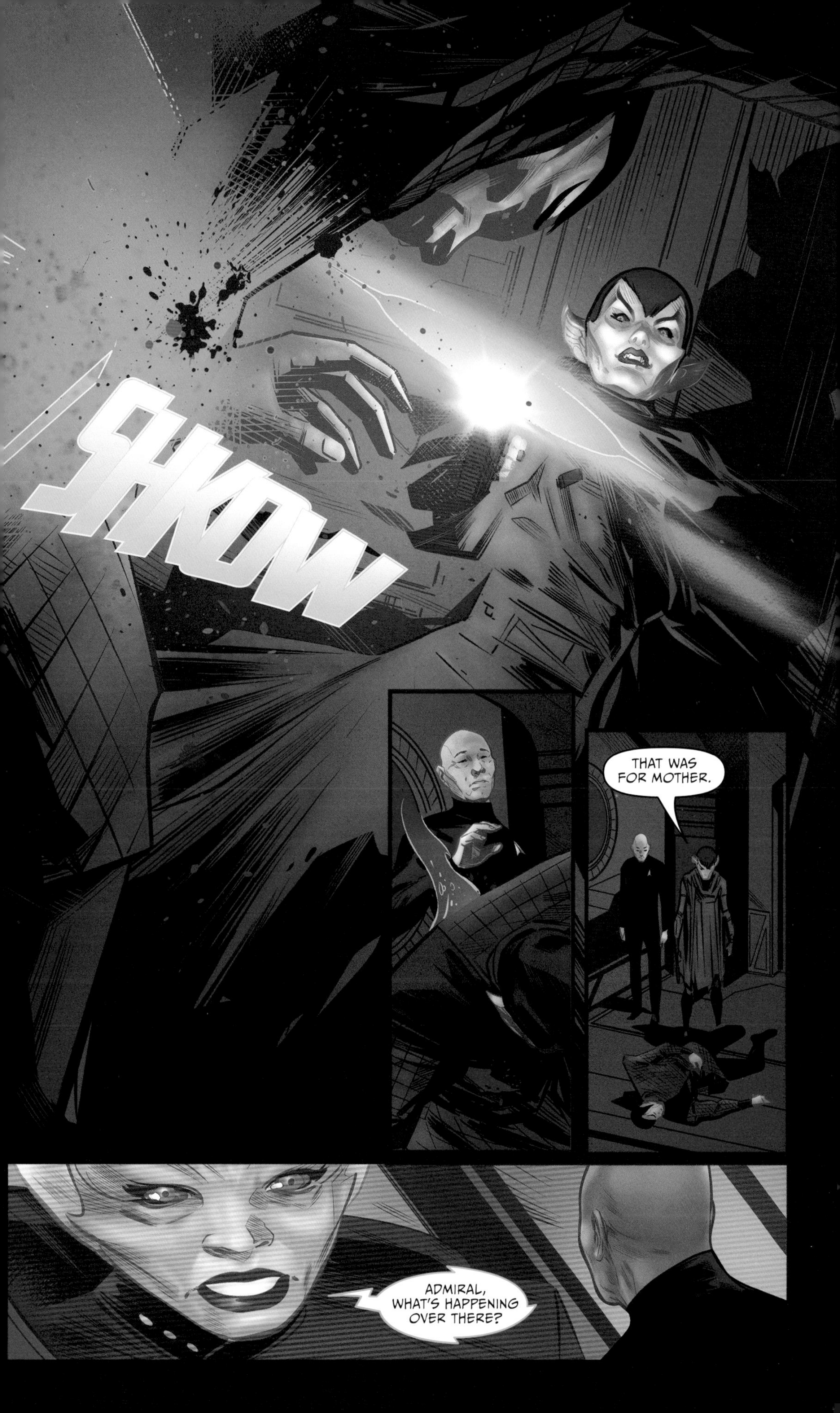
SHKOW
THAT WAS FOR MOTHER.
ADMIRAL, WHAT'S HAPPENING OVER THERE?

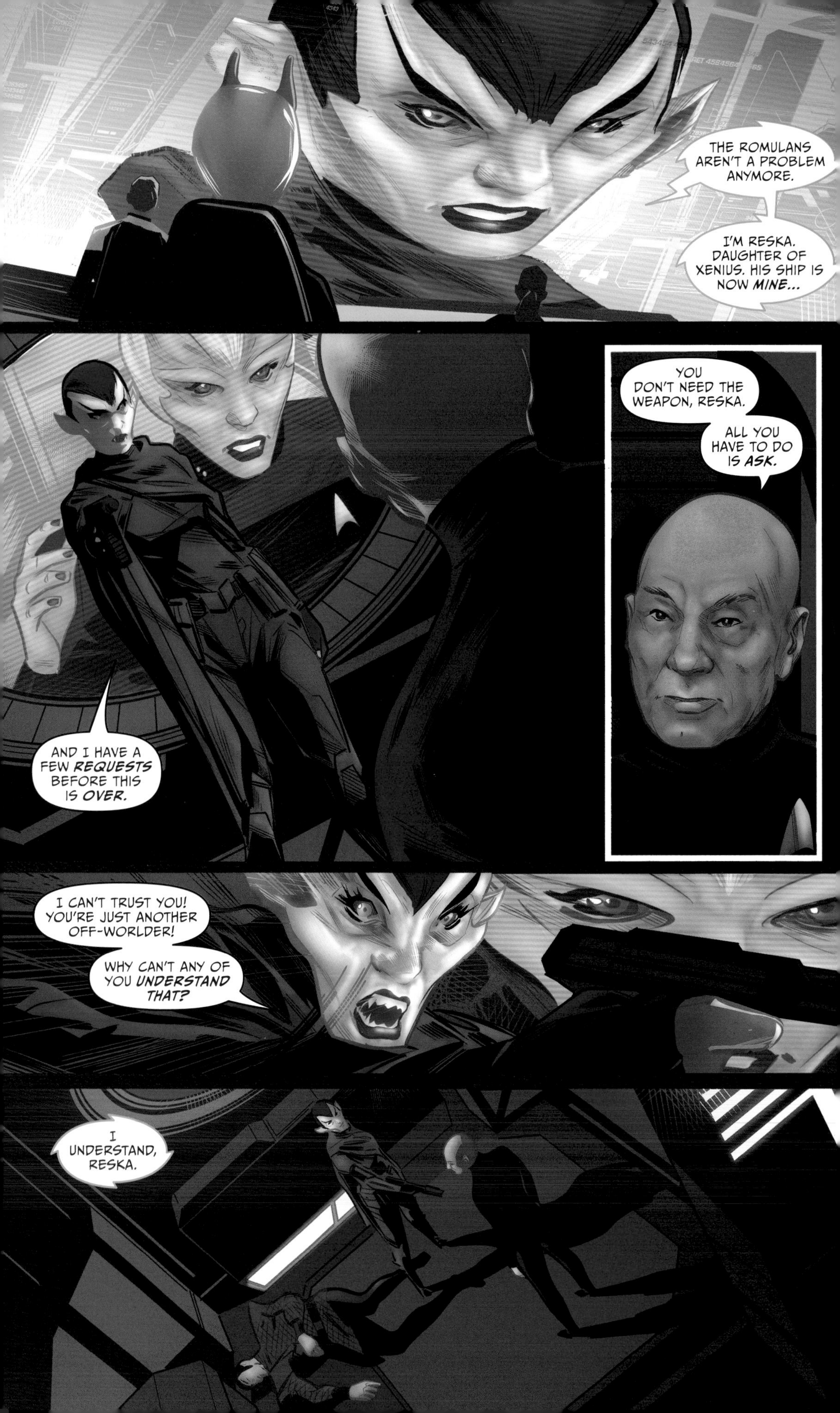
THE ROMULANS AREN'T A PROBLEM ANYMORE.
I'M RESKA. DAUGHTER OF XENIUS. HIS SHIP IS NOW *MINE...*
YOU DON'T NEED THE WEAPON, RESKA.
ALL YOU HAVE TO DO IS *ASK.*
AND I HAVE A FEW *REQUESTS* BEFORE THIS IS *OVER.*
I CAN'T TRUST YOU! YOU'RE JUST ANOTHER OFF-WORLDER!
WHY CAN'T ANY OF YOU *UNDERSTAND THAT?*
I UNDERSTAND, RESKA.

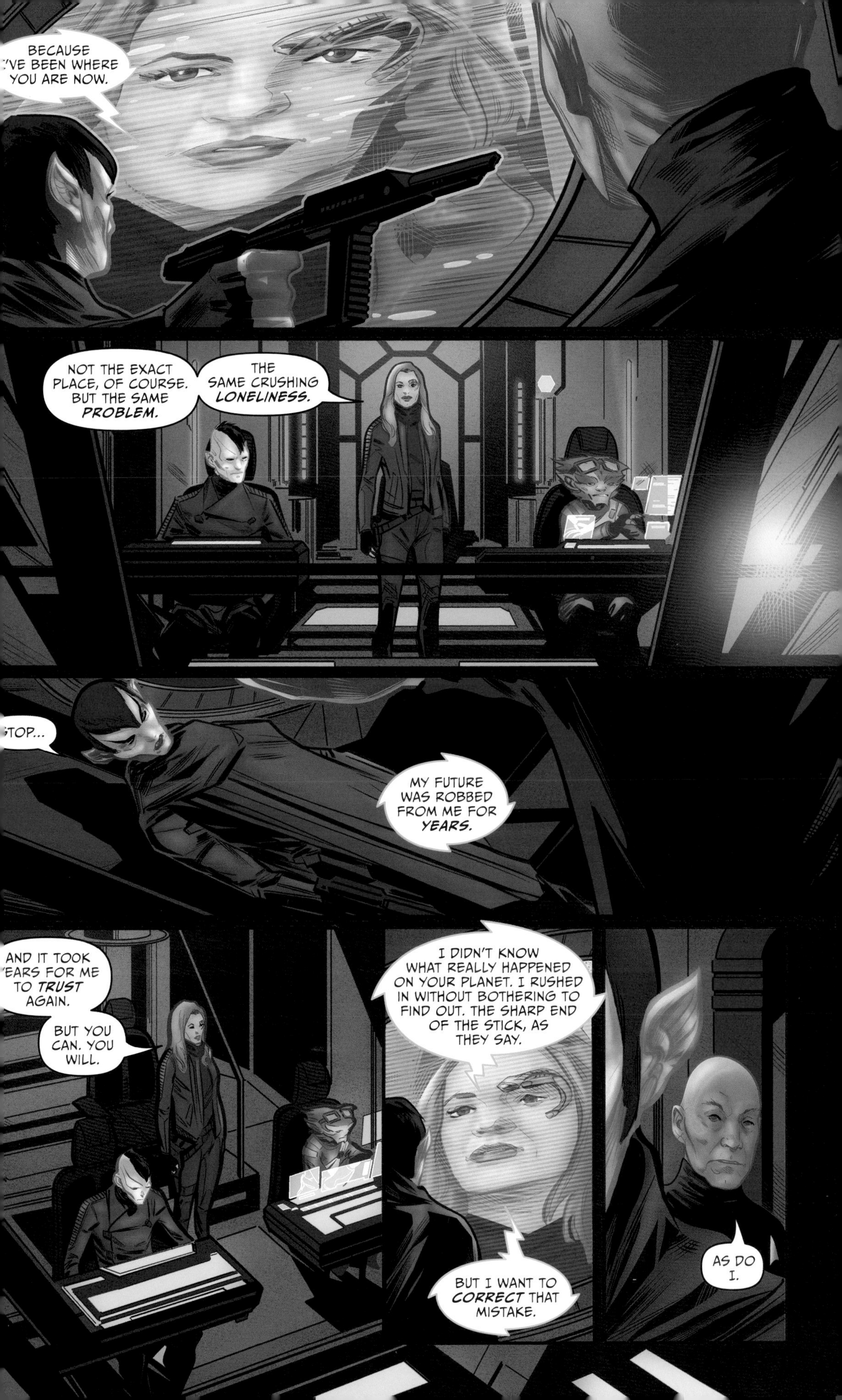
BECAUSE I'VE BEEN WHERE YOU ARE NOW.
NOT THE EXACT PLACE, OF COURSE. BUT THE SAME *PROBLEM.*
THE SAME CRUSHING *LONELINESS.*
STOP...
MY FUTURE WAS ROBBED FROM ME FOR *YEARS.*
AND IT TOOK YEARS FOR ME TO *TRUST* AGAIN.
BUT YOU CAN. YOU WILL.
I DIDN'T KNOW WHAT REALLY HAPPENED ON YOUR PLANET. I RUSHED IN WITHOUT BOTHERING TO FIND OUT. THE SHARP END OF THE STICK, AS THEY SAY.
BUT I WANT TO *CORRECT* THAT MISTAKE.
AS DO I.

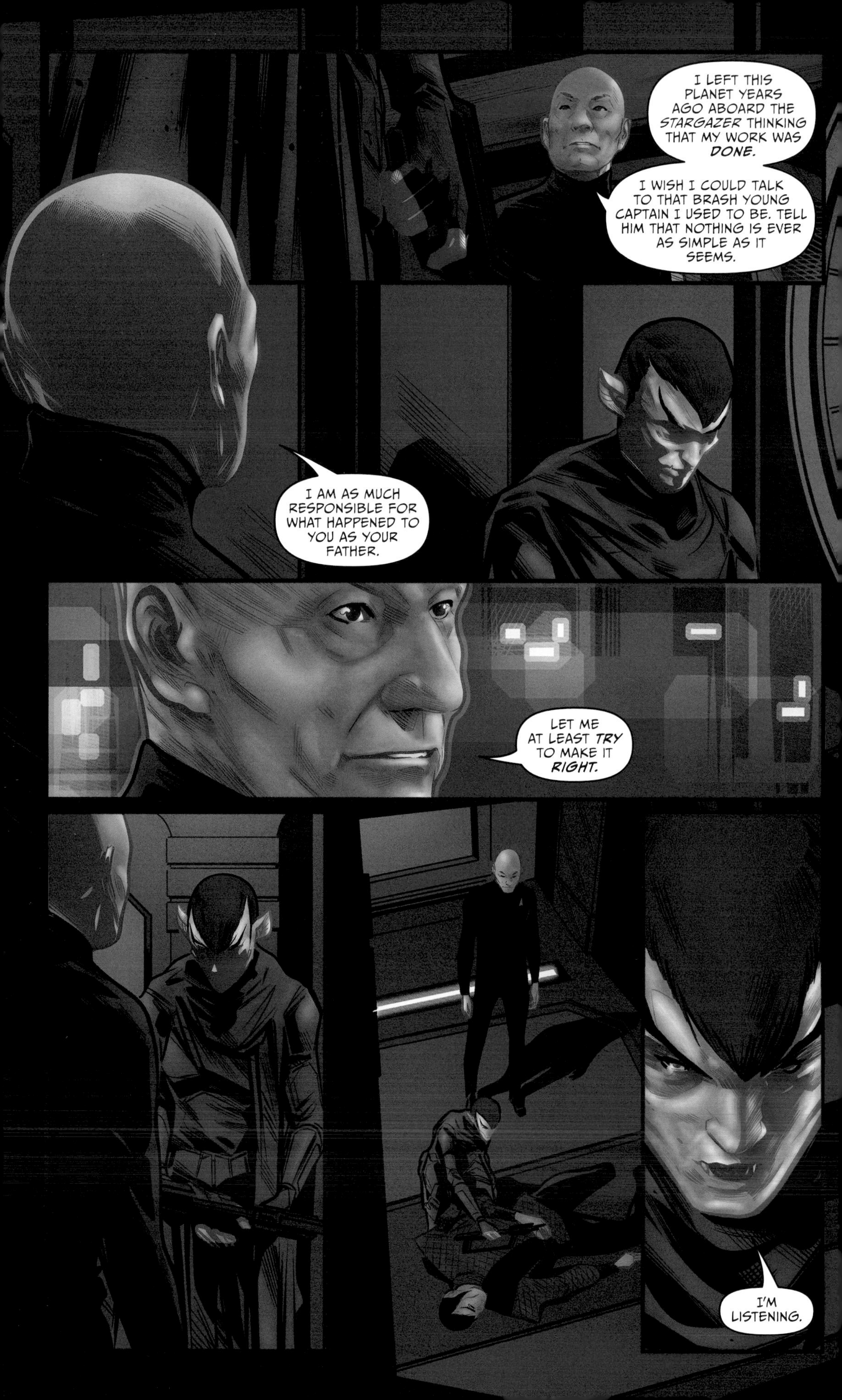

I LEFT THIS PLANET YEARS AGO ABOARD THE *STARGAZER* THINKING THAT MY WORK WAS ***DONE.***
I WISH I COULD TALK TO THAT BRASH YOUNG CAPTAIN I USED TO BE. TELL HIM THAT NOTHING IS EVER AS SIMPLE AS IT SEEMS.
I AM AS MUCH RESPONSIBLE FOR WHAT HAPPENED TO YOU AS YOUR FATHER.
LET ME AT LEAST *TRY* TO MAKE IT ***RIGHT.***
I'M LISTENING.

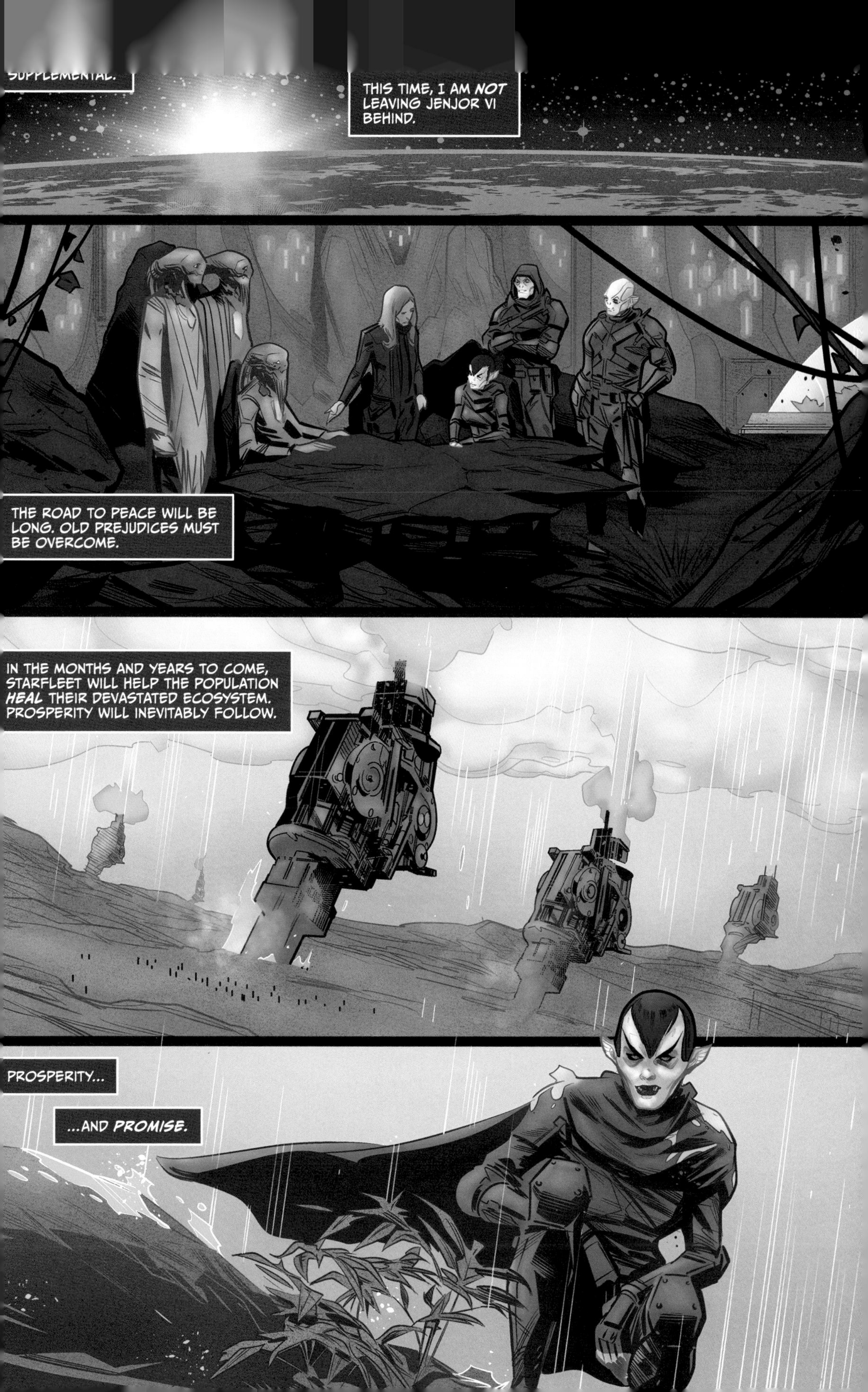
SUPPLEMENTAL.
THIS TIME, I AM NOT LEAVING JENJOR VI BEHIND.
THE ROAD TO PEACE WILL BE LONG. OLD PREJUDICES MUST BE OVERCOME.
IN THE MONTHS AND YEARS TO COME, STARFLEET WILL HELP THE POPULATION HEAL THEIR DEVASTATED ECOSYSTEM. PROSPERITY WILL INEVITABLY FOLLOW.
PROSPERITY...
...AND PROMISE.

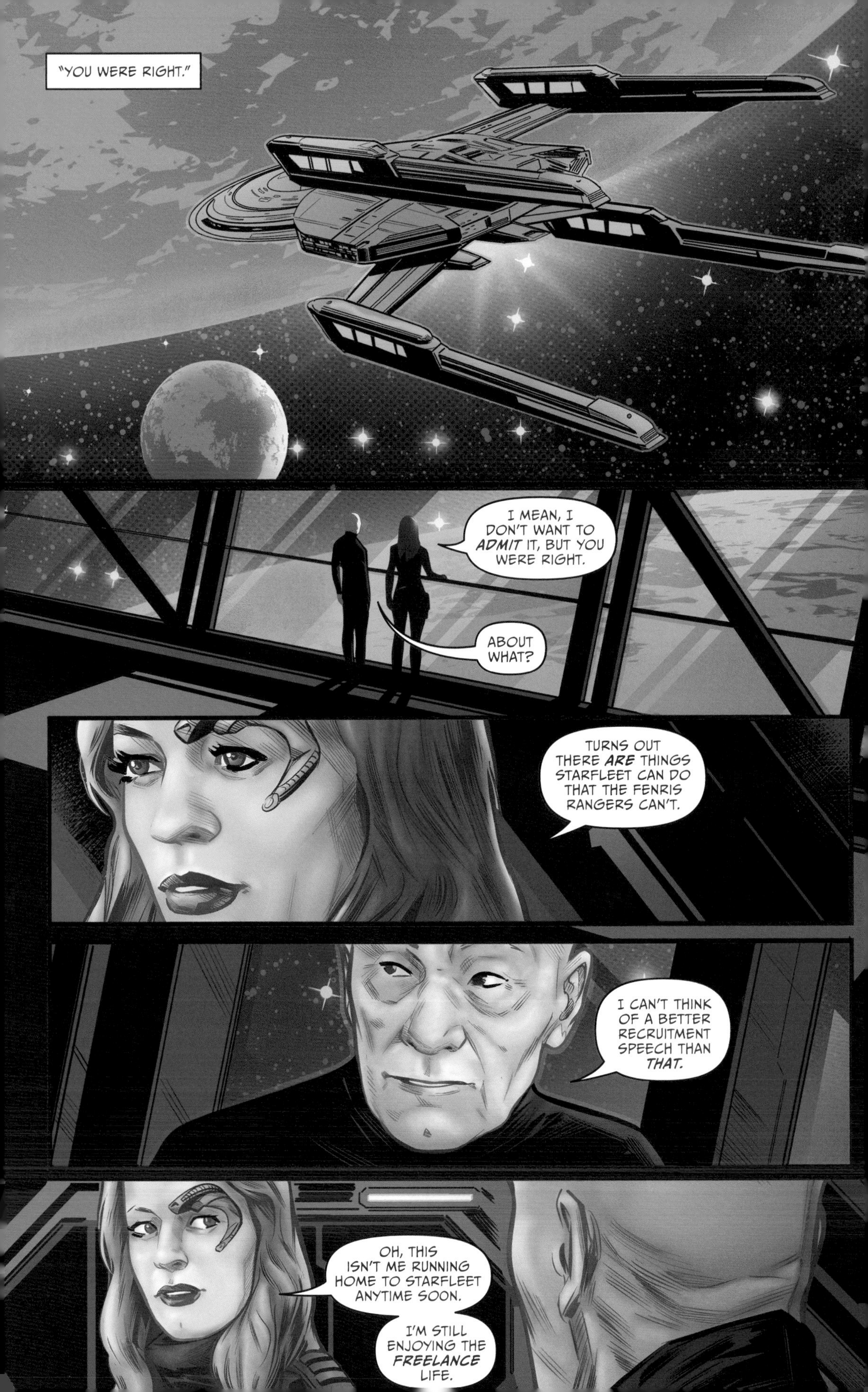
"YOU WERE RIGHT."
I MEAN, I DON'T WANT TO *ADMIT* IT, BUT YOU WERE RIGHT.
ABOUT WHAT?
TURNS OUT THERE ***ARE*** THINGS STARFLEET CAN DO THAT THE FENRIS RANGERS CAN'T.
I CAN'T THINK OF A BETTER RECRUITMENT SPEECH THAN *THAT.*
OH, THIS ISN'T ME RUNNING HOME TO STARFLEET ANYTIME SOON.
I'M STILL ENJOYING THE *FREELANCE* LIFE.

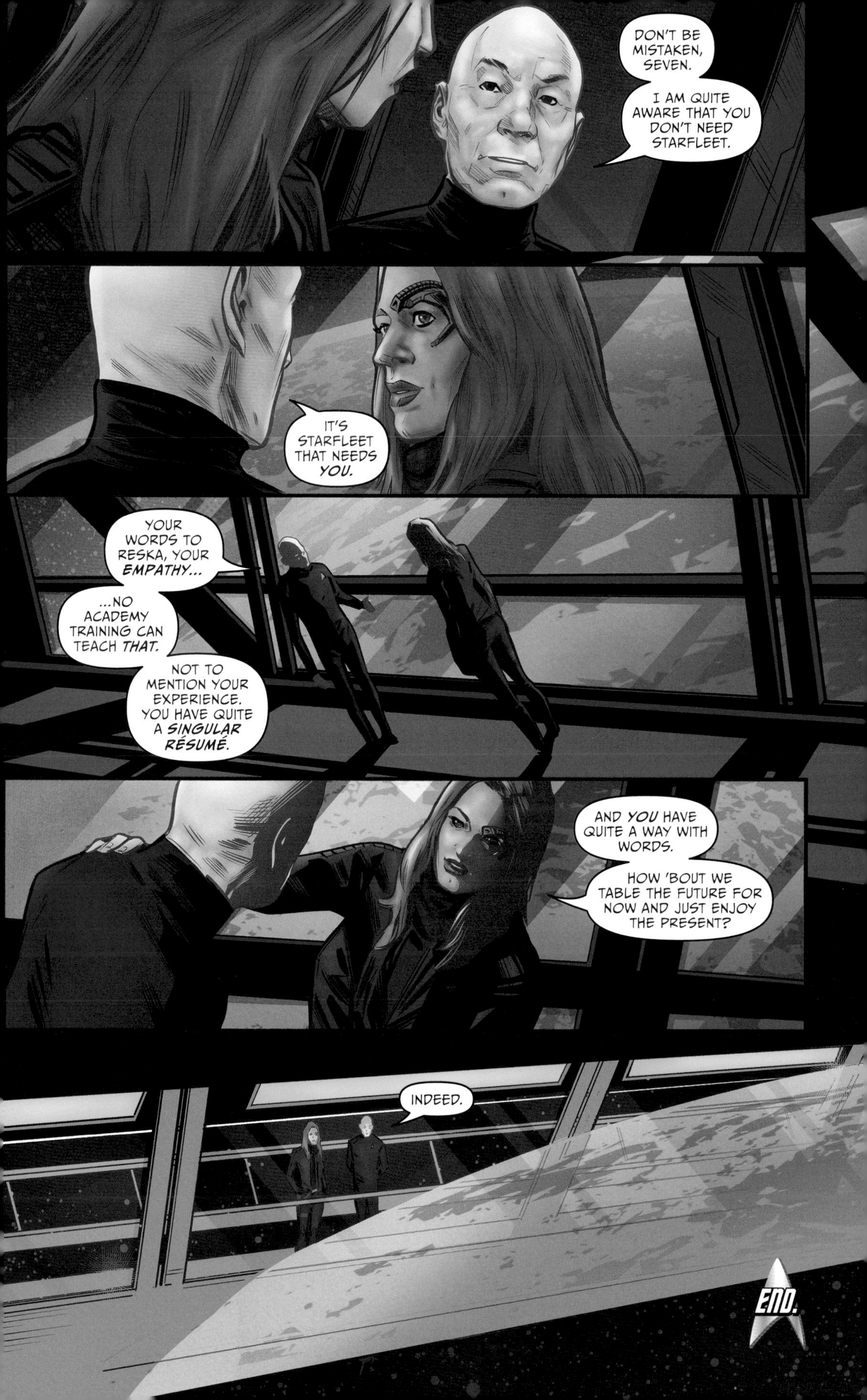

DON'T BE MISTAKEN, SEVEN.
I AM QUITE AWARE THAT YOU DON'T NEED STARFLEET.
IT'S STARFLEET THAT NEEDS *YOU.*
YOUR WORDS TO RESKA, YOUR *EMPATHY...*
...NO ACADEMY TRAINING CAN TEACH *THAT.*
NOT TO MENTION YOUR EXPERIENCE. YOU HAVE QUITE A *SINGULAR RÉSUMÉ.*
AND *YOU* HAVE QUITE A WAY WITH WORDS.
HOW 'BOUT WE TABLE THE FUTURE FOR NOW AND JUST ENJOY THE PRESENT?
INDEED.
END.

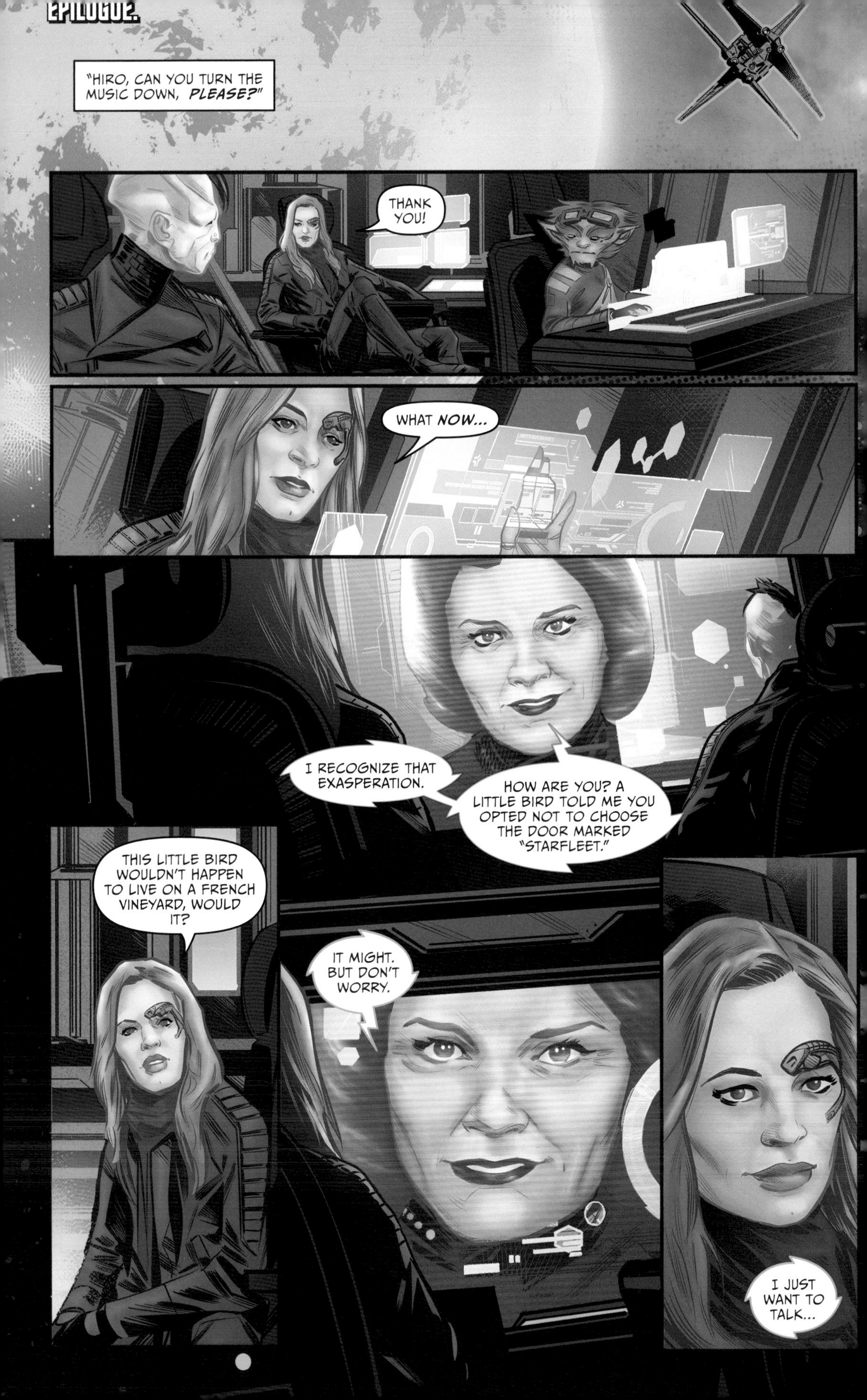
EPILOGUE.
"HIRO, CAN YOU TURN THE MUSIC DOWN, PLEASE?"
THANK YOU!
WHAT NOW...
I RECOGNIZE THAT EXASPERATION.
HOW ARE YOU? A LITTLE BIRD TOLD ME YOU OPTED NOT TO CHOOSE THE DOOR MARKED "STARFLEET."
THIS LITTLE BIRD WOULDN'T HAPPEN TO LIVE ON A FRENCH VINEYARD, WOULD IT?
IT MIGHT. BUT DON'T WORRY.
I JUST WANT TO TALK...

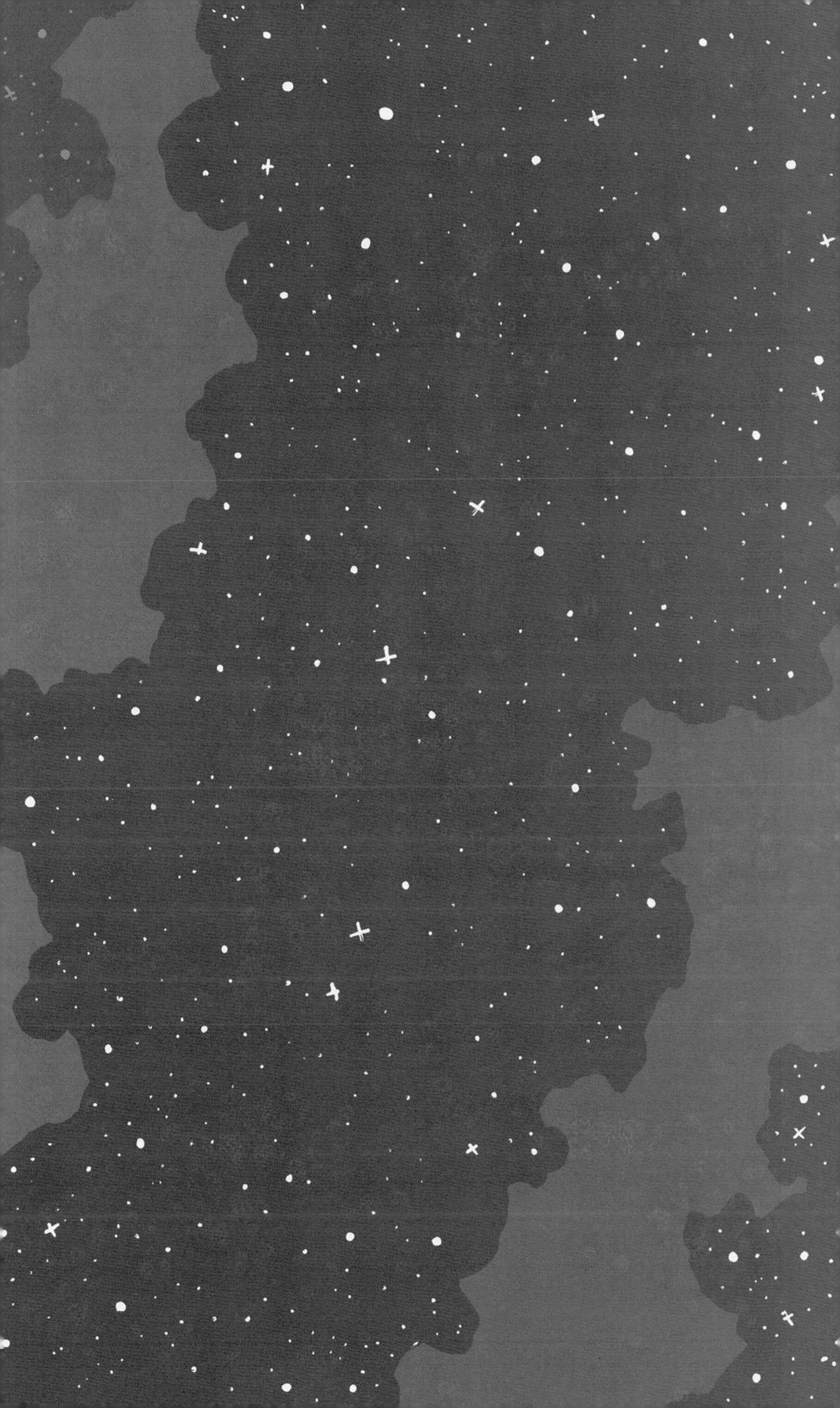

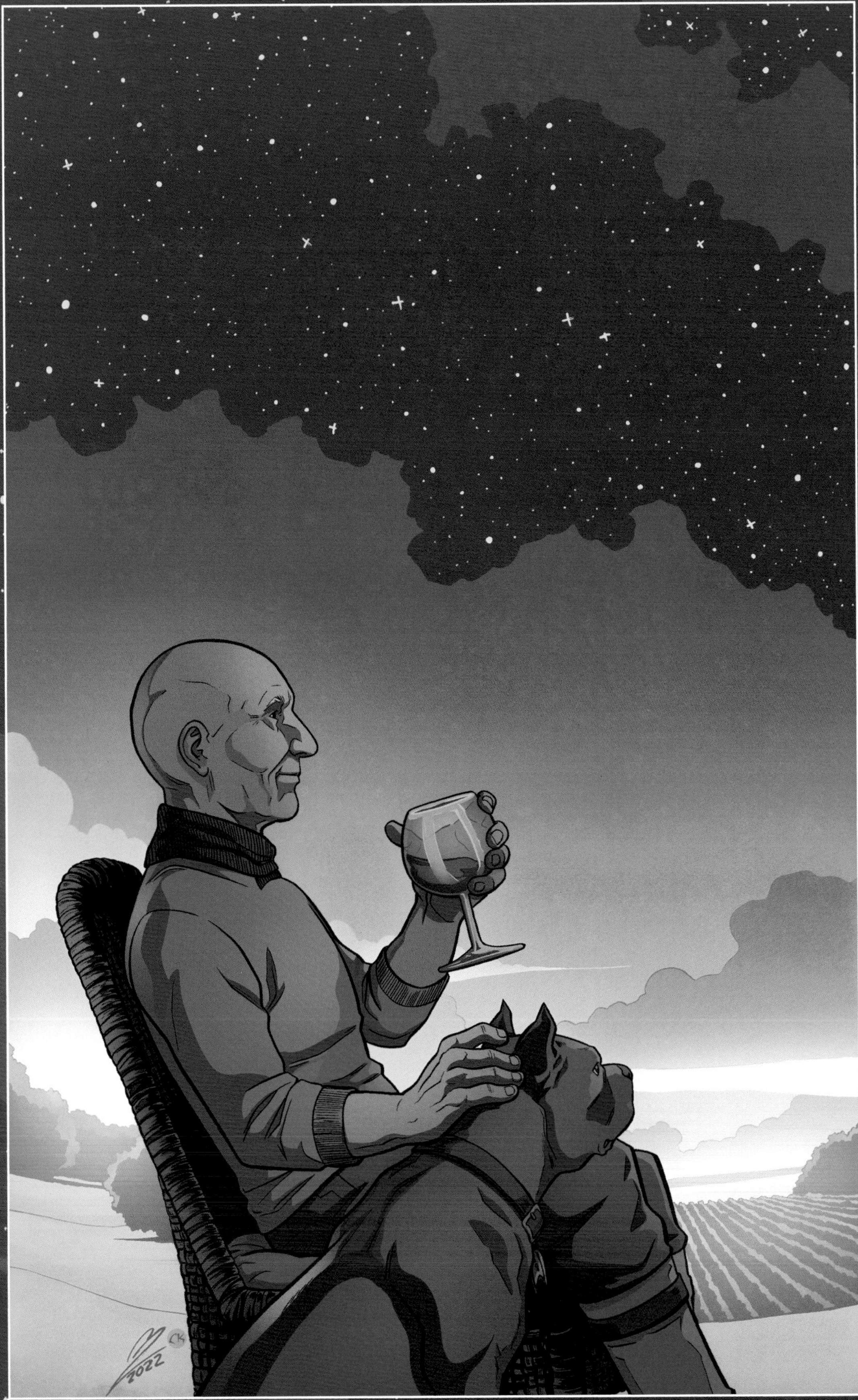

art by MEGAN LEVENS | colors by CHARLIE KIRCHOFF

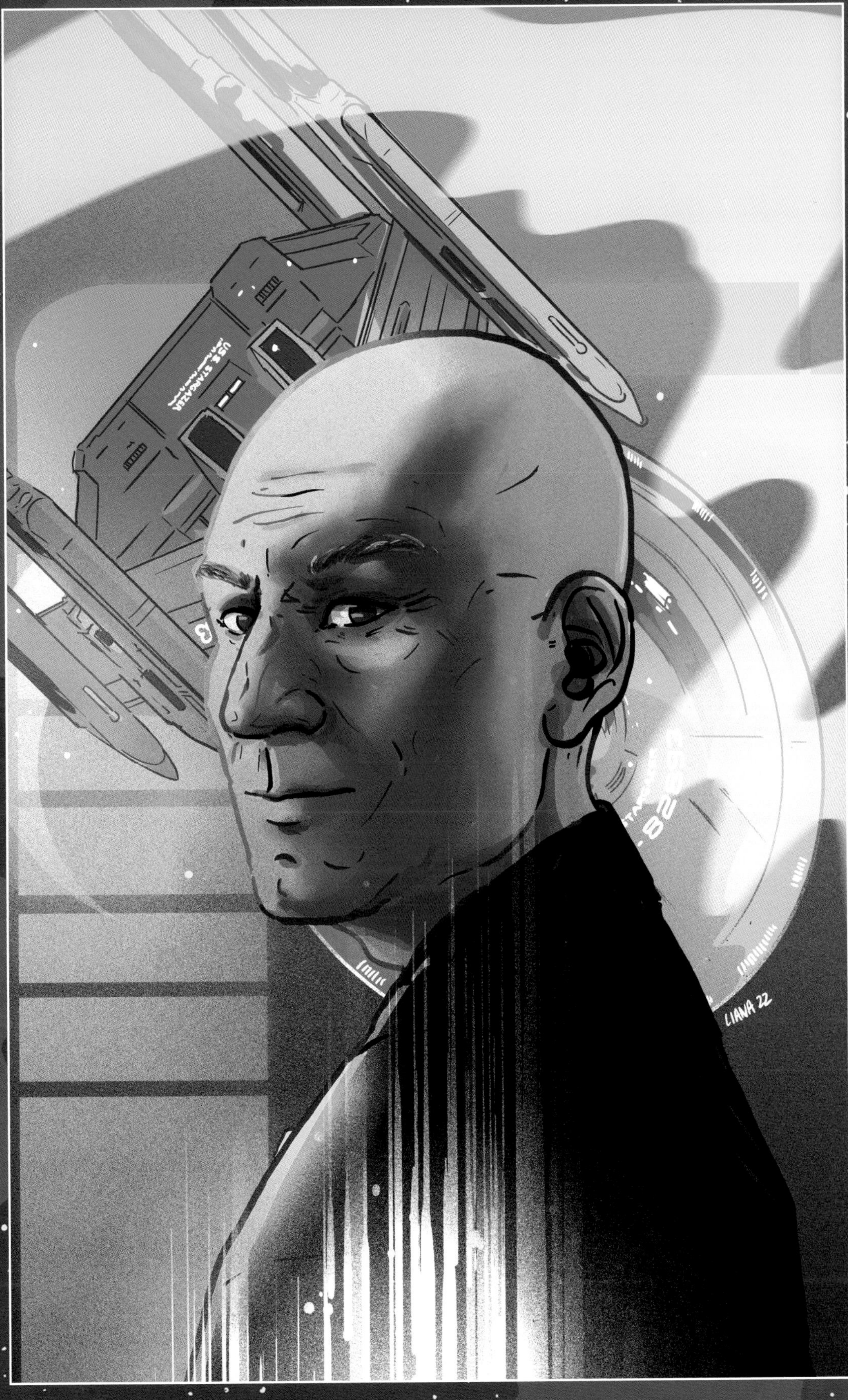
U.S.S. STARGAZER
LIANA 22

art by LIANA KANGAS

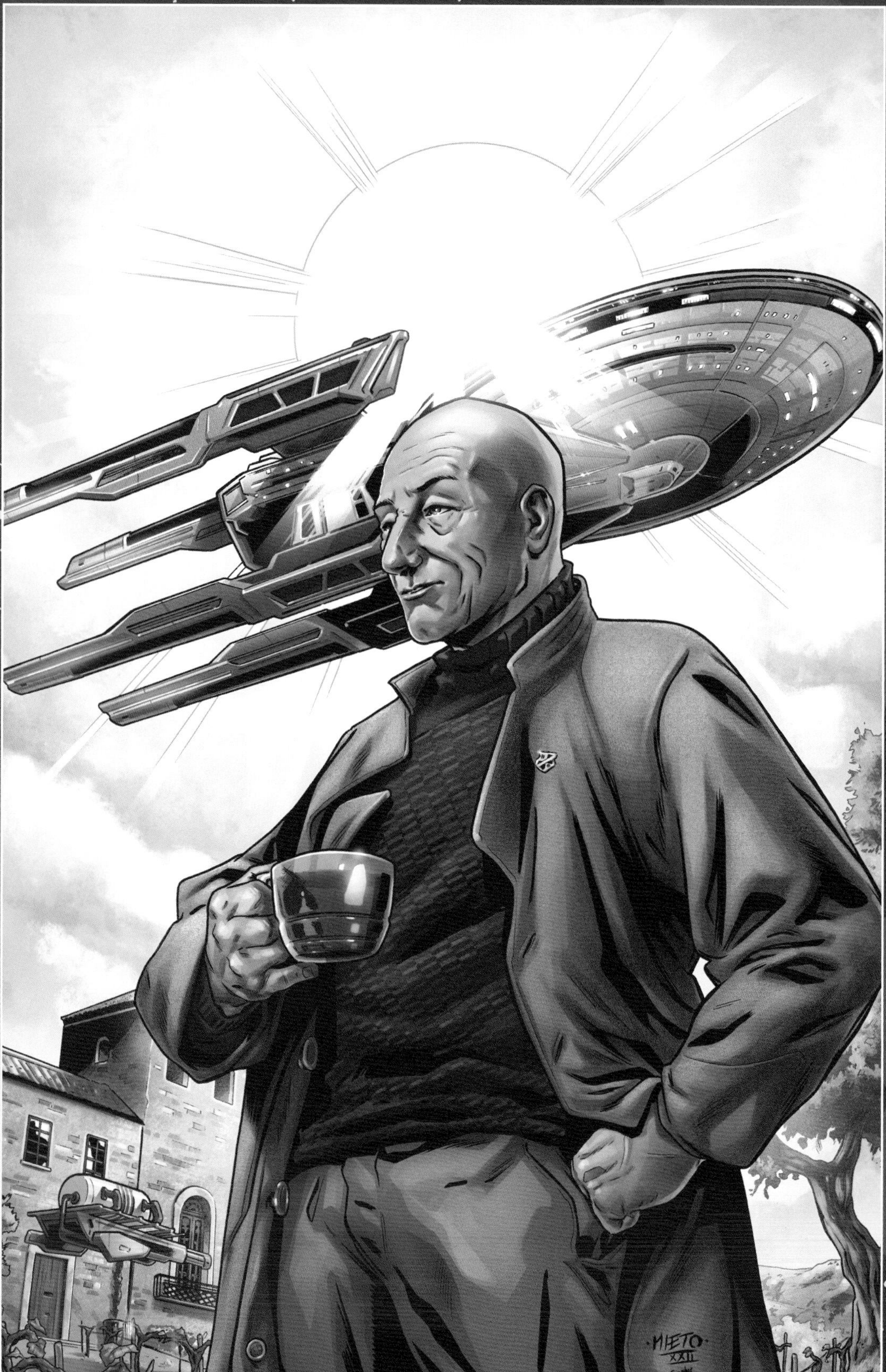
NIETO
XXII

art by CARLOS NIETO | colors by FRAN GAMBOA

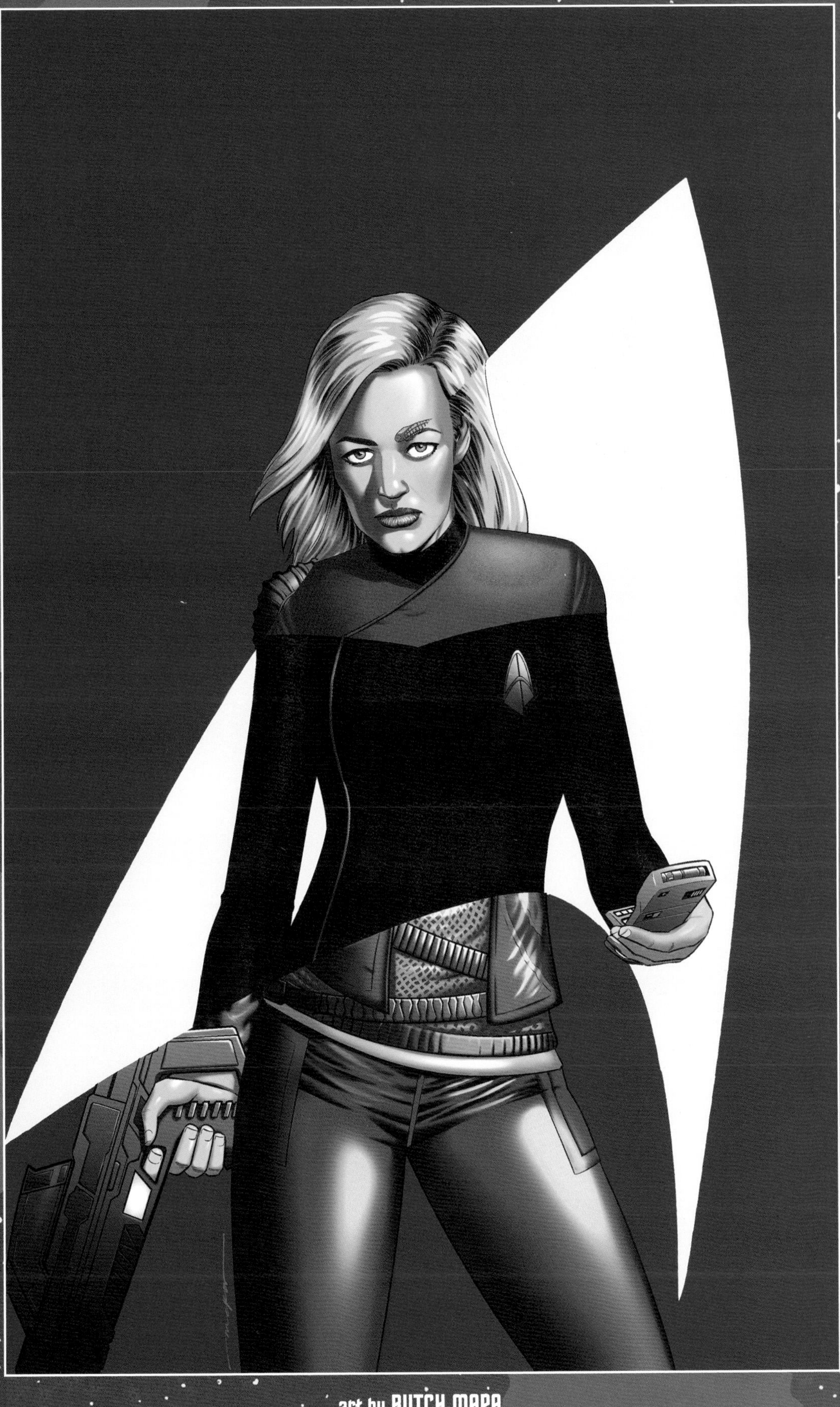

art by BUTCH MAPA

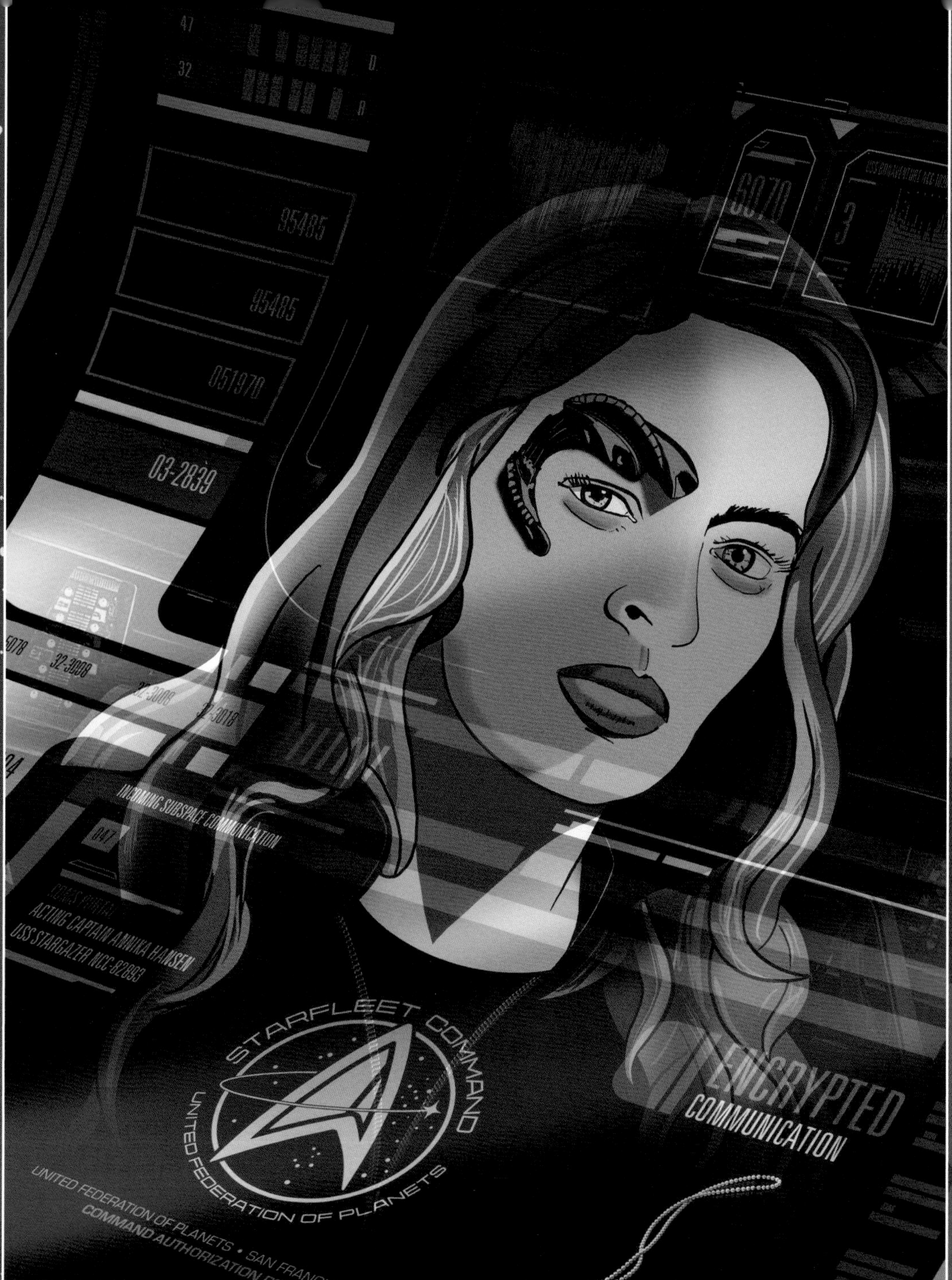
95485
95485
051970
03-2839
INCOMING SUBSPACE COMMUNICATION
ACTING CAPTAIN ANNIKA HANSEN
USS STARGAZER NCC-82893
STARFLEET COMMAND
UNITED FEDERATION OF PLANETS
ENCRYPTED
COMMUNICATION
UNITED FEDERATION OF PLANETS • SAN FRANCISCO • EARTH
COMMAND AUTHORIZATION REQUIRED
53-659
63-062

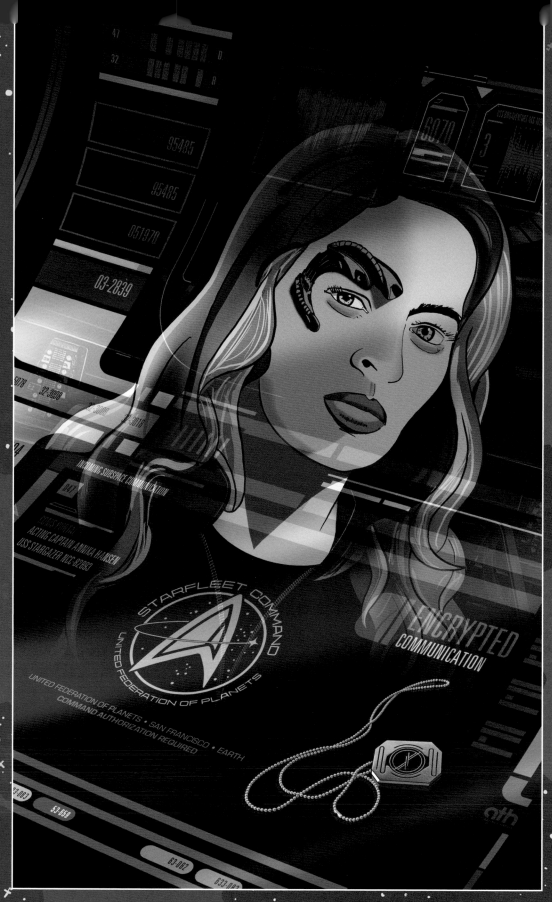

art by AARON HARVEY

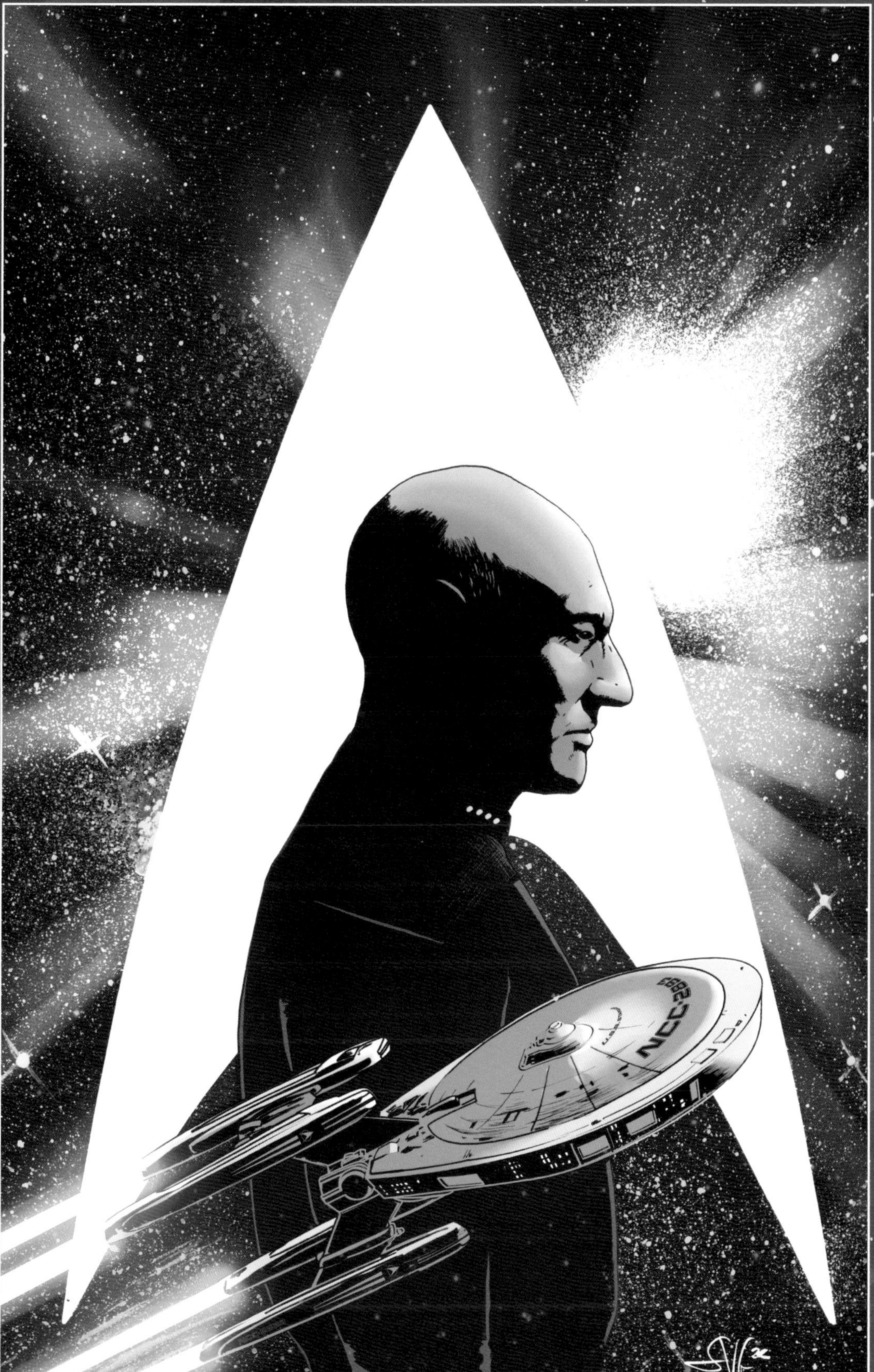
NCC-2893

art by SEAN VON GORMAN | colors by JOSH JENSEN

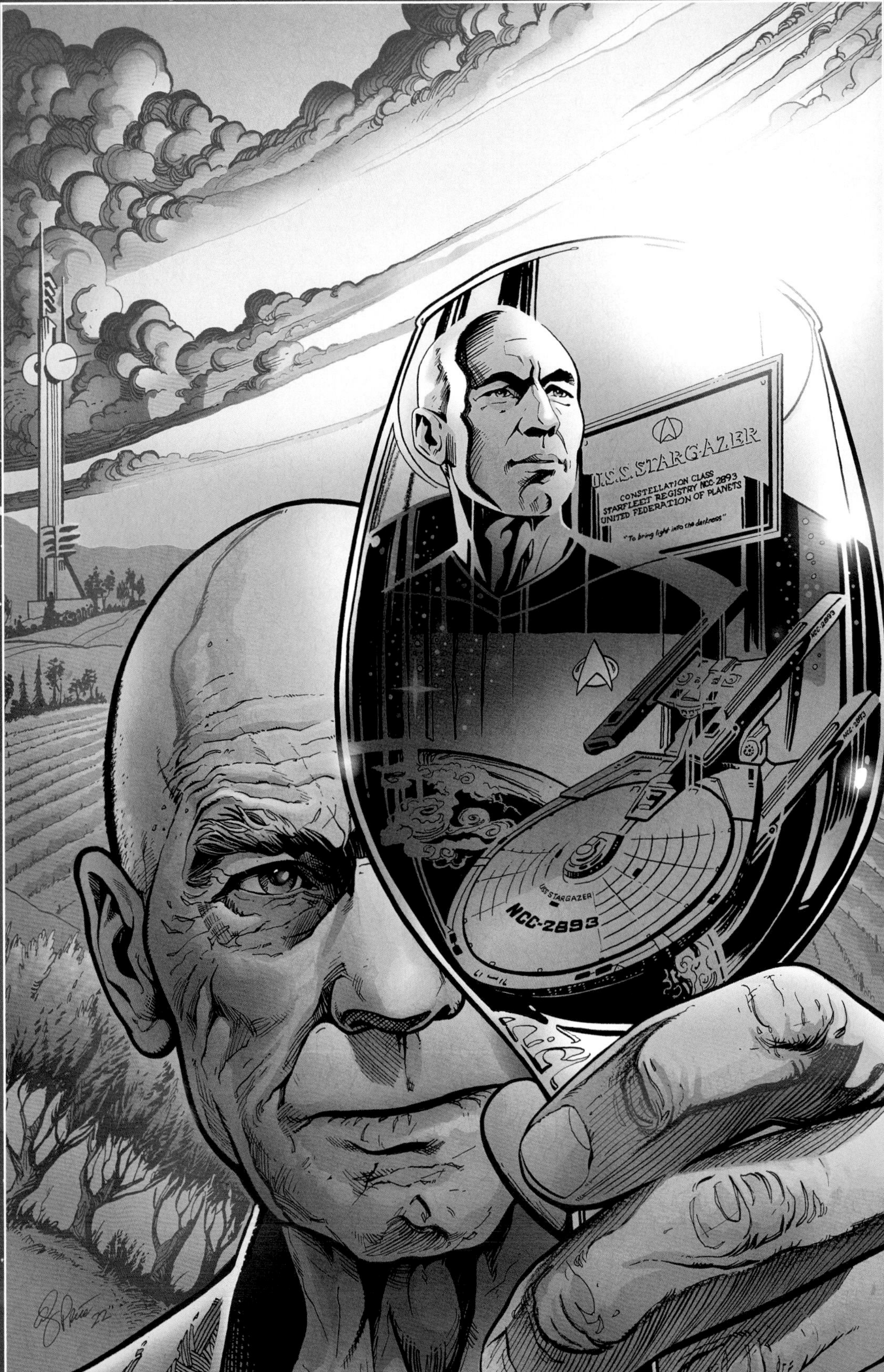
U.S.S. STARGAZER
CONSTELLATION CLASS
STARFLEET REGISTRY NCC-2893
UNITED FEDERATION OF PLANETS
"To bring light into the darkness"
U.S.S. STARGAZER
NCC-2893

art by ANDY PRICE

Star Trek: Picard—Stargazer Crew Interview

From *Star Trek: Discovery* to *Strange New Worlds–The Illyrian Enigma*, the Beyer-Johnson duo have created some of IDW's most iconic comic series tying into and bridging the gap between the comics and critically acclaimed TV shows. What is your creative process like? How has it evolved since your first collaboration?

Kirsten Beyer and Mike Johnson: Once we know which characters we'll be using, we like to start with a simple question: What would we like to see that we haven't seen on the shows? That could be a new location, a new threat, a new alien species, or delving deeper into a character we already know. We bat the story back and forth, and then Mike goes and writes a draft of the script. Kirsten reviews it, makes changes, we argue about them until we quit and vow never to work together again. Kidding! It's always an enjoyable process and has been since it started.

Angel Hernandez is a frequent collaborator on your *Star Trek* comics creations. What do you feel he uniquely brings to the stories you tell?

KB and MJ: Angel is the not-so-secret weapon of the *Trek* comics. And his superpower is his ability to draw anything. And we do mean anything! Our imaginations as writers are free to go as far out as they can because we know that Angel will make anything we throw at him thrilling and beautiful. And it's not just the spectacle he does so well! He excels at the quieter moments of conversation between characters that are such an integral part of *Star Trek*.

***Stargazer* leads up to the highly anticipated final season of *Star Trek: Picard* on Paramount+. Can you provide some insight into how you landed on this particular story? What does it reveal about Picard and Seven that will lend to viewers' experience of the Admiral's final voyage?**

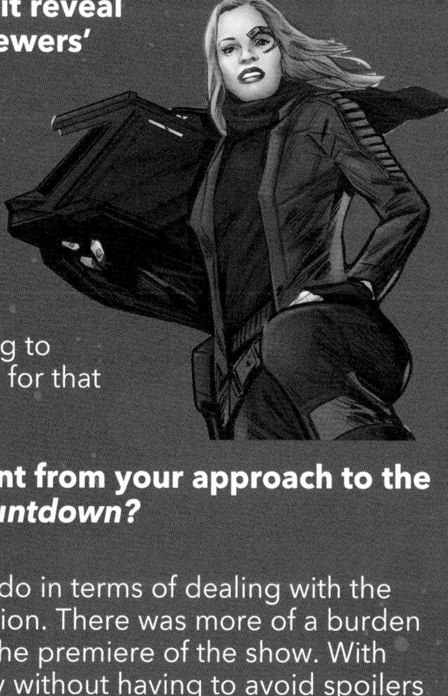

KB and MJ: We wanted to reach back into Picard's days as a younger captain and contrast that with where he is now, with decades of experience under his belt. We created the world of Jenjor VI as a way to give both the past and present Picards the same problem to wrestle with. In addition, we knew that Seven would be returning to Starfleet in Season 3 so we wanted to set the table for that by showing her evolution as a Fenris Ranger.

Was the approach to this comic any different from your approach to the *Star Trek: Picard* prequel series, *Picard–Countdown*?

KB and MJ: *Countdown* had more heavy lifting to do in terms of dealing with the vitally important backstory of the Romulan evacuation. There was more of a burden of proof with the series because it was setting up the premiere of the show. With *Stargazer*, we are able to tell a more personal story without having to avoid spoilers the way we did with *Countdown*.

What goes into writing Picard, one of pop culture's most prolific characters? Are there unique considerations when writing him for different media? TV series versus comics, for example? What are the challenges of writing his character?

KB and MJ: All the fans who have loved *The Next Generation* over the years can hear Picard's voice in their ears. The trick is capturing that voice on the page, be it for an artist drawing the character or for Sir Patrick Stewart himself saying the lines. Comics has it easier because there is no greater expert on how the character sounds than Sir Patrick, so the bar is higher writing for TV. But whatever the medium, the trick is to keep the character sounding true to the character millions of fans know and love. It can be challenging to avoid cliched lines like "Make it so" or "Engage," so they have to be deployed judiciously.

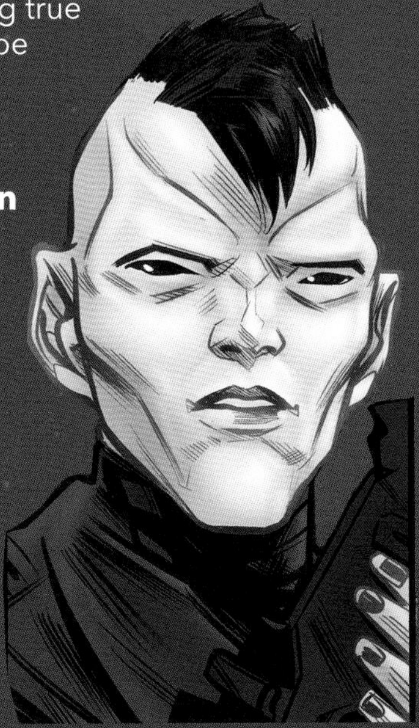

As readers may or may not know, Hiro is not an entirely new character as he stems from your *Picard–No Man's Land* audio drama. Is there a specific reason you felt it was time for him to make his comics debut?

KB and MJ: We needed more Fenris Rangers for the comic! We came to know Hiro and Deet so well in the audio drama that it felt natural to bring them into the story. It was a great opportunity for some cross-media pollination, and we thought fans of the audio drama would get a kick out of it.

Could you share some of the direction you provided to Angel for Hiro's and Reska's designs?

KB and MJ: Hiro was literally, "What if Paul Bettany was an alien?" We wanted a sleek look, elegant but ass-kicking, and Angel delivered. For Reska, the key word was *fierce*. She needed to have a look that could convey danger to Picard and co., but who wasn't necessarily evil. She's one of our favorite designs, and we hope we haven't seen the last of her.

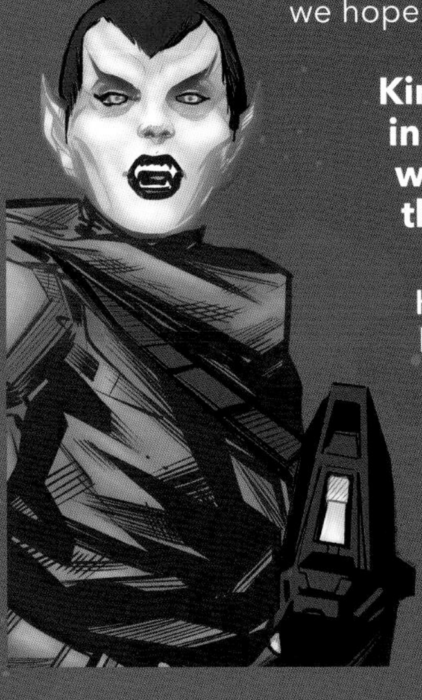

Kirsten and Mike, do you have a favorite moment in this series? Any moments you anticipated would go one way but changed once words hit the page?

KB and MJ: We both love the climactic scene with Reska, Picard, and Seven. Yes, the finale has the requisite action, but the story is ultimately resolved by the empathy Picard and Seven show Reska, and by Reska's courage in reckoning with her past. We also love the opening scene of the series with Picard's revamped Kobayashi Maru.

Are there any Picard stories you have yet to tell but would like to?

KB and MJ: Absolutely! There's no end to stories featuring Jean-Luc. More of his adventures on the original *Stargazer* would be a blast. We just need permission to…wait for it…*make it so.*

Angel, your work has become a staple of IDW's Star Trek comics, many of which are team-ups with Kirsten and Mike. What is it about their stories that keep you coming backing back for more? What do you think J.D.'s work adds to your art?

Angel Hernandez: From the beginning, from the first Trek project in which I participated, I felt really privileged, and even today, after many projects together, I still feel the same. Having the opportunity to be part of this great story together with great creators like Kirsten and Mike is a real honor to me. They make you feel comfortable in their stories, they give you space to fully develop your visual ideas, and it is very comfortable and pleasant to work like this. For me professionally, that is a necessity.

Each project is the sum of layers in which each contributor tries to add their best to the previous layer. In this case, J.D., has given life to my layer, with personalized color and style that, I think, have enriched it.

Can you give us some insight into your process for designing new characters?

AH: Typically, in the first stages of a project, the script describes the characters that are going to appear. Kirsten and Mike were very clear about the appearances they wanted to give to the new characters, and that was very helpful to me. Sometimes it is very simple because we already know what they look like since they have previously appeared on the show, but in other cases there is absolutely nothing, and at that time good chemistry between writers and artists is essential. Whenever I have the responsibility of designing a new character, I try to visualize them interacting with the members of the series. If I see that the situation looks natural, I know that I am on the right track. For example, in this case, a character like Hiro had to work very well alongside Seven at all times, and, at the same time, Deet—who doesn't have much space in this story—had to mesh well with the previous two. I always try to make each new species, each new character, seem like they've always been there. I hope I have succeeded in this.

What was your favorite scene to draw in this series? Are there any Picard stories you would like to draw but haven't had a chance to yet?

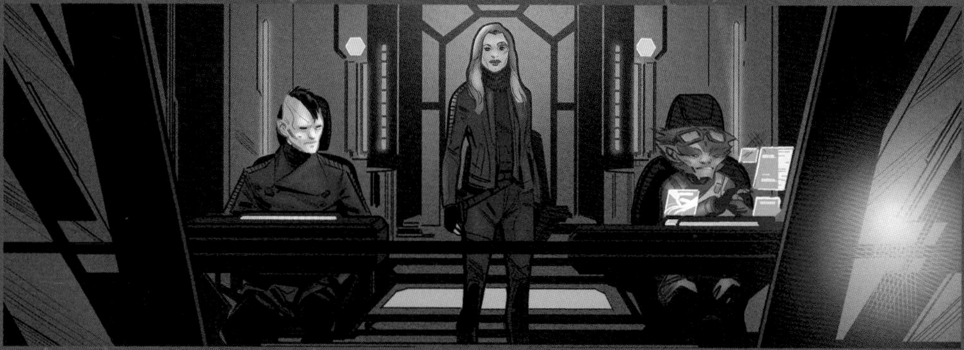

AH: In this series, I had the opportunity to work on many exciting scenes. If I had to choose one, I would choose the scenes of ships in space. I have always liked to draw frenetic space battles, and here I had the opportunity to work on some of the most spectacular ones I have done so far. I hope readers enjoy them as much as I did.

I've worked on several stories spanning Picard's life in Starfleet, so I would like to draw something from before, from his childhood, before entering the Academy. I'd like to understand his motivations, desires, and the small adventures that defined the character he later became.

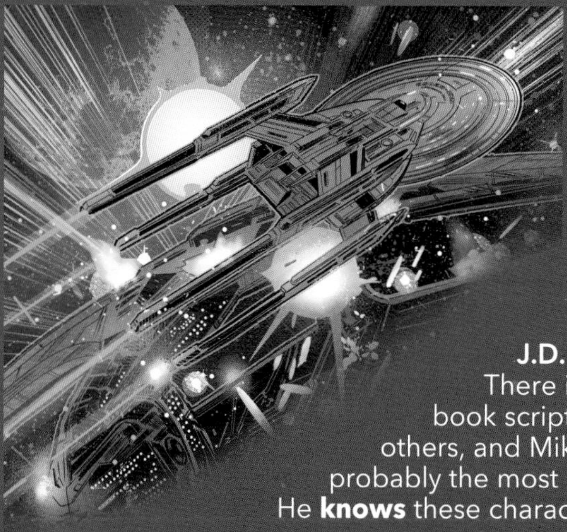

J.D., you've now teamed up with this crew on *Star Trek: Discovery* and *Star Trek: Picard*. What is it about Mike and Kirsten's stories and Angel's art that keep you coming back for more?

J.D. Mettler: I love Mike's scripts. There is no standard format for a comic book script. Some are better constructed than others, and Mike's are **always** a tight read. He's also probably the most prolific *Star Trek* writer in the industry. He **knows** these characters. Script is key.

Kirsten is one of the brilliant minds behind the shows, which I think are all fantastic. It was an honor and feather in my professional cap to get to work with her in the comic book format.

Angel Hernandez, IMHO, is one of the finest artists in the biz today. His line art is phenomenal to color. The layouts, lines, likenesses, panel flow, ink washes, VFX, etc....just beautiful work, and he's always on time (or early). He consistently produces the kind of pages colorists love to get their hands on!

Can you give us some insight into your process coloring this series? What considerations went into your landing on this specific palette?

JDM: Lots of channels, layers, custom brushes, etc. Trek gets all the shiny bells and whistles. This was definitely a heavy visual effects book. Blending modes, layer orders, brush settings, and opacities are where I reside. I dream in layers, modes, sliders, and opacity settings at this point. Photoshop will take over your brain after decades of use, kids.

We went with a pretty digitally painted look for these issues. Lots of colored ink lines. The palette was usually pretty saturated but also varied in hues, tones, and values depending on locations/lighting. Not photographic, but hopefully keeping with the look/feel of the show while embracing the comic book format and taking advantage of the different things we can do with these issues.

What was your favorite scene to color in this series? Are there any Picard stories you would like to work on but haven't had a chance to yet?

JDM: I love the space scenes! Anything that has star fields and nebulas and alien planets/surfaces. I can mostly just zone out and play on all the backgrounds and VFX stuff—cue Bob Ross' voice—"And maybe over here...some happy little space clouds below this quasar explosion...that's nice."

Really the coolest thing about comics (and *Star Trek* in particular) is that we have to be ready for anything/everything. One issue might be mostly caves and water, the next might be all tech, and the next a Western theme. There might be aliens and ships, an actor's likeness to match, a double-page spread of an advanced city, or pages of horses and trees. You don't know until you get that next script, and the Trek scripts keep an artist on their toes!

There is not a time in my life I remember not knowing *Star Trek*. I think my aunt made sure I knew the *TOS Trek* characters by the time I could say words/names. I love the Trek universe, even more so now that it has expanded. Working with Heather and Vanessa at IDW has been an absolute pleasure. I've said every comic book project was my last for years, but who knows? This crew is soooo good... I'll **always** be interested to see where they take it next!